Letterman

Simon Bramhall
and
Fionn Murphy

Scalpel Stories

ISBN-9781916191556

Cover design by: S. Bramhall and F. Murphy

Other books from Simon and Fionn

Trick or Treat?
Charity
Just Another Saturday Night
Dilemma
Deceitful Blood

Available on Kindle and in paperback from Amazon

Find out more at www.scalpelstories.com

for Fiona and Doug

CONTENTS

1

LETTERMAN

BEGINNING

A split second. A moment of madness.

CHAPTER ONE

If it had been anyone else, he might have smiled.

But this was Julia.

"It is an independently verified review. Julia. Your complaints about Alex Whiteley's lap chole have been thoroughly investigated, as the seriousness of the allegations required.

The Medical Director turned his attention to the document on his desk, pushed his glasses further up his nose and spoke even more quietly than usual. Julia was forced to lean forward to hear him.

"It seems that of all the surgeons in this organisation who perform laparoscopic cholecystectomy procedures, Alex has the lowest conversion rate, the shortest overall length of stay and no mortality."

"I don't believe you. It's not possible. I know – I work with him."

"The review concludes that the allegations made against him that he has a high complication rate and is converting too many to open procedures, are completely unfounded."

There was a pause. The man on one side of the desk glanced at his screensaver. The woman on the other side did not notice.

"It's a cover up. A scam."

He looked at her. She couldn't be serious.

Julia's eyes narrowed as she turned and left.

It was all about timing.

CHAPTER TWO

Midland Central Hospital

Number three operating theatre was brightly lit. People were coming and going, doors swung open and nudged shut, mobiles gave off text alerts, monitors hummed, hiccupped and occasionally beeped; machines clicked on and off and throughout it all the regulated breathing of the patient on oxygen provided a rhythmic backdrop to the activity. Once the initial incision had been made into the patient's abdomen and the procedure was securely underway, the surgical team, led by Alex Whiteley, had been talking about pets as they sliced, probed, picked and drained.

"Did I ever tell you about the time my dog blew all the fuses in the house?"

He had.

"It was cold so instead of sitting in front of the fan heater the dog sat on top of it. Of course, he blocked the vent so it overheated, exploded and blew every bloody fuse in the house. Dog never noticed."

He threw back his head and laughed loudly at the recollection, a deep bellied, throaty laugh that resonated round the room and seemed to bounce off the metal surfaces. The chat across the table could have been about almost anything – holidays, football, what was on offer in Tesco – but on this occasion it was Alex Whiteley's dog, Baldrick, an adored but out of control Jack Russell. Pets were a favourite and safe topic of theatre conversation and generally produced laughter, a relaxant in a charged situation. Non-controversial conversation was the norm but occasional black humour crept in. There was stress enough in the surgical procedure. Contrived informality was a strategy that senior surgeons used to reduce tension.

Alex owned the operating theatre and would have owned the whole hospital if he could. It was hard to believe that such sausage fingers could perform the delicate, intricate surgery of which he was master. He loved his patients and they, mostly, loved him. Junior staff trusted him, but ostentatious success had alienated many of his peers and fellow surgeons. Scalpels were drawn and ready.

This evening however, with the exception of consultant anaesthetist, Julia Voss, sitting beside the patient's head, Alex was with his team. Despite the riskiness of the procedure, he was enjoying himself. This was his world and he loved it. At 53 he was at the top of his game and now had his eye on a professor's post in the city's university – the logical next step in an illustrious and lucrative career. There simply were not enough hours in the day to accommodate his genius.

On the table before him was Tiger Lily Lacey, only twenty years old and far too young for it to be fair that she was suffering from cancer. Alex was the only surgeon prepared to undertake the complex, risky procedure to remove primary and secondary tumours from Tiger Lily's liver and bowel. Without the surgery her prognosis was poor, only three months at most. She and her partner, Fern, had fought and fought to reach the stage where surgery could even be considered. They had even paid for an unapproved drug when it was still being trialled, Avastin, to reduce the size of the tumours enough for surgical intervention. Then they had scoured the NHS for a surgeon crazy and arrogant enough to operate. Only Alex, who revelled in the glory associated with high-risk success was prepared to do it and, what mattered more, was sure it would work.

They had been operating now for nearly three hours. Tiger Lily had been squeezed onto the scheduled list at Alex's special request and he was more than ready to operate beyond the hospital's daily routine in order to treat her. He knew his team would share his dedication and so it had proved. He glanced around at them with an almost paternal pride: first assistant James McKenzie stood opposite, with the expensive Edinburgh-Morningside accent. In his late twenties he was evolving into a particularly dextrous cutter. Beside James was the scrub nurse who never needed to be told when to wipe his glasses, she always knew. To Alex's right was the second assistant - still so much to learn but getting there - and also on his right but not scrubbed up, one of the two runners. Hovering proprietorially in the background was the imperturbable theatre sister whom he had never seen flustered, not once. A treasure. Perched on stands behind him were a mixture of doctors and medical students observing the proceedings, their heads bobbing up and down like chickens as they strained to see over shoulders and the movements of the scrubbed staff. There was quite an audience despite the antisocial hour as this was an 'interesting case'. Another runner, the resident theatre staff, the porters and a trio of anaesthetists – consultant, junior doctor trainee and the operating department practitioner to draw up drugs - put up fluids, blood and the like.

The anaesthetists. Alex's self-satisfaction about his team abruptly imploded. Always three of them, like something out of a tragedy. Anaesthetists were the really clever ones in medical school, and they had a hell of a responsible job to do, no one would dispute that. But why did they have to be so supercilious? And you never knew what they were thinking.

He wasn't the only one who thought that; other surgeons said the same. Alex glanced surreptitiously over his mask at Julia Voss, queen of any one's coven. Calculatedly single, ambitious, hungry for recognition, not a strand of her expensively streaked blonde hair was out of place. That was so typical. She was always immaculate. Efficient and competent, perfunctory and angular. People felt uncomfortable in her presence which was unfortunate because she genuinely cared about her patients, although she cared about her medical career more.

Alex's attention was caught by the theatre sister´s mobile signalling the arrival of a text. She gave it a quick glance and hurried from the room. This was not unusual – it was her task to liaise with the office throughout the surgery but the expression on her face had assumed a grave expression and she had raised her eyebrows in surprise. That was not so usual. She was absent only a few minutes but, on her return had instantly passed a written message to him via the non-scrubbed runner who held it up for him to read. Hands embedded inside Tiger Lily's abdomen he peered at the message over his mask.

"Tell them please, Sister". She did not hesitate or alter the normal modulation of her voice as she made her announcement.

"Just to let you know that a major incident has been declared and we are now on Code Red."

For an instant time stood still, then fractured. The observing medics clattered from their perches and flapped away, clucking and consulting mobiles. Everyone else had stopped and was looking at Sister. She had anticipated the question and answered before anyone had time to ask.

"A light plane has crashed on the M42 in heavy traffic. Pile up and multiple injuries."

"Thank you, Sister." Alex seemed unperturbed. "We are in the middle of a complicated procedure which I don't need to tell you is at a crucial stage and mustn't be interrupted. Stage one is almost complete." Alex watched James carefully as cleaned up the inside the gaping wound, held open by sturdy metal clips. "We'll finish the job in hand and then deal with whatever comes our way."

He continued as if nothing out of the ordinary had happened. "That's it, James. Now, suck. Suck. There. Thank you. Good. That completes the extended removal of the right lobe of the liver and the secondary malignant growth. Well done, everyone. We'll send it for analysis. Let's go straight on into the next phase." He looked up at the clock on the wall opposite, next to the large screen so vital to keyhole surgery. "Five to ten. Hmm. Could be worse. Oasis, I think, to oil the wheels." One of the runners went over to Alex's MP3 player in its cradle on the other side of the room. The Bose speaker he had bought for use in theatre had been the idea of Lisa, his wife.

He addressed the room, calmly, almost casually, as if ordering a takeaway, "Stage two. Removal of the right side of the colon. Everyone ready?"

"Do we have to listen to this rubbish?"

Julia's question took him by surprise. Peremptory and in his face, this was clearly a challenge.

"Yes, Julia, we do. It helps me concentrate and perform to the very highest standard."

He was glad his pomposity would infuriate her.

"And we all want the best possible outcome for our patient, don't we?" He paused for a moment, then asked if anyone else had any objections to the choice of music. No one did.

Julia's face was impassive, but her eyes were thin.

Alex smiled behind his mask. My theatre, my rules.

A brief pause.

“Right, let’s start. Time as they say, is of the essence. James, you lead, and I’ll take over when we get to the tricky bit.”

CHAPTER THREE

The light aircraft had come down in a field close to the motorway. It was carnage, not least because although it had just missed the road, the drivers of the vehicles who had witnessed its descent had panicked. They had hopelessly knotted themselves together and were now being unravelled by the emergency services under the white glare of the hastily erected flood lights.

It had been comparatively easy to access the plane. On board were three people. The unconscious pilot at the controls was found to be alive – just - and was immediately despatched to the hospital. Of the two passengers, the woman, a nurse, was dead. The third passenger was a seriously ill man who was on his way to the Midland Central for life-saving treatment. Sedated and securely strapped on a stretcher, he had not the slightest inkling of the interruption to his journey.

The pilot looked exactly as he had done on admission except that now he was in a bed, his head propped up slightly on a low pillow and his arms neatly arranged on the white sheet covering his lower body. He looked – insignificant. Diminished. Eyes open, face grey, lips white and cracked below the oxygen mask attached to the ventilator keeping him alive. Even the bruises and blood stains on his face and chest seemed to lack colour.

Beside the bed stood the on call Critical Care consultant who was looking at his watch. Next to him was the on call registrar and a consultant anaesthetist who had abandoned a formal dinner to answer the Code Red call and was still sporting a bow tie.

The first set of brain stem death tests had been carried out on the pilot just over 30 minutes ago. They were now waiting for the results of the second.

There had been no reaction to the torch shone directly into his eyes or when the hyper sensitive cornea had been stroked with a tissue. The pressure applied to his forehead had been considerable, making the anaesthetist pant slightly with the exertion and he had pinched the nose hard enough to leave pressure marks but no response. The eyes did not move when ice-cold water had been syringed into each ear: tiny drops of water were still trickling down the man's neck onto the bedclothes. There had been no response to the thin, plastic tube threaded down into the windpipe to provoke gagging or coughing.

The anaesthetist looked grim and sighed.

"Cut the ventilator. We'll see if he makes any attempt to breathe on his own."

The registrar reached over and flicked the switch. At once the breathing machine's rhythmic, soothing pumping stopped.

They waited. The ICU consultant looked at his watch. They scrutinised the pilot's chest for the slightest sign of movement. The digits on the monitor moved on, the second hand on the consultant's expensive Breitling orbited his wrist, once, twice and then a third time.

"That's it, I'm afraid."

The quiet voice of the consultant.

"Brain stem death determined at..." he looked at the clock on the wall this time, "20.40 hours. Are we all agreed?"

They were.

"We'll sign the forms, then you know what to do?" The registrar nodded.

"He was a card-carrying organ donor. He's on their database so we've already got the information we need to get started."

"Next of kin?"

"Wife. She's on her way, from Cheltenham. Should be here any time now."

"At least she won't be using the M42."

The anaesthetist made a wry smile as he spoke and pulled his bow tie undone so that it hung like a limp moustache round his neck.

"The police will blue light her through the traffic. OK. Call me if you need anything."

And with that they departed, in different directions, to tend to the living.

The registrar stood for a moment in the presence of death, looking at the man's face, eyes now closed, utterly still. Was that it? The great mystery. They knew so much about the living and preserving life, but nothing about what happened afterwards. Death was as much a part of medicine as life, but something you hoped you would never get used to.

Turning away from the body she was already scrolling down her mobile for the contact number of the Blood and Transplant Centre as she walked towards the Intensive Care office. They transferred her directly to the on call SNOD – the acronym for Specialist Nurses in Organ Donation which they bore with characteristic good humour.

"Sally Crowther. SNOD. Can I help?"

"Hi. I'm the ED Registrar. We've just confirmed a brain stem death on a 55-year-old male who's on the organ donor database."

"You're in ICU now?"

"Yes".

"I'm on my way".

CHAPTER FOUR

In theatre number three the surgery on Tiger Lily was going well. James was leading again. Alex's close but unobtrusive supervision gave him confidence and to his surprise he had found that the low volume Oasis playing in the background really did help concentration. He was aware of Alex standing opposite, watching his every move.

"Nice and neat, James. Good. We'll make a surgeon of you yet." There was a snigger around the table but more of a snort from the top of it, where Julia was sitting beside the patient's head. Alex's calm voice continued,

"A little more suction. Try a squidge. Works like a turkey baster."

There was a louder snigger and another snort as James said "Squidge" to the scrub nurse at his side and she enthusiastically squirted normal saline onto the operative site then slurped up the consequence from the open wound.

James was enjoying himself.

"Excellent! Suction now, that's it and... swab. A little more suction. Thank you, Squidge."

The scrub nurse squealed in delighted mock fury and everyone except Julia laughed, Alex throwing back his head and steaming up his glasses. The scrub nurse, whose name was Penny, would now be known at the MCH as Squidge. The story would spread like bacteria through the hospital, a hotbed of gossip and rumour.

Alex looked approvingly at James. That was just the kind of camaraderie a successful surgical team needed; he would be a good surgeon once he overcame his nerves and gained the confidence that came from experience. If only Julia was not such a po faced cow, Alex thought. He glanced furtively at her to find her staring at him, unblinkingly, through gimlet eyes. His good humour vanished.

In ICU Sally was assessing the dead pilot.

"Road traffic victim?"

"No, the pilot of the light plane that came down."

Sally paused for a moment.

"Any others on board?

"One fatality on site and another passenger who's in intensive care. Apparently, he's a famous actor, Carlos Cardoso, who was being flown here with acute liver failure."

"Never heard of him."

"No, nor me."

Sally was scrutinising the pilot as she spoke. He was a slim man who obviously worked out regularly with no comorbidity. An idea was forming itself. She had already registered him on the NHS Blood and transplant database where all his information was stored and she consulted it again with interest. He was 55, a little old perhaps for the plan she had in mind, but physically in excellent shape and he met all the other criteria. Organs were in such short supply; demand far outstripped availability. Perhaps if they could split the liver into two unequal parts, the larger for an adult and the smaller for a child, then both lives could be transformed?

She saw that the pilot's next of kin was his wife, Amanda Mallaburn, aged 45. The same age as her. Surely as a pilot's wife she would be aware of the risks her husband had regularly faced and would be emotionally equipped to cope with his death? But you just never knew, and you could never take anything for granted. In the ten years she had been doing this job, Sally had seen more grief and joy than most people witness in a lifetime.

She scrolled through the contacts list on her mobile. Important to get the right person to break the news of the death then, someone else to deal with the consent for donation. There must be no confusion or misinterpretation about the two. God! She was reminded of an occasion a few years back when the relatives of a young man had agreed to donate his organs then retracted permission, saying that they'd been too blinded by grief to think straight and hadn't known what they were agreeing to. All hell had broken loose, and then the tabloids had got hold of the story. Just the recollection of it made her shudder. She'd also need to talk to the transplant surgeons and contact the Recipient Coordinator, John Hardman. So much to do. So much to gain if she got it right. No time to waste.

"Leave it with me. I expect you've got your hands full in A&E."

The registrar smiled. It was called the Emergency Department now but everyone still referred to it as A&E, especially those who had worked in the NHS for a long time and the general public, who never thought of it as anything else.

"Let me know how it goes and if I can help," she said. As she headed back to the ED, her stomach growled with hunger. She'd get something to eat later. If she was lucky.

Amanda Mallaburn was alone in the relative's room. She scrutinised the pale green walls, the framed print of Constable's 'Haywain', the cheap rug, all doing their best to be soothing and restful. Not quite so comforting were the chirpy notices reminding everyone to use sanitising hand spray (freely available throughout the hospital) after using toilets; not to visit if you had diarrhoea or vomiting, as if they were fashion accessories; how to prevent Norovirus, Shingles, Flu, Chlamydia and STDs; the availability of obesity clinics, how to breast feed, how to give up smoking and, if all these failed, the services of the Samaritans were available night and day. Being informed that Oesophageal cancer was a burning issue and that a visit to the doctor was recommended the instant you discovered blood in your stools seemed somewhat gratuitous from where she was sitting.

She pictured her husband lying motionless and silent in the stark hospital bed in ICU. So unlike him she thought. Always doing something, always active – he couldn't sit still for a second, even in the cockpit. How often had she berated him for it and what did he always say?

"But this is me. You know it is. I can't be anything else", and they had laughed, because it was the truth.

Outside the night sky was alive with light and sound. Just like Peter, she thought, standing up and pulling the curtain to one side so that she could gaze out. Light and sound.

Behind her the door was gently pushed open and Sally Crowther stole into the room. She looked at the new widow, ready to read her expression and reaction.

Amanda turned slightly and saw the tall, big boned woman who had greeted her when she had arrived at the hospital.

"Hello again."

Sally spoke calmly.

"Can I get you anything? Tea, coffee? Not from the machine, I promise! I have access to a kettle and even biscuits."

Amanda smiled but shook her head.

"No thanks. I'm fine. Really", in answer to Sally's unspoken question. "I always knew this might happen one day. We talked about it, Peter, my husband", her voice faltered for just a second, "and I. It's about what happens next, isn't it?"

"Yes. But only when you're ready Mrs Mallaburn."

"Call me Amanda, please. But not Mandy – Peter hated that."

"Amanda."

"I've made up my mind. Well, there's nothing to decide really. It's what Peter wanted so, yes, let's do it."

"I'd like you to talk to our specialist requester, Amanda. It's a big decision and she has all the advice and information you might need."

Sally knew that the organ donation protocols had to be strictly observed. She was not going to take any chances. Too much at stake.

"Of course. But the decision's made. I know what I have to do."

In the kitchen of a two-up two-down Victorian terraced house on the outskirts of the city centre, Jason Orchard sat in darkness at a table, a cold mug of tea in front of him, the milk congealing on the top. Upstairs, his young son was asleep in the small back bedroom, with the glow in the dark stars scattered about the ceiling above his bed. In the front bedroom his wife, Meghan, should by now, have fallen into a troubled doze now that the pain killers had kicked in. Outside, Jason could hear the drone of the endless traffic.

He and Meghan had been awoken by the roar of a helicopter overhead and then hundreds of sirens bursting out all over the city. Something big was going on and if he put on the telly no doubt, he'd find out what, but he couldn't be arsed. Enough going on in his own life without everyone else's problems. He sighed heavily, then thought of Meghan and felt guilty. Her suffering was constant and apparently endless.

Their only hope was a liver transplant but they'd been waiting for years. Even now, although they were at the top of the list, there was always someone else more urgent ahead of them or the donor liver wasn't suitable. Always bloody something. They didn't even know for sure what had caused the liver disease in the first place. It had just started to fail soon after Jack was born, five years ago.

"Jase".

Meghan was calling feebly from upstairs. "Where are you?".

"Coming love."

Jason got up straight away and moved to the stairs. "What is it?"

"I can't stop the itchin'. It's drivin' me mad."

Jason loved his wife's soft Welsh accent – you could take the girl away from the Rhondda but never the voice. It had been love at first shy blush: the assembly hall, Year Seven Induction day, Rhondda Community College. No other girl for him, then or now.

"I'm comin', annlwyd."

This was about as much Welsh as he spoke; there wasn't much call for it in the Midlands. He hastened softly upstairs but his brow was furrowed. If the itching was overcoming the painkillers that was another worry. It could indicate something worse. He'd have a close look at the whites of her eyes for bleeding and redness, signs of a sub conjunctival haemorrhage. That in itself wasn't too bad but he'd also check her abdomen to see if it was more swollen than usual. If it was ... he sighed ... then he'd call Mr Whiteley's secretary at exactly 8.01 am when he knew she would just have sat down at her desk. She was never late. They'd drop Jack off with the neighbour, be in the hospital by 9.30 and would take it from there, whatever 'it' turned out to be.

CHAPTER FIVE

The operation on Tiger Lily Lacey was going well; textbook so far but the very tricky bit was yet to come. Alex watched James working his way through the layers in her abdomen, cutting, pinning, suturing and sealing with elaborate patience and care.

"Good teamwork".

Praise from Alex was often given. However,

"Let's not get complacent. Still lots to do. Nifty work, James. Have you been practising?"

"Aye. On grape skins, chicken breasts and chicken feet..."

Alex rocked with laughter then they both spoke, in unison,

"...for skin, veins and tendons".

Everyone stared at them.

"Standard med. school advice for trainee surgeons," Alex explained, "Everyone gets told that all the time and it's what I tell my students. I'm going to use you as a teaching model, James. Fair play to you."

James beamed as he sweated his way through another

membrane on his slow way out to the skin, which would be stapled not sewn together Quicker, stronger and less prone to infection.

Alex's smartphone suddenly broke into a synthetic rendering of Madness's 'Our House', drowning out Oasis and conversation. As lead surgeon and on call consultant his was the only phone not on silent but even so, a call through to theatre was unusual and he knew it would be important. His heart jumped for a second. Was it Lisa? Was she OK? She had been seriously ill a few months before and he had nearly lost her. Much as he loved his patients and profession, he loved his wife so much more. Beyond reason really.

The runner was there, answering and listening on his behalf. Who the hell was ringing him here? However, as the runner did not look unduly perturbed, it could only be hospital business. Alex realised he had been holding his breath and exhaled deeply as the runner came over and held the phone up to his ear. As he listened, he held his blood-stained gloved hands up in the air away from the table and away from possible contamination but never once took his eyes away from the table.

"Mr Whiteley? It's Sally, the on call SNOD. Sorry to interrupt but it's urgent."

"Hi Sally. No problem. What is it?"

Alex was watching James' every movement as he spoke.

"We've got an organ donor in-house and I'm wondering if we can split the liver?"

Alex's eyes gleamed above his mask.

"Tell me about the donor".

He listened intently as Sally told him about Peter Mallaburn and barely hesitated before replying.

"Yes."

He said it with enthusiasm.

"Yes, I agree. We'll split it between a child and our patient at the top of the waiting list. Who's our recipient?"

Throughout this conversation, Julia had been watching Alex's face and straining to hear what he was saying. Everything about Alex Whiteley was of interest to her - and might be useful. She wanted to hear exactly what he was saying. Behind her the theatre sister was talking to the porter and second runner in an animated conversation that seemed to centre round the porter doing a job he felt was not his, and he didn't mind who knew it.

"Will you shut up?"

Julia had spun round in her seat to address the trio who were shocked into silence.

"How the hell am I supposed to concentrate with all this bloody racket? As if it's not bad enough with this musical cacophony."

Pointedly oblivious to the fracas, Alex continued his phone conversation. Julia could now hear every word that he said and was satisfied. The porter, theatre sister and runner however, were not. The hospital grapevine would be buzzing enthusiastically with all the salacious details of her outburst by the time Julia had removed her scrubs.

"Excellent. She's been waiting a long time."

Alex was still talking.

"Who's the Recipient Co-ordinator? ... John Hardman? Brilliant. Will he tell them or you? ... Obviously if someone comes in on the urgent list it'll change but let's set up for Meghan Orchard."

Again, he was listening intently, then confirmed,

"Yes, I'll lead."

He looked around the room and then directly at James

opposite. "Can we use my team?"

He was asking Sally but everyone was listening. "Most of them are here with me so I'll ask. It's their choice of course, any one of them can say no. It's already been a long night."

He was looking at them as he spoke but he, and they, already knew that they would agree. However, Alex deliberately avoided looking at Julia, knowing that she would refuse. The others could only hope. The tacit understanding of a united team. Agreement. They signalled their assent. Still talking to Sally, Alex was planning ahead.

"We'll need another Consultant Anaesthetist and assistants". Yes, they would. The existing ones confirmed this with decisive nods of the head and Julia looked murderous, outraged at Whiteley's arrogance. The presumption of the man! Speaking not just for his team but for hers as well. It was intolerable. And he was still speaking ... he was insufferable.

"Yes, straight from here into the liver transplant if we can. Couple of hours? Good? ... Keep me updated. Thanks Sally. Love to those dogs of yours."

Sally was the proud owner of two labradoodles that Alex secretly coveted. He knew that Baldrick would be delighted, but Lisa might not be so keen. He'd have to work on her.

CHAPTER SIX

"Meghan!"

Jason was almost screaming.

"They've got a liver for you!"

He'd been upstairs when he heard his mobile ring. Damn. He'd left it in the kitchen, on the table. Stumbling as quietly as he could out of bed so as not to disturb his wife, he had raced downstairs and reached the phone just as it rang off. "Bugger" he had muttered and jabbed at the missed call button.

The call was from John Hardman. John Hardman! The Recipient Co-ordinator! "Oh, please God", Jason had murmured as he hit the return call button and held his breath. John had answered at once.

"Jason Orchard? Husband of Meghan Orchard?"

"Yes, yes, that's me, that's her I mean. Yes, I'm Jason." And yes, he could confirm her date of birth and yes, he could tell her, and yes, yes, yes, they would be at the hospital within the next two hours.

Yes they could they go straight to Critical Care where they would be expected and would meet John there. They'd see him as soon as they could. Sooner if possible.

“Meggie, it’s going to be alright, annlwyd. It’s going to be alright.” They were both sobbing as he helped her lever herself painfully into a sitting position and then out of bed, swinging her legs over first then slowly forcing her itching, aching body upright into a standing position. He woke Jack to tell him what was happening even as he was phoning the neighbour two doors down. Latisha was a like a second mam to Jack and would simply absorb him into her own family, as she had done so many times before. Meghan had put on a shapeless tracksuit over her nightdress – everything would be replaced by a sterile hospital gown once they arrived at the Unit, then Jason virtually carried her downstairs.

As he opened the front door that led straight out onto the street pavement, Latisha was on the doorstep in her pyjamas. Clutching his lucky football Jack was enfolded in her dimpled arms and carried off into the night, already half asleep against her enormous low-slung breasts and soft belly. Her husband, Nev, was waiting outside in the street in his ancient Renault with its engine running. He would drive them, erratically, alarmingly and swiftly through the back streets to the hospital. Nev always knew a short cut after his days as a taxi driver. Now he drove a bus, which everyone reckoned was why he drove so inconsistently – always stopping and starting. Neither Jason or Meghan cared how he drove, just as long as he got them there.

In Intensive Care the ICU Consultant, Hepatologist and Critical Care nurse were studying Carlos with grim expressions and tight mouths. The Hepatologist was a man of few words and untidy appearance, well known for wearing ludicrous socks and trousers a couple of centimetres too short for his scuffed leather trainers - so useful for jogging to work and then trekking endlessly around the hard hospital floors.

However, his un-ironed, crumpled appearance and bumbling, preoccupied air was a sham. He was an unassumingly distinguished Cambridge graduate with an incisive intellect, invariably the first choice of senior consultants for informed analysis and decisions. He tugged at his unruly hair and crooked tie as he studied the notes on the whiteboard chart at the foot of the bed, clicked his tongue and conferred briefly with the ICU consultant. Then the quick dial on his smart phone was pressed and he was speaking to a colleague in the blood analysis lab. He spoke briefly and tersely – no time to waste on words and pleasantries – ending with,

"Call the Recipient Co-ordinator. There's serious cause for concern. I've put him on the super urgent liver transplant list."

Carlos was extremely yellow and comatose, tied by tubes and wires to drips and monitors. His chest was bare but draped with lines attached to electrodes. The monitor at the side of his bed was humming and pulsing, tracking every vital movement.

Suddenly it stopped. Hiccupped, and stopped again.

"Flat line!"

The nurse was slamming the palm of her hand against the red emergency button on the wall before she had finished speaking. People and machines appeared from nowhere.

"Respiratory arrest."

The ICU Consultant spoke rapidly but very clearly: no margin for error.

"Ventilate. Central and arterial lines and a urinary catheter. Intravenous fluids with crystalloids to start. Then Noradrenaline to strengthen the heartbeat. What's his bp?"

The Hepatologist had stood back to give the ReSus team room to manoeuvre themselves and the portable equipment that had slid into place around the bed. The ventilator was already rhythmically breathing, linked to Carlos' mouth and nose by a tube like a mechanical elephant trunk that swayed slightly with each manufactured breath.

"Low."

It was not clear who replied but it did not matter. Team work. The consultant continued, his face a mask of concentration, studying the digit on the blood pressure gauge.

"If it drops any lower we'll give him some colloid – human albumin solution – to increase blood volume and get the pressure up to speed. Check his urine output to monitor his responses to the fluids and do his bloods to assess renal function. Asap."

He looked at the Hepatologist who nodded and said,

"I'll do it myself."

The consultant gave him a tight smile and looked at the efficient nurse channelling blood from Carlos' arm into four small phials that she sealed, put in a plastic bag and handed to the Hepatologist who padded noiselessly out in his scruffy shoes, his trouser bottoms flapping.

"He's back with us."

All eyes were on the monitor which had hiccupped again and was now beeping and humming as if nothing had happened.

"Good. But we need to watch him for acute renal failure. Stand by with the dialysis catheter just in case. Let's hope something comes in for him before it's too late.

Meghan and Jason arrived at the Intensive Care unit just as a pale streaky dawn started to smudge the glassy sky behind the MCH towers. John Hardman, was waiting for them outside the ward and had no difficulty in recognising his patients as they came down the corridor. Meghan was in the wheelchair, yellow skinned, hollow eyed, exhausted. The thin, angular man with the intense expression and wispy goatee pushing the wheelchair with such vigour and determination would be her husband, Jason; he was carrying a worn backpack and a loving look in his eyes as he spoke to his wife. Although he could not hear what was said, John could guess at their conversation and would have been right. He was an old lag, had been in the NHS man and boy all his working life and now had only another four years to go before he could retire on a full, very hard earned, pension. He hoped it would be enough to fund all his postponed dreams.

"Meghan and Jason?"

Yes, of course it was.

"John Hardman, Recipient Co Ordinator. We spoke on the phone." This to Jason. To his wife, a gentle,

"Hello Meghan".

He offered her his hand and she lifted hers, with languid effort, to briefly touch his before letting it drop onto her lap.

"This way. Let's get you settled in then I'll tell you what's going to happen and answer all your questions. I'm here for you every step of the way and some."

His soft Brummie accent was reassuringly ordinary and familiar, a reminder of normality for desperate people in pain and fear. Jason pushed the wheelchair through the double doors which swished as they entered uncertainly into the ward. It was Arctic bright; white with artificial light in the absence of windows and vibrant, alive with the murmurs and whispers of the sophisticated technology that cradled and sustained the quiet, docile patients in their care. As John led them towards the bay that would be Meghan's they made way for a dishevelled looking man in trousers too short for his legs, clutching a plastic bag with what looked like tubes of blood in it. He was striding purposefully towards the exit with a preoccupied expression and hardly noticed them. John smiled and chatted.

"Consultant in Bloods; works on a level all his own. Nice man. Best there is I'm told."

A middle-aged woman came forward, introduced herself as Barbara, Meghan's assigned ICU nurse, then spoke very quietly to John in an aside that only he could hear. As she spoke, he turned, abruptly, to stare at her. Aghast. He then looked directly at Meghan being helped out of the wheelchair by Jason.

John's face was a study of self-control as he told them, nonchalantly,

"Barbara'll look after you while I step out for a minute. Just to sort out some admin. I'll be back before you know it."

And he was gone.

Behind the closed doors of the ICU main office a full-scale row was in lava flow. John was appalled. The ICU consultant was unmoved.

"There's no choice. Cardoso has to have it or he'll die. That's why he's been put to the top of the list."

"But she's been told. She's here! Out there in ICU, with her husband, right now, expecting a new liver. She's been waiting months and months; how do we know that she won't die?"

"We don't, but she's not going to die today if she doesn't get a transplant and he will. It's a question of priorities."

"John. Face the facts. We've got one liver and two patients. They can't both have it. It's bad enough that we can't now split it and save a child as well as an adult but that's the way it is. The Children's Hospital has already been told. Carlos Cardoso has to have a transplant or he'll die within the next 48 hours and you know the protocols as well as I do. The choice of recipient is based on immediate need."

John's face was ashen.

"But she's here. How the hell are we going to tell her?"

The consultant, who genuinely shared the dilemma, considered, rubbing both eyes with the palms of hands as if trying to clear his way to an answer.

"We need to speak to the Hepatologist, and see what the blood analysis has come up with. Then we'll contact the NHSBT Duty Office and check the protocols but you and I both know that ultimately it has to be an MCH decision. Who is down to operate?"

John consulted his notes. "Alex Whiteley."

"Then I think we need to speak to him too, although I know he'll go with what the blood men say. As the operating surgeon he has to. In the end it has to be a clinical decision based on the best possible outcomes."

The consultant lowered his voice.

"Don't you think you should tell Meghan Orchard what's happening? So that she knows?"

"Yes, I do," John retorted sharply, "but I really don't want to. Would you?"

The consultant was abashed.

"No. Not really. Look, we'll do it together if you like."

John was touched, but professional. "Thanks, but no, I'll do it. It goes with the job and it won't be the first time."

"Or the last. I'll go to Hepatology now and find out what's happening while you break the bad news. She's almost certainly not going to get her transplant today, not unless there's a miracle and a second donor turns up."

Calm now and resigned, they opened the office door. John walked reluctantly towards the Orchards while the consultant sped away in the other direction, as much to escape as to talk to Alex Whiteley and the Hepatologist.

CHAPTER SEVEN

In theatre three the procedure on Tiger Lily Lacey was in its final stages and there was an air of general satisfaction - a job well done as she was being stapled and sealed. Only Julia seemed less than pleased, as if she resented the success of the operation. Not for the sake of the patient, of course, but because it was a battle gain for Whiteley in their ongoing war. There had been another phone call for him a few seconds ago but, despite shifting forward in her seat and then handing over her position completely to her assistant, she had been unable to hear anything but,

"He must have the final say".

Whiteley had then looked tragic (what melodramatics) and murmured, "she'll be devastated", whoever she was. Julia did not know but would speculate about with Garth later. Garth Mahendran was the second in department to Alex's first and essential to Julia's long-term plans.

There had also been a message via that supercilious theatre sister to say that the organ retrieval was well under way in an adjoining operating theatre if Mr Whiteley wanted to assess the condition of the liver. 'Mr Whiteley' indeed! Since when did he deserve such deference and respect from a jumped-up theatre sister? As a consultant anaesthetist she was always, of course, Dr Voss, but Whiteley was only a general surgeon in spite of his delusions of grandeur. As she removed her mask and scrubs outside the theatre while Tiger Lily was being wheeled into the recovery room, Julia's expression was one of repressed fury. Always a good-looking woman, with high cheek bones and a slightly too thin but still attractive Roman nose, she would age well if she could offset the emerging lines of discontent around the corners of her mouth. Botox would take care of her eyes and forehead.

Everyone else was chatting animatedly as they peeled off their disposable gowns and gloves and threw them in the yellow contaminated waste bin, washed their hands and sluiced the blood off their theatre shoes at the scrub up sink. She had detached herself from them and moved away as far as she could without actually leaving the room. All the better to hear and not be seen.

The Hepatologist had listened intently to the ICU Consultant outlining the problem with the donor organ. He had clicked his tongue, twisted his tie and tugged at his unruly hair so hard that he seemed to be trying to lift himself off the ground. Now it stood up in tufts and his tie had virtually disappeared under his crumpled collar, but his face was clear and determined when he finally spoke.

"It has to be Carlos Cardoso. There's no other choice. I'm sorry for Mrs Orchard, but we can't let a man die when there's an organ available to save him."

The consultant nodded in agreement. He had known it was a foregone conclusion, but they had to be sure and be seen to have explored every available avenue. Dealing with the Orchards was going to be a serious problem, but it had to be done. Hell. Sometimes doctoring seemed like the cruellest profession in the world. He set off back to ICU with footsteps heavier even than his sense of dread.

John was sitting on the edge of Meghan's bed. She was lying down, not quite flat but with a low pillow under her head, the only position in which she felt bearably comfortable. Her stomach was distended; her eyes were closed. The consultant stopped some way off and watched the scene unfold – a tale of tragedy and despair.

The Co-ordinator had finished speaking and for an instant everything froze, outside all time and place. Then it smashed apart as Jason exploded into a maelstrom of sound and fury. His screeching anger reverberated around the ward, crashing into the monitors, equipment and other patients, bouncing off the walls and ceiling then ricocheting from the floor onto the man who had uttered the fateful words:

"The donor organ has to be given to someone who needs it more."

There was no point in arguing, protesting or even speaking. Jason had every right to be angry; he would have to blame someone and that someone was, of course, the person who had delivered 'the death sentence' as Jason called it.

While Jason raged, John watched Meghan. What he saw shocked him more than any amount of noise, anger or violence. She was completely impassive. Her complexion had paled and was a sickly combination of grey and yellow. Her eyes were still closed but silent tears were unevenly pooling down her cheeks and around her mouth. Her top lip had all but disappeared, sucked inwards over her lower lip into which her teeth were so firmly clenched that she had drawn blood. The blood and tears had entwined. A watery red puddle was silently forming in the shallow cavity where her collar bones met.

CHAPTER EIGHT

In the corner of the sluice room outside the operating theatre Julia was on her phone.

"Nightmare."

She was almost spitting.

"Typical bloody look-how-wonderful-I-am Alex Whiteley. Throwing himself about as per usual. Forcing us to listen to his appalling music. God, he's such a Philistine. He might be a good surgeon but, oh, don't we know it?"

She barely paused for breath before she continued.

"Where? What time?".

A cursory silence and then her mouth became slightly less rigid and there was almost an upward curve at its edges. A smile? Not quite. She despised gratuitous expressions of emotion; so vulgar.

On the other end of the phone Garth was rapidly calibrating: tell Mariyah his comfortable wife of seventeen years that something had come up. Wouldn't be home tonight. So sorry; mortified: knew she would understand; she always did. What would he do without her?

He answered Julia.

"Your place?"

Yes. She would see him there.

In the theatre coffee room Alex and his team were taking the compulsory, brief break before they began the lengthy transplant procedure on Carlos. Alex glanced at his no-nonsense Seiko watch and then at his team, heading off for coffee and whatever they could find in preference to the ping ping burgers in the vending machine outside the closed canteen. Just enough time to call Lisa, see Tiger Lily's partner, Fern, then maybe grab a coffee himself. He spoke into his phone as he walked down the corridor towards the patients' waiting area, leaving behind him a disappearing trail of footsteps from his clean but damp theatre crocs. Speed dial took him straight through to his wife's voicemail.

"Hi Lisa. It's me. Just finished and about to speak to the family. A super urgent has come in so it's an all-nighter. Love you. Big hugs for my boy. See you later."

He was clicking off the phone as he arrived at the waiting room. An uncomfortable room in which to wait: once smart it was now shabby with hard seats lined up like condemned prisoners awaiting execution, a low table in the centre covered with a bedraggled army of magazines that had been skimmed repeatedly but never read. Fern was perched on the edge of an uncomfortably bright blue plastic chair and looked up anxiously at him as he opened the door. She was holding the edge of the seat with both hands for emotional support as she stretched up her head and neck, her eyes wide with the unspoken question.

"She's fine, Fern. Textbook. There's every reason to assume an excellent outcome."

Fern's pale face was stripped by the brash illumination from the overhead strip light, her short-cropped hair like a spiky bleached coronet framing eyes purple with tiredness and fear.

She said nothing but her face suddenly crumpled and her body slumped. She cried like a baby, body racking sobs woven into shuddering inhalations of air and noisy gulps. Alex smiled and let her cry for a moment or two. He had dealt with so many reactions. Relief was easy.

“She’s in recovery and you’ll be able to see her when she’s back in Intensive Care. Someone will come and get you.”

Fern nodded her head vigorously but said nothing, too emotional to speak.

“I’m due back in theatre now but any problems or concerns contact me. You’ve got my mobile number.”

Fern nodded again, still sobbing violently as Alex left the room.

CHAPTER NINE

They were in the same operating theatre again, number three, and with the exception of the anaesthetists it was the same surgical line up. There had been a slight delay as Alex had slugged down a strong black coffee hastily cooled with cold water and tasting of metal, but he needed the caffeine. Caffeine – the lifeblood of the NHS. It ought to be on prescription he thought as he wiped his mouth with the back of his hand before scrubbing up.

Now they were all in place. Alex looked around at each one of the team to assess their readiness. Well used to his system they nodded assent as he caught their eye and waited until he gave the go ahead to make the first incision, always a tense moment. In the background the runner had put on Simon and Garfunkel and the patient, never thought of by name when on the table – too personal and emotional – was smeared with pink antiseptic, eyes taped, face masked, breathing rhythmically through the ventilator, measured, marked, oblivious and ready to cut.

"Everyone ready?"

Yes.

Wielding his knife like a pen, Alex pressed into Carlo's upper abdomen from the bottom of the right rib cage down to the right flank and pressed very gently – just enough to break through the skin in a curved line like a sabre blade. There was not much blood - just a few drops. Quite normal.

"Diathermy blade".

The scrub nurse handed him the high frequency electrosurgical blade that cut and coagulated the small blood vessels simultaneously as it passed through the yellow fat. It produced a whiff of smoke as it incised, and a smell of charred flesh like cooking smoked bacon rose into the air. Appetising, in different circumstances. Alex knew that due to the deranged clotting of those with fulminant liver disease like Carlos, there was a real risk of excessive bleeding. They would have to watch out for that, particularly in the later stages of the procedure.

"Counter traction please, James".

The tissues below the layer of fat were gently parted using swabs by he and his assistant working in tandem until the milky sheath surrounding the muscle was prised apart and divided. Alex was concentrating but relaxed; routine, standard procedure so far. He glanced at James who was equally comfortable. They had done this so many times together now. With the diathermy blade he began to work his way slowly through the dense muscle then clipped, divided and tied off the sickle shaped ligament. At this point he stopped, stood back slightly, blade poised and looked around him.

"Let's see what we've got shall we?"

This was always a profound moment, poised as they were at the threshold of a virgin cave, never before exposed. Since the day he entered the world 43 years ago Carlos' naked body had been mothered, cuddled, fondled, bathed, explored, sun tanned and displayed but never once had anyone turned the inside out before this moment. Alex strained forward and creased his eyes in concentration to get a better view of the trials and tribulations that might lie ahead. All the scans in the world could not fully reveal what lay before them now. Alex marvelled at the wonder of the human anatomy. Everyone different yet alike in structure and form; the detail of the world within, closed and unseen until opened up by sharpened metal blades wielded by intruders. Swords, sabres, knives, scalpels. The intention might differ, but it all amounted to the same invasion. Then there was the pathology, the way disease affects us as all, changes our bodies, minds and lives. A medical Pandora's box.

As always at this point Alex felt both humbled and empowered. It did not do to think about the responsibility; too intimidating. He stopped staring into the soft pulpy cavern and called for the Stieber rib retractor – £15,000 worth of highly engineered metal – that would enable them to wind open the wound, lift the ribs and give maximum exposure to what lay beneath.

The liver. In a healthy person it would be brown and smooth, roughly the size and shape of a kebab pitta bread but much heavier. The one he was looking at was small, shrunken, pale and lifeless. He could almost see the dead cells with a few patches of less damaged ones looking slightly pinker. What mattered now was the swift, efficient removal of the damaged organ in order to replace it with the healthy one, currently enthroned in a container of ice.

No one was talking much. They were tired. Already they had been operating for over two hours, not to mention the eight hours plus procedure on Tiger Lily, and there would be at least another two hours to go, barring complications, before there was any chance of successfully completing the transplant. None of it was easy, but removing the diseased organ was usually less fraught than the insertion of the new one. Conversation had waned. It was just a question of getting a slow, painstaking, critical job done as quickly as it would safely allow.

Alex was adept at removing livers. It was something of a speciality of his and, had opportunity presented itself, could have been something of a party piece if such a party could ever be found. Once the blood vessels had been tied off and the diseased liver had been detached, he inserted one hand into the cavity, placed it under the offending organ and plopped it out, whole, with a watery sucking slurp. A satisfied sigh from Alex, an admiring glance from James and it was slopped into a metal bowl to be taken away for analysis. So far, so good.

Time for the donor liver to be brought in. The efficient theatre sister had already pre-empted instructions from Alex and two porters were carrying the large plastic container in through the swing doors as Carlo's own liver was being taken off to the lab. It took two people to lift the box which was about the size of a couple of dining room chairs and heavy with ice. Close to the surface, nestling snugly in the chill was a bowl full of fluid, sealed in sterile bags and vacuum packed. In the fluid, like an unborn baby in a sac, was Peter Mallaburn's healthy, life-saving liver. Immeasurably precious; Meghan Orchard would have given a kidney for it. There was a faint whiff of aviation fluid about the box, or was that their olfactory system playing tricks because they knew the source? Alex had once received a liver in a box stained with fire-suppressing foam after it had been retrieved from a traffic collision en route to the theatre. He could have sworn that it smelt of petrol and burnt rubber.

As the dead pilot's liver was being unpacked, as gently as un-swaddling a baby, its distinctive metallic aroma invaded the operating theatre giving off a smell not unlike roast beef.

"Ready for stage two?"

Alex looked around again, and again, everyone nodded assent. It was critically important to prevent potentially fatal high portal blood pressure so a portocaval shunt had to be inserted – intricate and complicated – to create a new connection between the main blood vessels and to control the blood flow.

Then they could use a piggy back technique to graft in the new liver.

Alex bent over the table, completely focussed. James had inserted and fixed the large, imposing, side-biting clamp which was effectively closing the inferior vena cava, the huge vein that returned the blood to the heart from the lower part of the body. Now the new liver could be put in without dangerous loss of blood. Once it was in and the connection made then they could open up the IVC again and the blood flow would be restored. In theory, straightforward, but in practice unbelievably fiddly and demanding requiring strong hands, delicate finger work and self-assurance. James might have had the skills to perform it but did not yet possess the necessary confidence. It was always a question of being able to cope if something went wrong; that was the sign of the real expert. Suddenly the scrub nurse was removing his glasses to wipe them. Alex was surprised and paused; he had not realised he was sweating. She slid them onto his nose above his mask and he regained focus. Then, with a twist and just a hint of pressure, the new liver was in place. Yet to be affixed and fully connected, but in place.

Alex straightened up and stepped back just a fraction from the table, bloodied, gloved hands in the air like a surrendering soldier or an artist standing back to inspect a newly completed masterpiece.

"Flush the new liver with warm 5% dextrose, James, then vent the vena cava to get the blood flowing nice and clear. We need to keep everything moving and make sure there's no potassium in there. That's it. Good... Do you want to continue the portal vein suture or shall I?"

The younger man looked at him over the table.

"I'd like to, aye."

Alex was pleased: James was doing well. He smiled briefly.

"When you're ready then. We'll tie the knot to allow a stretch but before we do, just release the vein quickly... and stop. That's it. We don't want any clots. Good. Bleeding?"

"No. None".

This was the signal for Alex to address the consultant anaesthetist beside Carlos' head.

"Ready for me to clamp off?"

The next step and one of the most difficult. The portal vein had to be clamped and controlled by hand before moving on to connecting the artery. It was up to the anaesthetist to do battle with the variable blood pressure and to keep the patient stable, breathing and hydrated. Once stability had been secured, the operation could move on. The anaesthetist gave the briefest of assenting nods. The tension was palpable. Alex was calm, but uncharacteristically formal. There was an air of expectant trepidation, a frisson in the room.

"Music off. More light. Can everyone see? Move for a better view if you need to. Magnifying loops – 3.5x please."

The same runner who had brought him his phone so many hours ago removed Alex's glasses which the scrub nurse replaced with magnifying loops. Now he would be able to see in minute detail every movement, every tiny suture, every delicate manoeuvre.

"Arterial clamp".

James obliged swiftly and silently to close the pulsating artery as he watched Alex's fingers squeeze, tug, twist and thread. Subtle but sure, the result of years of experience and practice. Millions of pounds worth of training and learning in those finger ends behind the well-trimmed nails inside the flesh-coloured latex gloves. No wonder they were so heavily insured. Alex was giving a running commentary on his actions:

"I'm patching the recipient artery into the donor arteries and connecting them with a very fine prolene stitch for durability.

Scissors."

He delicately cut the thread.

"Swab."

The scrub nurse dabbed and cleaned the suture site. Alex breathed out audibly.

"Right, a quick bleed out to make sure there are no clots and we should be there. Clamps off."

There was a moment of silence.

"James, clamps off".

Alex's voice was very slightly louder.

"They are."

James' reply was firm but edged with fear.

"Hell. There's no flow."

Everyone was looking at Alex as he spoke.

"Re-clamp. I'm going to do that anastomosis again."

No one spoke. No one except Carlos seemed to be breathing. The monitor charting his life pulsed and beeped preternaturally loudly in the otherwise silent room.

Alex was once more bent over the table, pressing, pulling, threading and twisting his fingers, repeating even more carefully the once failed procedure. He then nodded to James who released the clamp. They all prayed for a sign of the blood flowing into the liver. The clamp came off and there was a weak pulsation but no fluid thrill. Nothing.

Now there was real fear in the room; fear you could smell and taste. Above their masks all eyes were wide, pupils dilated. Even the theatre sister was biting her lip. Alex was calm and controlled but worried. This was a life-threatening situation. If blood could not reach the liver from the recipient's main artery via the donor artery attached to the liver, then it would die and so would the patient. They simply had to connect it. He would have another try.

Even as he was unsuccessfully attempting the connection the third time Alex knew it would fail and was desperately trying to work out why. There was nothing wrong with the way they had inserted it, of that he was certain. It had to be a problem with the liver from the way it had been retrieved from the donor. He spoke his thoughts aloud:

"It's an intimal tear. It's got to be. There's a tear in the donor artery which creates a false passage for the blood flow. I'm going to have to cut the donor artery right back to remove the defect. I just hope I don't have to go too far or there won't be enough left to connect it to the patient's own artery."

There was no need to ask for quiet. Time froze into an endless, suspended eternity, beyond dimension. It seemed to last forever. Nothing existed except the need to make the single connection that would restore blood flow, life, hope; the present as well as the future.

Freely sweating into his gown, Alex continued to probe and scrutinise the gristly tube at his fingertips. He peered closely, sucked his mask into his mouth as he inhaled extremely deeply and then made a steady-handed dissection. Without saying a word, he then began the reconnection procedure for a fourth time. It was obvious to everyone that there was not much artery left to work with. The anaesthetist was looking anxiously at Alex, the clock, the monitor, the blood pressure readings and then back at Alex. Not difficult to read now – he was clearly very concerned. They all were.

"Yes!"

Alex bellowed and reality bounced back into the room.

"Thank God. Clamps off."

As James removed the clamp there was a combined sigh of relief as the blood flowed bright and red and viscous.

"Beautiful," sighed the scrub nurse.

Still controlled but visibly relieved Alex explained what had occurred, as much for himself as the others. He needed to rationalise his stress.

"A tear like that is an injury caused by traction on the blood vessels during the retrieval operation - when the liver was taken from the donor. Thankfully it doesn't often happen. Sorry it's been stressful everybody. Soon be there."

He knew that exhaustion was now a very real problem and a natural reaction to the tension they had all been under. Once the adrenaline rush subsided they would all feel shattered. It was essential to complete the operation before that happened. They were his team and he cared about them; it was up to him to get them through as well as the patient. Only the bile duct to join and then, ironically, it was uncontrolled bleeding that they now had to watch for so it was vital to seal the blood vessels before they tidied up and worked their way out towards the skin and closure.

"Time zero biopsy please, James".

As the Scot took a tiny sample of the new liver for ongoing analysis and monitoring, Alex asked for the argon beam coagulator – the ABC. The inert argon gas, that marks but does not burn and leaves the end of the diathermy wand as a column of blue gas like a hybrid of something out of Harry Potter and a light sabre. It had to be tested on the liver before being used to seal off the vessels. A series of small dots would be enough to check whether or not it was working. Preoccupied, Alex directed the current onto the right lobe of the liver. The blue gas contrasted strangely with the visceral pinks and reds; it glowed eerily and left a superficial brown mark like a strip of sun tan. If wiped it would disappear, but when Alex stood back from the table the marks were clearly visible – two letters, comprised of dots but still recognisably forming his initials – AW.

Only James did not see; he was busy preparing the biopsy

sample for dispatch to the lab. The anaesthetist stood up, ostensibly to stretch his legs but to get a better look. He half opened his mouth as if to speak but then shut it again and sat down. Alex seemed oblivious. Still focussed on the table and by now sealing the blood vessels he simply smiled to himself and was heard to murmur,

“For a job well done.”

More loudly he then said to James, by now back at his post,

“You close, James. Nice and neat.”

CHAPTER TEN

As they stripped off their scrubs in the sluice room and washed away the procedure, the exhaustion assaulted them. At first no one spoke; everyone was preoccupied with their own thoughts and immediate needs – hunger, thirst, tiredness. Alex had disappeared to find a coffee and then the theatre office to log his report and details of further treatment for Carlos. In his absence there was an unacknowledged acceptance about what had happened. His team trusted him. The anaesthetists however, were huddled together in an exclusive scrum leaving the others to edge around each other in the confined space. Should something be said? Or not? And if it should, who would say it, and who would they say it to?

Anaesthetists apart, they were a close team and it was tacitly understood that what had happened was crossing a line, but it was understandable, and no harm had been done. Every liver transplant surgeon had their own unique pattern of trademark dots so what was the difference between those and initials? It all amounted to the same thing. The initials would disappear of their own accord within a week on a healthy liver and had they been wiped, would have gone already. Alex was their surgeon; they were his team. They looked out for each other.

And that's the way it would stay.

Squidge, the scrub nurse was the first to speak.

"He's not the only one. Or the first."

The second assistant surgeon looked at her.

"Oh yes. It's what one of the surgeons who used to work here did all the time. Once he played noughts and crosses with the first assistant."

"On a donor liver?".

"Yes. And there was another time when he wrote 'up' on it because one of his colleagues had put in a left lateral lobe upside down."

The second assistant began to smile, and then laugh. He put his hand to his mouth to suppress what he felt what might be inappropriate mirth but all the others were smiling.

"I know" continued Squidge, giggling, "it's not supposed to be funny of course but no harm was done and the marks all disappear anyway. It made everyone much more relaxed in theatre, that's for sure!"

It's hilarious!" announced the second assistant. "God, I wish I'd been there!"

He was still chuckling as he flung his soiled scrubs into the yellow bin and strode off towards the coffee machine.

James was oblivious; his mind was elsewhere. An ex-girlfriend – his only ex-girlfriend - had once described him as having all the sensitivity of a brick. The relationship had been short lived and since then he had preferred to worship from afar. As he slubbed down the windowless grey and white corridor in his shapeless cords and faded, scrumpled 100% cotton checked shirt towards the canteen in search of breakfast, he relived the moment of exultation they had all shared as Alex finally connected the artery. The experience of pulling someone back from the brink of death thrilled him. The drama, the tension, the uncertainty and the sense of power was intoxicating. Addictive?

The corridor was getting busier as people arrived for shift changes and another day at the office. It must be warm outside he thought as he noticed that those not in uniform were wearing short sleeves, summer frocks and sandals. On the walls the pictures of landscapes and sea scenes were designed to soothe and calm; Constable's 'Haywain' was there along with the ubiquitous Turner. James had worked in a provincial west country hospital a few years ago where the corridor walls were peopled with portraits of eminent former consultants and patrons – dark, unsmiling Victorian patriarchs who glared out of their frames at modern medicine, intimidating patients, nurses, medical students and probably even consultants, especially if they were female. Female! The sound of their combined intake of bewhiskered breath at such an outrage was almost audible. Thank God some things were different now.

He glanced at his watch – nearly 7.00 a.m. but the canteen might be open. If not, there was a vending machine outside where he could get something to eat. He hoped it would not have to be a ping ping burger.

CHAPTER ELEVEN

The taxi organised by the hospital arrived outside the Orchard's house as the rest of the world was getting ready for what was promising to be another ripe sunny day in the school holidays. Jason helped Meghan out of the back seat and onto the pavement where she rested, breathlessly, supported by the taxi driver while her husband unlocked the front door and pushed it open. The house was largely in darkness, the curtains closed, but the hall light was on: feeble and unnatural in contrast to the daylight filtering in through the open door. Meghan had not spoken since they had been told that there was no liver for her. She too, was feeble and unnaturally yellow.

"Want a hand with the stairs, mate?" the taxi driver addressed Jason who shook his head.

"No, ta. We'll manage. Thanks."

He took Meghan's weight as she leaned into him and they entered the house. The driver pulled the door shut behind them, returned to his cab and slowly drove away.

Alex also was on his way home. It was a beautiful morning so he had opened the driver side window of his top of the range

Land Rover Discovery, the one with leather seats and charcoal oak veneer dashboard. The air was refreshing after the intense, sterile operating theatre; it felt good to feel the breeze, to smell the real world, to hear life as it roared past the black roof and Firenze red four by four. Madness were hammering out 'Our House' from the MP3 player as he signalled left and turned into the secluded, suburban avenue where he lived. It was definitely an avenue and not a street according to the estate agent who had sold them the house ten years before. All to do with the trees along one side apparently, but not on their side. Lisa liked light so while trees opposite were a social asset and pleasant to look at, they did not cast too much shadow over their front garden or prevent sunlight from cavorting on the diamond leaded window panes.

The house was a bay-windowed statement of 1930s Tudorbethan respectability. It still had its original leaded windows and solid oak front door. There was a boot scraper set into the quarry tiled steps leading up to an arched porch framed by fake black beams, white stucco walls and ornate brickwork. Quite the period piece smirking behind a sturdy wall. Large electric double gates protected a gravel drive leading to a double garage, equally period in appearance but an entirely modern add on.

Lisa was the gardener in the family; generous borders and flower beds bulged with lavender, hollyhocks, delphiniums and roses in the old English style. She let the lawn grow too long because she liked the daisies and the buttercups, the early morning dew on spider's webs latticed across the blades of grass. It was joy to walk barefoot on the cold wet sunup grass and to leave a trail of footprints behind her. Only when Baldrick left a continuous line of flattened grass where it had been crushed by his low sung undercarriage would she allow the grass to be cut. Alex would have liked to do it for her, but did not have time. He paid the someone else who also cleaned the windows.

The gates were open in expectation and Alex pulled into the drive a little too fast so that the pea gravel spat from under his black wheels. He pressed the button just above the rear-view mirror below the glass roof and watched the gates begin to close behind him. Then he cut the engine, slammed the door, locked it with the key fob and strode – almost bounded - towards the front door. He loved coming home. As the front door was opened, a tan and white salvo of badly-behaved Jack Russell ricocheted off him before another more successful assault and lodging himself in Alex's arms, stumpy tail dobbing from side to side. Alex failed to avoid the tongue which ended up in his ear.

"Ugh. Baldrick. Stop that". He did not mean a word of it.

"One word from you and he does what he likes."

Lisa, small, feisty, direct undisputed master of the household was on the doorstep.

"I thought you weren't supposed to be eating sweets?" Alex looked perplexed, innocent, aggrieved and then busted. Baldrick had retrieved a packet of extra strong mints from the top pocket of his suit jacket and was consuming them, foil and paper included.

"Hello, darling. How was it?"

Lisa stretched up to kiss him briskly while she extracted with one finger the slobbery mess from the dog's mouth. She would have made an excellent surgeon he thought. Better than me.

"Long. Tricky. Over now. Is there nothing this dog won't eat?"

"Not much. What about you? I assume you're not staying?"

Lisa knew her husband and accepted his obsessional dedication, most of the time. Sometimes she rebelled and that always shocked him.

"Shower, clean shirt, slice of toast and back for the ward round?"

She smiled as she spoke. They both knew he adored her, but only she recognised his absolute dependence on her.

“Something like that.” He too was smiling.

“Don’t tell me, busy day ahead?” she said, mimicking his deep voice in the last three words. He threw his head back and roared with exuberant laughter. Baldrick barked.

“I’ll put the kettle on.”

She held the door open as he carried the dog across the threshold and then shut it behind them with a very firm hand.

CHAPTER TWELVE

On the other side of the city and much closer to its fashionable centre, Julia was fixing her hair in front of an uncomfortable dressing table mirror, all glass and white wood. Her townhouse flowed over three floors, with more ensuite bedrooms than she would ever need, a bijou decked balcony instead of a garden and an integral underground car park and exclusive convenient off-street parking. The complex was gated so she could leave her white Mercedes convertible on view. No one there knew anyone to speak to of course, but she had scrutinised the cars of her neighbours before buying the property and decided that it was a suitable place for her to live. It had class, style and was expensive.

She was not there for the company; an occasional nod of greeting or acknowledgment of recognition was all the social interaction required. But it had prestige and it was a substantial investment which sat well with her growing property portfolio. Her bedroom was predominantly white and almost totally impersonal. Like the rest of the house, it was a monument to elegance rather than comfort. Everything had been chosen and placed for effect; it was beautiful, unwelcoming, pristine and perfect. Julia loved it.

The door buzzer sounded as she was teasing apart the strands of her highlighted fringe. Garth was never late; one of the better things about him. What she liked more were his Bollywood good looks: chiselled features, dark eyes under silky long lashes for which a woman would have paid a fortune. Yet he managed to seem masculine, despite enviably high cheek bones. He was tall and slender, firm rather than muscly and since she had taken him as her lover had learned to pay more attention to the way he dressed. There was the wife, of course, and the inevitable children – expensive and time consuming – but they were of no consequence to her. His family, his problem.

The buzzer sounded again, more insistently this time. Good. She would make him wait. Fire up his need for her then make him wait some more. Sometimes they never made it beyond the entrance hall before they farrowed, but the Italian marble floor could be rather cold. Better against the wall.

Eventually she went downstairs and opened the door. Garth forced it aside and immediately started to kiss her as he slammed it shut with his foot.

"I wish you'd give me a key" he muttered, biting her ear lobe and tugging her blouse up out of her skirt. He brushed across her nipples as he reached for the front fastenings.

"Don't pull. It's a Valentino."

He took no notice and tried to push her to the floor. She slapped him in the face.

Only then did she let him in.

Afterwards, when they were sitting in the kitchen at the breakfast bar sipping cold Chablis from impossibly fragile glasses, did Julia regale him with the events of Tiger Lily's surgery the night before. She was vitriolic; Alex was the enemy. Spite made her eloquent and witty. Garth was entranced; mesmerised by the movement of her mouth and dilating pupils as she spoke, the wisp of blonde hair that she repeatedly twisted and put behind her ear while she sipped the wine between increasingly venomous comments.

"It's all his fault."

Julia stopped talking.

"Are you listening to me Garth?"

"Of course. What is?"

Julia glared at him.

"Alex bloody Whiteley is the reason I was refused funding for my research project. He was the one who persuaded the finance committee to turn down my application. He knew perfectly well that that research would have made me famous so he deliberately blocked it. Bastard. I'll never forgive him."

She drained her glass, delicately, moist lips gleaming.

"But I'll get him back."

"How? What will you do?" Garth was captivated. He stroked his face where the slap she had given him was still tingling.

"Revenge is a dish best served cold" Julia murmured.

She studied the empty glass in her hand, held it up towards the window and turned it round so that the light was refracted and distorted through its curves. Then she smashed it violently onto the surface of the counter. Garth recoiled, shocked, from the shards of splintering glass and stared at her.

"What are you doing?"

"That's what I'm going to do to Alex fucking Whiteley."

Julia looked straight ahead.

"I'm going destroy him."

CHAPTER THIRTEEN

Six days later.

Carlos lay prone and still, eyes closed, cracked dry lips slightly apart as if about to speak but suspended in mid-sentence. He would have been appalled at the sight of himself – he, the almost famous actor – with a tube up his nose, sunken cheeks, dark shadows around his eyes and a sickly, pale, yellow complexion. Around him was an audience of mute machines, following and charting his every move but seeing nothing. Almost as bad as an empty auditorium.

There was a rustle of feet and an untidy gaggle of medical students approached the end of the bed to inspect the whiteboard at its foot, as if studying a theatre programme. They were quiet, whispering to each other as they awaited the arrival of the star turn, Garth, who was leading the ward round. He had stopped to take an important phone call from someone in Italy who was performing a complicated transplant procedure and urgently needed advice. Garth always stressed the importance of being available for one's international colleagues at any time of the day or night. He felt most strongly that experience, knowledge and skill should always be shared. It wasn't about the surgeon, however eminent, but the welfare of the patient.

“He looks a bit yellow for someone with a new liver.”

One of the young women spoke, in low tones, brave enough to venture an opinion but only in front of her peers. Students were tolerated by most consultants on a strictly seen but never to be heard basis and they in turn were suitably intimidated. Their opportunity would come, in time. Until then, they were novices and never allowed to forget it. The ICU nurse assigned to Carlos was waiting with the students and overheard the comment.

“Yeah. He is.” she said. “He should be pinker by now. And sitting up and taking notice”.

“When did he get the new liver?”

Another intrepid student had dared to speak. Nurses were generally much more approachable and invariably knew more than anyone else about ward life.

“Six days ago. An urgent. He was on the plane that came down on the motorway.”

“Thank you, nurse. I’ll take it from here.”

Garth was back and everyone retreated into silent obeisance. He was scrutinising Carlos’ notes.

“His colour isn’t good. Too yellow. Hmmm. Surgery was six days ago. Where are his most recent blood test results?”

The nurse silently pointed them out on the chart and he sniffed.

“Abnormal. Well, I’m not surprised judging by the colour of him. I’ll arrange an ultrasound and er, er, an urgent CT angiogram if necessary. We need to watch him very carefully. It looks to me as if the new liver is failing.”

Tiger Lily on the other hand was thriving. Pink cheeked with health and pleasure she was now on Ladies Surgical in a bed beside the window with a view of the sky, the third tower and, if she peered downwards, a small courtyard with one tree valiantly pressing the cause of nature in the face of overwhelming urbanisation. The curtains were open and the brisk, wide-eyed morning made the internal lights look old and tired. Her bed was a riot of colour and untidiness to the despair of the nurses and the amusement of those doing ward rounds who read her cards and ate her home-made fudge with enthusiasm. Fern made the fudge, brought in the cards, tissues, books, MP3 player, hand lotion, elderflower cordial, wet wipes, fruit, trail mix, magazines, beginner's guide to knitting kit, clean clothes and endless laughter. Flowers were not allowed as the pollen interfered with the sterile ventilation system otherwise the bed would have resembled the wild card entry at the Chelsea Flower Show. She radiated love. Tiger Lily - Tilly - was her life. Her whole world, beginning, middle and without end. Now and forever. Amen.

When it had looked as if Tilly might die Fern had resolved to fight. She had coaxed, shouted, cried, mortgaged and argued her way into the Avastin drug trials for her beloved and miraculously, the tumours had been reduced enough for Alex Whiteley's surgical intervention. That crazy man had agreed to operate when everyone else had refused, fearing uncertain outcomes and dangerously high risks. And now here was Tiger Lily, almost ready to go home. The staples in her abdomen would be removed by the community nurse on one of her daily visits. Fern had plans for those staples. Until then, Tilly's movement would be restricted but at least she could get out of bed, walk to the shared bathroom, sit up - with difficulty - kiss and be kissed. The day she had announced that she would scream if her hair wasn't washed had reduced Fern to tears. Tilly was always in a foul mood if she had dirty hair and usually washed it in the shower every morning. She was getting back to normal. She would soon be her usual obnoxious, adorable, intense self.

"No! I'll do it!"

Fern screeched as Tiger Lily tried to lean over towards the table on wheels beside the bed for a tissue. The three other women in the ward ignored the noise; they were getting used to it.

"I can do it myself!"

Tiger Lily hated the fuss. She glared at her spiky-haired, short-legged lover in shapeless trousers and yesterday's T-shirt, saw her exhaustion and climbed down.

"Sorry. Yes, please, you do it. Thanks."

Fern beamed, handed her the tissue, and kissed her on the mouth.

"Welcome back. Can't wait to get you home."

In ICU Carlos was semi-conscious with his eyes half closed against the stark lights. Not actually sitting up, he was propped vaguely upright by pillows resting against the raised top half of the remote-controlled bed that minutely vibrated to prevent bed sores for inert occupants. He had been extubated but looked little better than before. Perhaps worse because now he could remember his illness, distended abdomen and loneliness. He gazed in soft focus through his partially closed eyelids. There was a motley collection of what looked like medical students and more senior doctors standing at the foot of his bed but none of them seemed to notice him. They were ignoring him. Why? What was so terrible that they dared not acknowledge him?

There was a good-looking, dark-haired man in a suit who seemed to be in charge and was speaking with loud authority as the others listened. Some had notebooks in which they were ostentatiously scribbling while the ward sister and his own designated nurse watched. Those two he recognised but had no idea what they were called. Shouldn't they be taking notes too? He was obviously very ill and his treatment had to be complex, important, critical even. Why else would they be taking notes?

"A CT scan has confirmed a hepatic artery blood clot after an, er, liver transplant six days ago. We're going to have to, er, open him up and replace the liver which is starved of blood. He's been relisted as super urgent. James, you were at the, um, first transplant?"

The dark-haired man was now addressing a younger man dressed in a limp check shirt with a stethoscope snake round his neck.

"Aye, Mr Mahendran. An intimal tear made the arterial connection very difficult. It took Mr Whiteley several attempts to establish the blood flow."

Carlos listened as intently as his opioid painkillers permitted. He recognised the name of the surgeon who had given him the new liver but what was this about a tear? He strove, unsuccessfully, to fully open his eyes and focus on this chap with the soft, Scottish voice.

Mr Mahendran was off again.

"It is most unfortunate that despite the er, heroic efforts of Mr Whiteley, our er, illustrious head of department, it appears that this patient ... " he consulted his notes and glanced up at the smeary whiteboard above Carlos' head, "Carlos Cardoso, aged 43, remains critically ill. Hmmm. I intend to perform a second transplant therefore, as soon as a liver becomes available. He is at least in a more stable condition than when first admitted and for that we must, um, thank Mr Whiteley. The patient has been designated as a super urgent case so will qualify for the next available donor organ and take precedence over everyone else on the sadly extensive waiting list. Donor organs, as you know", this was directed at the students hanging onto his every word, "are in extremely short supply. Sadly, most people don't even make it to the waiting list before they er, die. It's a very topical debate that you would do well to study before your exams."

The students all nodded vigorously as they noted this down.

"Anyone who wishes to watch the transplant procedure when it occurs would, er, be well advised to do so. When it will happen of course, is unknown and depends on the availability of a donor organ. That, in itself, represents a tragedy for someone else but, as physicians, you will have to accustom yourselves to the close proximity of life and death. It's something you may, er, encounter on a daily basis. Be prepared for it."

The students all nodded, sagely, and were suitably sombre. No one ever argued with Mr Mahendran, especially when he was on an ethical soap box. They would all be present at the transplant procedure whenever it occurred though, knowing full well that the suggestion that had been made was not so much an invitation as an instruction.

"James, I'd like you to, er, assist."

Another instruction to be accepted with overt gratitude.

"Thank you, Mr Mahendran. Of course."

James would go far, with or without a girl-friend.

By now, exhausted by the effort of concentration and the attempt to understand what was happening, Carlos had slumped into another dreamless Tramadol-induced slumber so did not hear the conversation between the consultant and the ward sister.

"We'll need the consent form signed for the second transplant, Sister. Obviously, he's in no fit state at the moment. Let's wait until he's awake and I'll come and see him. Explain what's going on, preferably in the presence of someone close to him. Does he have a wife or partner or, er, someone?"

"There doesn't seem to be anyone. He's had no visitors or calls, except from the medical insurance company to check on his progress and I don't think that counts."

Garth looked surprised.

"No family?"

"There's a nephew but the contact details are incorrect. The insurance people are on to it but so far, no luck."

"That's a shame."

Garth meant it.

"Well, I'll have to come back when he's sitting up and taking notice. Let me know as soon as he is. There's no knowing when a donor liver may come in."

CHAPTER FOURTEEN

The same day, the same city but a different world. The real one, outside the hospital.

Jason was pushing Meghan in a wheelchair along the park's grey paths while Jack dribbled his football alongside on the scratchy grass. Meghan was silent and inert but watching and listening. The extreme sensitivity of her body had distorted her heightened senses. Above her she could hear the clouds moving and taste the noise of the wind as it rocked the leaves of the wrinkled elephant skinned oaks. Their voices were louder than those of the people around her, the dogs barking, the excitement, the pleasure and laughter of a summer afternoon in an overcrowded city forgetting its cares. Over her legs the fleecy blanket was soft and quiet, gentle where it enfolded her pain, as if trying to smooth it away.

Jason took such good care of her. What would he do when she had gone? Would Jack remember her as anything more than an invalid? She listened to the trees talking to each other in breathy ancient voices, an eternal lullaby sung over time but heard only by those who knew it was soon to be over. She sighed, exhausted by her life. Disappointment was bearable; it was the hope that was killing her.

The wheelchair momentarily halted then plunged forward as

Jason kicked the football to his son.

"C'mon Jack! See if you can get that!"

Skinny legs and elastic knees in shorts took off in pursuit of the scuffed football, blocked it and thudded it back towards the wheelchair which it just missed.

"Gooooaaal!"

Jack roared and set off after it. Jason leaned over his wife's shoulder to speak to her as he pushed.

"He's good, isn't he? Be playin' for Cardiff City before y'know it."

A pause.

"You OK, Meggie?"

Another pause, then the slightest of nods from Meghan, too ill to speak. Everything was so difficult, so exhausting, such an effort. She closed her sunken eyes to better cope with her husband's forced enthusiasm.

"We could get a dog when you're better. What about a sheepdog to keep Jack in line? A Welsh Collie'd be nice, like you had when you were a kid."

Meghan tried to smile. Jason never gave up.

"It'll happen, sweetheart. When you least expect it. There'll be a phone call and we'll have you in and better in no time. Don't give up. Me and Jack, we need you. We love you, annlwyd."

It was a good thing that he was behind her and could not see her tears.

CHAPTER FIFTEEN

Two Days Later

Theatre number three again, with a different team, an entirely different atmosphere but the same patient.

Carlos had already signed the consent form and when the donor liver had been delivered by special organ courier just a few hours earlier, had only to be informed and prepped before he was ready for his second transplant. He had been incredibly lucky in that a viable organ had become available. One man's luck; another family's loss. Timing was everything, the essence of comedy and tragedy.

Garth was leading the surgery assisted by James, as ordered. The other members of the operating cast were well used to Mr Mahendran's methodical, careful methods but for James this was a new experience and he was a little nervous. All senior consultant surgeons had their own modus operandi and Garth had a reputation for severity. There was very little conversation as such over the table but a constant, analytical, mostly running commentary – Garth occasionally stuttered self-consciously - about the procedure for the benefit of the huddle of students on the platform behind the action. James felt self-conscious and exposed: gladiatorial, a spectacle in an amphitheatre. Over his mask Mr Mahendran, as he liked to be called by less senior doctors, even in private, was scrutinising the abdomen pinned open before him. Other than his voice and the reassuring hum of the monitors and machinery, it was very quiet. Before the procedure had started, he had asked the Consultant Anaesthetist if she would like music on in the background or not. Rather endearing, old-fashioned courtesy James had thought. Dr Voss – another one who did not encourage first name usage between senior and junior staff – had been very definite about not having any music whatsoever anywhere near the theatre: she could not abide it.

"An unnecessary distraction and flippant" she had stated in a tone of voice that ruled rather than reasoned and Mr Mahendran, whom she alone called Garth in their hearing, had acceded without demur. He had seemed more than happy to oblige, which struck James as considerate and solicitous. Perhaps he wouldn't be too severe after all. He'd ask around. Discreetly. Rumour had it that Garth sometimes lacked confidence in theatre which caused a kind of well=behaved panic. He glanced up at him to see if he had noticed but Garth was engrossed in a particularly resistant piece of ligament, so that was OK. James looked round the room and met the fixed, questioning eyes of Dr Voss who saw everything. She could overhear ten conversations in a room at once. He dropped his gaze back to the table and felt himself go hot and shiver at the same time. Then it was up to him to detach the ligament, so he forgot about her.

Julia had watched the young man with pretensions to surgery and had not been impressed. His focus had wavered, only for a moment, but that was all it took. Fortunately, Garth was in control. Yes, he would make an effective head of department – much better than Alex bloody Whiteley. She criticised Garth for being indecisive but that had to be preferable to the current overbearing autocracy. God! Anyone would think that

Whiteley was the Medical Director himself. His abuse of power was scandalous.

Their current Medical Director was a friend of Garth's, Hari Shah; they had gone through Med. School together. Oh my God! Did Alex Whiteley have ambitions in that direction? The idea of him as her line manager and on the board of the hospital trust pinched her throat and she gagged.

"Everything alright, Julia?"

Garth was peering at her over his mask; liquid eyes.

"Fine, thank you. Tickly throat."

"It's the chemical atmosphere. A glass of water for Dr Voss, please."

The runner obliged. Would a paper cup be acceptable to Dr Voss? Yes, it would have to do. A gracious thank you as she was handed the water and the procedure continued.

Julia had taken great care with her appearance that morning. There was nothing contrived or artificial about her carefully arranged natural look, the light make up and tidy 'just swept back' hair twisted into a sophisticated chignon in the nape of her neck. Useful too, as the strings of the mask did not interfere with it while her patrician profile was displayed to advantage. Well-arched brows heralded deep-lashed blue eyes beneath, a legacy from her father along with the nose and the trust fund. She and Garth were a handsome couple. It was a pity that they had to keep it to themselves, but that would change.

She listened to him describing his actions as he probed tentatively and meticulously towards the failing liver. He tended to stutter when performing before an audience due not to nerves but an anxiety to be correct, beyond all possible dispute.

"Fortunately, this is an, er, unusual occurrence and this patient has been extremely lucky to find a second donor in such a short time. I am now about to expose the first donor liver which I fully expect to present as markedly discoloured and patchy due to the blood clot. It will also be, er, considerably enlarged. An image would be a useful so I think we'll have a picture of it."

He signalled to the runner who had fetched Julia's water and she went to the side of the room and fetched his smartphone, well used to Mr Mahendran's fondness for photographing items of surgical and medical interest, oblivious to the rules of consent. He had built up quite a collection over the years. Apparently, he planned to write papers for erudite journals and would publish the images to illustrate the more complex points. Once, she had inadvertently scrolled into his photo archive and had been astonished at the complete absence of personal pictures – no wife, children, pets; nothing. Such dedication seemed weird to her but hey, he was the senior consultant and she was just a runner.

"Thank you" he said to her. "We'll have a close-up photo of it, please. Lean over from the other side. That's it. James'll move aside."

James sidled to his left as Garth and the camera lens peered into Carlos' gaping abdomen.

"Here we are and, as I predicted … "

Garth stopped. There was a sudden silence. Nothing moved, not even the camera shutter.

Garth was staring at the liver, frozen, speechless. Everyone else was staring at him.

"What is it?"

Julia spoke for them all. Garth slowly raised his head and looked at her. Still, he said nothing.

"Garth, what is it?"

Julia's voice had risen in tone and her alarm was close behind.

"Look!"

Garth pointed at the liver and they all leant over into the confined space to see. Julia stood up for a better view and almost rested her elbows on Carlos' prone body as she stretched forward down the table. The observing students craned and contorted themselves to try and see ... what?

On the right lobe of the liver two letters about 1 cm high were just visible, a little uneven and discoloured, but unmistakeably forming the outlines of an A and a W. Julia's eyes were wide with wonder and disbelief. She looked at her lover then, with astonishment in her voice, exclaimed out loud,

"He's put his fucking initials on it."

No one spoke but Julia.

"Photograph it" she told the runner.

CHAPTER SIXTEEN

Later the Same day

Hari Shah was 49 but there were days when he felt twice that. Days when he mistook the dark eyed, balding man in the bathroom mirror for his father. However, once dressed in one of his eye-dark sharp suits that passed for bespoke, he again inhabited his own skin and felt he could front the world. Slight, energetic and lithe minded, he liked to charm his way ahead - ruthless, but never impolite.

This medical directorship was something of a poisoned chalice and there were times when he heartily regretted having fought so hard for the post. The aluminium plate outside his opaque glass office door confirmed that he was, indeed, the Deputy Chief Executive Officer, whether he felt like it or just Hari the Cardiologist - the physician, who enjoyed his clinical work more than any other aspect of his current role. Besides, it helped him liaise with the real life of the hospital which gave him an edge in the boardroom. He could link policy to people as well as to white papers, government directives and balance sheets.

The assertive rapping on the door was an unwelcome intrusion. Outrageous nursing overtime costs concealed in full sight on an emailed spreadsheet on the screen in front of him had required two espressos before he could even bear to open them. However, Trust policy was 'my door is always open even when it's closed' so he called

"Come in"

with as much chirpiness as he could muster. On seeing Julia Voss appear in the doorway he felt like cursing.

"Ah! Julia! Come in. Always a pleasure. And Garth! What can I do for you?"

Both were dressed in scrubs which surprised him. Julia particularly. He had never seen her outside theatre in anything but her intimidating executive suits. Garth had never been known for his sartorial prowess, especially at Med. School, but lately he had smartened up Hari had noticed. No bad thing. Perhaps Mariyah had had a word. Lovely woman, Hari's wife. He was a lucky man. Julia was clutching her smartphone like a Faberge egg and had a facial expression that filled Hari with a sense of dread. He hid it.

"Take a seat"

he said jauntily and waved them in the general direction of two chairs on the opposite side of his desk. Garth sat down but Julia pulled her chair right up the edge of the desk, all the better to see him. Hari unconsciously leant back in his swivel chair as she invaded his space, and closed the file on the computer screen. He pushed the mouse to one side and prepared himself.

"What can I do for you?" he asked.

There was a silence, which Hari had not expected, especially from Julia. She and Garth were looking at each other and he could not quite read what they were saying. Garth seemed uncomfortable and ill at ease and Julia appeared to be willing him to speak but he was stubbornly silent. A few seconds passed then Julia spoke in her prim, privately educated voice,

“We have something you must see.”

Hari eyed her quizzically. Then looked at his friend as if for confirmation. Garth avoided his gaze. Leaning over the desk she was already scrolling down her phone until she found an image. It took but a moment so she must have known exactly where to find it. She handed the phone to Hari who studied the photo on the screen.

“What is this?” he asked.

“Exactly what it looks like.”

“A liver?”

Hari was incredulous. What the hell was this? Julia nodded her head in assent but said nothing. Hari studied the image more closely and blinked as if waking up from a deep sleep. He enlarged the image with finger and thumb for a better view.

“With the letters AW on it?”

Julia nodded her head again, more vigorously.

“Where’s it from?”

By now Hari’s sense of dread was overwhelming. But how bad could it be? Julia’s eyebrows were raised as she resisted the inclination to make a facetious reply about the author of the penmanship and merely answered

“Transplant theatre number three. About four hours ago.”

No need to ask whose initials they were. It was about as bad as it could be. Maybe worse.

Hari regarded Garth enquiringly.

“You found it?”

Garth nodded, but he was grim faced. While he could not deny it, he so wished it had not happened; why did it have to be him who exposed it? Julia’s glee was, frankly, distasteful. Alex was his colleague; his boss. It was all so ... unfortunate.

"Um ..."

Garth fixed his eyes on Hari.

"Perhaps we could, er, pretend that we haven't seen it."

"What?" Julia screeched.

Garth kept his eyes on Hari's.

"What are you saying, Garth?"

"We could, er, get rid of it. The photo I mean. Delete it. Then they'll just fade away – the letters I mean, on the er, liver ... "

He faltered and stopped. Julia had moved very close to him.

"What the hell are you thinking?" she hissed. "What's the matter with you?"

"No harm will have been done and he's a good surgeon and well, we've all been there. Haven't we?"

Now Garth dared to look at her.

"No."

Julia moved as sharply away from him as her reply.

"Yes" Hari said, "But we don't get caught. Photographed."

He sighed deeply, blinked, then resigned himself to reality.

"Believe me Garth, there's nothing I'd rather do but we can't. I presume that the photo was taken without patient consent?"

Again, Garth nodded.

"And it has been seen – witnessed – so it can't be expunged. Of course, if you hadn't shown it to me and had deleted it yourself it would be a different story but now, unfortunately, I have no choice but to take appropriate action."

"Unfortunately?" Julia snorted. "Alex Whiteley has committed a crime. You have to take action. For all our sakes. Think of the hospital!"

Garth sighed and watched Hari's reaction. He appeared to be in a state of shock. The landline on his desk started ringing and at first, he ignored it as he stared at the image on the phone, and then at Julia. Suddenly he seized the receiver, shouted "Not now", slammed it down and galvanised himself into the action of which he had spoken.

"Email it to me" he ordered Garth, devoid of all geniality, "and give me a full written report. Today."

Then, more politely, "What about the patient?"

Julia replied.

"Garth successfully completed the transplant and he should be out of recovery and in ICU by now." Garth nodded in agreement and added,

"Yes. No problems, er, apart from ..."

"Quite."

Hari was the Medical Director and Deputy CEO once more.

"You'd better go and get changed. I'll be in touch."

They were dismissed and got up to leave. As they were crossing the floor to the door Hari called after them

"I want all the details. Names, witnesses, times. The lot. Report and photograph by the end of today. Please." He punched out the last word like a bullet into a corpse.

As soon as door shut behind them Hari contorted his face into a silent howl as he threw his head back and inhaled deeply. Then he exhaled himself back into role, pursed his lips and reached for the mouse. One click, the screen activated, the cursor danced and the train started to roll out of the station.

CHAPTER SEVENTEEN

Tiger Lily's departure had become a royal progress. In her wheelchair of state she was paraded along the corridors towards the main exit, waving and smiling, saying little but enjoying the attention. Fern was propelling the chair like a thoroughbred, proud, prancing, eyes shining. Following behind was a retinue of one nurse and a porter laden with the accumulated paraphernalia of a fortnight in hospital. Who knew there could be so much? He longed for days of yore when he could have accepted a tip.

Fern was loud and talkative, chatting to her Tilly and anyone else she encountered. It was clearly superfluous to explain that they were on their way home but that did not stop her sharing the great news. Hari was waiting outside the lift doors on the ground floor when they emerged. He used his hand to block the door's sensor mechanism so that they had enough time to tumble themselves out into the main concourse. It was impossible not to smile; everyone was watching, sentimentally oohing and clucking as if Tiger Lily was a baby in a pram on her first public outing. Hari smiled, in spite of the cold weight in his stomach as he stepped into the empty lift behind them and pressed the button for the first floor. The management floor. He had rung ahead and was expected. The Chief Executive Officer of the Midland Central Hospital NHS Trust had cleared her diary and was waiting.

In her glass-sided corner office, the only air-conditioned office in the building, Patricia Shelton was indeed waiting. It was not often that she received a call so serious that her PA had to rearrange her appointments but Hari had been insistent, even though he absolutely refused to explain why over the phone. He was an intelligent, shrewd man and she trusted his judgment. There were few enough people, especially men, that you could say that about. It wasn't that by nature she was suspicious; she spoke from the experience of having been repeatedly shafted by men as she had climbed the management ladder. Well. Here she was, she thought as she surveyed the main hospital through one glass wall and the competitor Trust Women's Hospital through the other. It was her name on the door, her portrait on the wall, her smiling image in the photographs of eminent politicians and dignitaries coyly distributed around the room to impress and remind. She was indisputably in charge and what was more, in control.

She glanced at her expensively discreet watch, an impromptu present from her husband (what had he done this time?) and moved towards her over-sized desk. Hari would be here in about a minute. As she sat down she, as ever, smiled at the wallpaper on her computer screen. Yes, there she was, standing outside the main entrance of the hospital shaking hands with Tony Blair. Patricia – Pat to only a carefully chosen few – and David, her husband, had entertained the Blairs a few times.

Not many people in the hospital seemed aware that she was married. She had always worked under her maiden name and remained discreet about her political connections, not to mention the fortune her husband had made in road haulage. It did not do to flaunt one's wealth so she rarely wore jewellery other than quietly costly stud earrings, the plain watch and a platinum wedding band that looked like silver. And never pearls.

She struggled with her weight and her propensity to plumpness was irksome. Fortunately, she could afford to dress in high end suits in dark colours with long jackets that covered her hips and created an impression of slenderness. She also wore elegant shoes with slightly too high pencil heels to boost her height and confidence. Often her feet ached at the end of the day but that was a small sacrifice for the elegant superiority it gave her over men in flat shoes and medics in unsightly crocs. Really, the money she spent on achieving such an imposingly humble exterior was worth every penny. Impressions counted for so much, especially if you were a woman.

She was smoothing down her jacket when Hari knocked at the door and entered the office, even as she was inviting him to come in. On this occasion she did not object. He walked across the carpeted floor to one of the wood and steel chairs in front of her desk, sat down, stood up briefly as he pulled it closer to the desk, sank heavily into it and leaned forward.

"What's going on, Hari? This is all very cloak and dagger. Should I be worried?"

"Yes. Have you checked your emails recently?" She looked at him as she clicked the mouse and brought up her inbox.

"From you?"

"Yes. I've sent you an image."

She was intrigued. An image? Of what?

It took a second to download and then appeared, filling the screen. She stared at it. Then she stared at Hari.

"What is this?"

She was incredulous.

"It's a liver. And yes, before you ask, those are letters on it. They're initials. Made with argon gas during a transplant operation by, obviously, A.W."

Hari hardly dared look at her as he spoke.

"A.W."?

"Yes."

"Alex Whiteley?"

"Yes."

"Our Head of Liver and Upper Gastrointestinal Department?"

"Yes".

Patricia continued to stare at the screen, deadpan, to disguise her escalating emotions.

How should she react?

With the first rule of tactics - when in doubt, throw it back.

"What do you propose to do?" she asked.

Hari responded at once, a little too quickly, desperate not to assume any responsibility.

"I think that is up to you and the Board" he said.

He was right and she knew it. Damn. Fine. So be it.

"He'll have to be suspended of course."

"Yes".

She wished Hari would stop saying yes; it was becoming irritating.

"There will have to be an inquiry."

"Yes."

She glared at him.

"And a disciplinary hearing."

"Yes, I know."

Patricia was genuinely perplexed.

"What was Alex thinking of? He's an excellent surgeon. The MCH Liver and UG department has an international reputation. He's at the top of his game. Why would he do such a thing?"

Hari replied as a doctor rather than an executive.

"Well, he'd been operating for hours and was tired. It was an extremely difficult procedure. There are mitigating circumstances – stress, cognitive overload … "

But before he could finish Patricia flashed back with venom,

"I don't care. He shouldn't have done it. No one else does."

Hari twisted uncomfortably in his angular chair and looked at the wall.

"Do they?" insisted Patricia.

"Well, it's not unknown. I know of at least one French surgeon who did. Ophthalmic surgeons use lasers to sign their initials on retinas and Orthopaedics sign the cement after hip replacements. You remember Jack Belton, Alex's mentor and trainer, recently retired? He's been known to play noughts and crosses on a liver while waiting for the swab count. Transplant surgeons are required to test the site area with the ABC. The Argon Beam Coagulator" he explained for the CEO who clearly had no idea what he was talking about. She continued to carve him with her gaze. "They have to test it before they can use it. Most surgeons have a trademark series of test dots."

Patricia raised her eyebrows, challenging, daring him to go on. He flung himself over the cliff.

"No harm is done and the marks fade quickly as the liver heals".

"Dots" she spat. "Not initials. And this is the NHS, not France. Or an amusement arcade." she added sourly. "So, because the liver didn't heal, they didn't fade and now we know all about it? … Does the patient know?"

Hari shook his head. "No. Not yet."

"Then you had better tell him. As soon as possible."

There was an awkward silence as Hari hesitated before he spoke.

"Does he have to know? No harm was done."

Patricia's fury was barely concealed.

"We are bound by a Duty of Candour, Hari, as you well know. We have no choice. Remember Stafford? What Alex has done is bad enough without making it into an even bigger scandal by trying to suppress it. And anyway, that never works. There's always some chancer who'll leak a story like this if they think they've got something to gain. Julia Voss for one. She's just the sort who'd go to the press and then the GMC will be all over it - and you."

Hari was ashen. She pushed the knife in further.

"How do we know he hasn't done this before? And then there's the question of the photograph."

Hari looked puzzled. She was exasperated.

"Think about it, Hari. Data protection! The liver was photographed on a personal mobile without the patient's consent. Is that legal? Justifiable? Or a breach of inviolable patient privacy? Here we are looking at an image of a patient's insides that he knows nothing about and which he certainly hasn't given permission for... I'll have to get the Trust lawyers on to it."

For a moment she paused and then she raged.

"Damn! There'll have to be a public statement."

Her cool demeanour had slipped and now slid to the floor.

"The Press are going to crucify us."

"Not us. Him. A.W."

It was small comfort but all Hari had to offer.

CHAPTER EIGHTEEN

Three Days Later

Hari knew he was well paid by NHS standards, but today he was going to earn every penny and still it would not be nearly enough. He had read the report submitted by Garth and Julia which was fulsome, detailed and damning. It was also partial and personal and would have to be completely redrafted before the lawyers got their beaks into it.

So thought Hari as he stood outside the closed door of Carlos' side room on the window side of the Liver and Upper Gastro. ward on the 7th floor. He tapped, reluctantly, quietly, respectfully on the door. Perhaps Mr Cardoso would be asleep, or in the en suite bathroom? Or out? No. Chance would be a fine thing and anyway, where would a patient recovering from a second transplant go?

"Enter!"

Hari breathed in, turned the handle and pushed open the door. It was a lovely room with a panoramic view across the city. Light, modern, decorated in soothing cool colours with none of the forced cheerfulness of the thin curtains on clattering metal rails that failed to provide privacy in the general wards. A flat screen TV eyed the patient from the centre of the wall opposite the bed but could not compete with the view and big skies. Sitting up in a chair beside the window, basking in the summer light flooding through the glass was Carlos, brightly illuminated on one side of his body and deeply shadowed on the other. He looked like the battle between good and evil thought Hari.

"Mr Cardoso?"

"The same."

"I'm Hari Shah, the Medical Director here. Delighted to meet you."

Hari's hand was outstretched and Carlos shook it, languidly, graciously. He did not stand up.

"How are you feeling?"

"Very much better, thank you, Mr Shah. I haven't felt this well for years."

It was true and it showed. Carlos was pink in colour, alert, his eyes were bright and his cheeks had begun to fill out, setting off his enviable facial bone structure. His features were sculptural and chiselled but now softened, which gave him a distinguished sensuality. Ideal for an actor. His agent would have recommended a hair trim but Carlos rather liked the way his fringe draped over his eyes. It had given him the opportunity to adopt an unselfconsciously-conscious habit of brushing the hair to one side to reveal his trademark green-grey eyes. He resisted the temptation to toss his head as he did so though. Such a cliché. His designer stubble was once more that and perfectly suited the 'looks and feels like silk' Paisley dressing gown he was wearing over slate grey pyjamas to match his eyes

"Please, call me Hari."

Carlos nodded his acknowledgement and closed the copy of

'Cloud Atlas' on his lap.

"A little light reading. I find it hard to concentrate at the present moment" he offered apologetically. Picking up a small bottle of Evian from the table beside the bed, he unscrewed the top and took a small, delicate sip.

"It's been quite a time for you, Mr Cardoso."

"It has indeed." Carlos agreed, fervently.

"May I?"

Hari gestured to another chair in the room and made to sit down. Carlos gestured assent with the bottle of Evian before he took another sip and replaced the top. Now that they were both on the same level Hari felt more able, loathe as he was, to continue the conversation.

"I hope you're comfortable in here?"

Carlos looked critically around the room before replying.

"At least I have my own bathroom. And a television, although there is so little worth watching."

Hari did not like to tell him that this was their most luxurious side room and usually reserved for private patients. Carlos had only been moved into it from a general ward because he, as Medical Director, had ordered it so.

"And you are being well looked after?"

Carlos considered.

"No real complaints" he said, "Apart from the food."

Hari smiled wryly; he could not argue with that. Nothing could ever compensate for what the kitchen did to vegetables. There was an uncomfortable silence. Carlos looked expectantly at his visitor. Why was the Medical Director calling on him, and so ingratiatingly? It was flattering of course, and very pleasant, but there must be more to it than that. As if a mind reader, Hari committed suttee.

"Mr Cardoso, there is something I'd like to talk to you about."

Here it comes thought Carlos and sat back in his chair to listen.

Well, it could have been worse thought Hari as he descended in the crowded lift to the first floor. Visiting hour was beginning and the hospital corridors were vibrant with noisy colour. His face was on auto smile as he walked but his mind was on the meeting with Carlos and the report he would have to give to Patricia. She had never invited him to call her Pat.

Mr Cardoso had obviously not taken the news well, which was to be expected, but his general reaction had been rather unexpected. There just hadn't been one. No hysterics or anger or outrage. Just a kind of blank bewilderment that had rendered him speechless. As Hari had left the room Carlos had remained in his chair, clutching his bottle of Evian, breathing heavily (but rhythmically so no respiratory complications to worry about) and pulling at his over-long fringe like the chain on an anchor. As the lift tipped him out onto the first floor Hari wondered whether this was a phoney war, the lull before the storm and whether his pension pot was full enough to enable early retirement.

CHAPTER NINETEEN

Alex had come straight from the ward via a departmental policy meeting to start his afternoon clinic. Not the most exciting part of his day but he enjoyed the interface with (mostly) walking, almost always talking patients. It was a chance to get to know someone before they became a body on the table. Alex used medicine to communicate – a kind of lingua franca – and to overcome a natural reserve that might have surprised his enemies.

It was the afternoon of the week when recent referrals arrived: new people, old problems but sometimes something unusual and unexpected. That frisson of surprise that shortened time and accelerated the pulse. He waved to the receptionists as he strode into the main Liver Outpatient's reception area on the ground floor on the left of the central concourse. The summer sun had filtered down from the high glass roof of the tower and was flirting with shadows and corners, forcing people to blink and squint at the flat screen announcement boards flickering on the walls. It was busy. it was always busy during the day but at night was coffin quiet as life, death and noise were confined to the higher floors. Patients were crowded around the central check-in columns thumping on the touch screens to register their arrival. New patients were recognisable by their tentative fingers and gentle taps which gradually became the thumps of the regulars who knew it was the only way to get a response. Once they were 'in' they sat, a rapt cinema audience, watching for their name on the flat screen which was the signal to move into the next phase – the main Liver Reception area. Only two more steps before the inner sanctum of the Consultant's corridor and the hallowed chambers of the consulting rooms.

Patients had to be just that, thought Alex as he clutched his take-out coffee with compulsory lid (one of the more sensible health and safety directives) and headed for the double doors to waiting rooms A and B. He was almost there when the receptionist called after him.

"Mr Whiteley! Something for you!"

He turned, smiling, and headed back to the desk. The queue parted as he approached one of the windows and peered in. The overweight receptionist was bending down behind the counter and then reappeared, red and a little flustered, holding a small parcel in gaudy wrapping paper sellotaped to an oversize card. She passed it to him through the window.

"Another conquest, Mr W!" she joked. The admin. staff liked Mr W. He valued them and even said thank you. They knew it was probably his wife behind the tins of sweets at Christmas but he still got the credit.

"You're always first in my heart" he responded and she laughed at the blatant insincerity. The waiting patients loved it too. What a nice man you could hear them thinking, and him a consultant!

"Aren't you going to open it?" the receptionist asked.

"For you, anything." Alex winked. He put his coffee on the

counter, the patients moved to one side for a better view and he carefully peeled the Sellotape away from the parcel to detach it from the card.

“Card or present first?” he asked his audience. Medicine is such a performance he thought as he spoke.

“Present!”

Of course. Always the present. He probed the parcel for an unobtrusive opening and expertly lifted a flap of paper from each end. Maximum access, minimum damage. Just like surgery. Inside was a Superman tie, blue, red, gaudy and so in your face that Alex loved it. He held it up for general inspection.

“Another grateful patient!” the receptionist said as he was opening the envelope of the card then reading its contents.

“A lovely lady and her partner” replied Alex, visibly touched. It was from Tiger Lily and Fern.

“I’ll wear it now”.

His existing tie was already unknotted and sliding from under his collar. Superman was immediately settled medallion-like on Alex’s chest.

“There!”

Everyone tittered, a few applauded and someone wolf whistled as Alex beamed as broadly as his chest and surveyed the room for further approbation. He spotted James emerging through the main doors.

“James! Look what our lovely Avastin drug trial lady with the colonic resection has given me! By rights it belongs to you as well. Perhaps we should have a rota for wearing it!”

James was taken aback. The rumours circulating about him were prolific and shocking. It was said he had branded a donor liver during a transplant in which he, James, had been present. Yet James had seen nothing and persistently said so, except no one seemed to believe him. He shifted his expression to one of polite pleasure and laughed, a little awkwardly.

"Aye. Very smart, Mr Whiteley."

He almost said, "It suits you" but the recollection of the gossip and rumours about the 'branding' as it was becoming known strangled the comment before it was born. Alex noticed his awkwardness and put it down to either public embarrassment or problems with that pink haired registrar with whom James was known to be infatuated. An unlikely pairing but he'd seen stranger. James ostentatiously looked at his watch, made an 'if I don't go now, I'll be late' face and moved on towards the double doors.

Alex took the hint, picked up the card, coffee, wrapping paper and old tie and set off in the same direction. He had taken no more than one step when his pager went off like a gun in his pocket, insistent and urgent. He read its message and his face changed. The smile died. Without looking up or uttering a word, he changed direction and left the room the way he had come in, still striding but head down, eyes focussed on his inner thoughts.

CHAPTER TWENTY

Patricia sat at her desk and read through the fifth and what she hoped was the final draft of the Press Statement. The Communications Department were effective up to a point but this was way out of their aegis and they seemed to have no understanding of the extreme sensitivity of the issue. In the end she had assumed the responsibility for writing it herself; it would be released in her name anyway so she might as well put words into her own mouth. At least she would know it was properly written.

The statement was due to be released at 1.00 pm, and she was dreading it. She was almost ashamed to admit, even to herself, that when she awoke that morning to the dulcet tones of the Today programme she had been hoping for an international tragedy, a terrorist outrage, some appalling climatic event, the gruesome death of an A lister – anything that might detract from the impact she feared the announcement about Alex Whiteley would have on the reputation of her hospital. It was not so much her career she feared for, although that was a serious consideration, but she felt a huge responsibility to the Trust of which she was the CEO. Then there were all the implications for the NHS, the medical profession, medical ethics, her Queen's birthday honours nomination.

Pointlessly she asked herself, yet again, why the hell he had done it? And on her watch? When he had arrived at her office yesterday, he had seemed genuinely amazed by the allegations. She had shown him the report that was to form the basis of an inquiry and inevitable disciplinary hearing; it was a much more anodyne, objective version of the original submitted by Garth and Julia but was still, nevertheless, damning and derisory. Hell! He had even said he did not remember doing it! Well, he certainly could not deny that they were his initials and clearly no one else had done it. Was he in denial? Senile? Lying? She really had no idea and that added to her irritation. She was not a woman who liked mysteries and conundrums unless they were of her making and she had access to all the answers.

The Director of Communications had suggested that the statement be strategically leaked to a sympathetic local reporter before a general press release. It felt a little underhand and she was not convinced of the outcome but it was worth a try. Anything to mitigate the role of the hospital. And the Press reaction to Alex? That, thank God, was not her problem. He was due to arrive at her office as arranged yesterday, in five minutes she noted, looking at the time on the desk top screen before she put it to sleep. The Trust lawyer would arrive any minute now and together they would issue the official notice of suspension. Alex would be escorted from the premises by the lawyer and then the TV reporter would arrive.

A knock on the door, the lawyer presented himself and settled into a chair beside Patricia on her side of the desk, although she remained in the centre. He was uncharacteristically empty-handed as all the paperwork was already on the desk in an unmarked A4 envelope so he fiddled with his cuff links instead. The suspension process would be incisive, brief, decisive. Alex would be expecting it. He was an intelligent man, a strategist, a departmental head and he would have to accept that there was no alternative.

Another knock at the door.

"Come in!"

Alex did so. Smartly suited, as always, with an immaculate white shirt and a dark tie. Thank God for that. When he had arrived yesterday, he had been wearing a ghastly, polyester, gimmicky thing sporting an image of a comic book hero. She did not have children and did not go to the cinema so she could not be sure but it had looked like Superman, or Spiderman or some other such travesty of popular children's literature. Utterly tasteless and so inappropriate. Tacky.

She indicated the chair placed in front of the desk and Alex sat down, as angular and straight backed as the chair. He looked directly at her and then at the lawyer at her side, whom he tacitly acknowledged. They knew each other well, but not today. Patricia cleared her throat and regurgitated a brief, well-rehearsed patter, a little too fast.

"Thank you for coming Mr Whiteley. Following our meeting yesterday and in accordance with the disciplinary procedures of the Midland Central Hospital NHS Trust, the allegations made against you are of a sufficiently serious nature that I have no choice but to suspend you from your post with immediate effect, pending an inquiry and a disciplinary hearing. You will remain suspended on full salary until such time as a full investigation and likely internal disciplinary hearing has taken place and a decision has been made about your future here."

She paused and looked at him, not unkindly.

"Have you anything to say?"

Nothing. Nothing to say.

"Any questions?"

No, none. She stood up, picked up the envelope and handed it to him.

"Your formal, written letter of suspension. The conditions of your suspension are outlined in the accompanying paperwork. There must be no contact with the Press, the hospital or anyone working here. The Midland Central Hospital Trust lawyer will escort you from the building to your car and ensure that you leave the premises immediately."

Again, she paused, then said,

"Thank you for your co-operation, Mr Whiteley."

Now he stood up, turned, went to the door and departed, even more angular and straight backed. The lawyer scuttled after him. When she had seen them leave the room, Patricia sat down and sighed. Eyes focussed on the door she leant down to the right and stealthily opened a lower drawer from which she lifted an open packet of Hobnobs. Sod the diet. She needed a sugar rush. Just time for one before the reporter was due, maybe two if she ate them quickly.

A knock at the door. She almost choked on the wedge of biscuit in her mouth as she attempted to swallow it while gargling "Just a minute" in response. Fortunately, the visitor got the message because she had time to wipe her mouth and clear the crumbs from her suit jacket before a second knock.

"Come in!" she called as the Hobnobs were stuffed into the drawer, the desk was wiped with her hand and the computer screen woken up.

In walked Malcolm Piggott, Midland Eye TV local reporter and health correspondent, short, slim, Middle England, middle of the road. Inclined to wear narrow collared shirts buttoned up to the neck without a tie and unbuttoned jackets with gaudy linings over casual trousers. Very media. He had initially accepted the role of regional health correspondent because his mother had been a radiographer and no one else was interested, but it was turning out to be more rewarding than he had ever expected. Cutbacks in the NHS, suppressed scandals, Stafford, financial mismanagement and now what? If the CEO of the MCH wanted to see him it would be juicy. They had met, briefly, a few months ago at a press conference; it would be interesting to see if she remembered him.

"Mr Piggott? Thank you for making time to see me. I know how busy you are. We've already met, I think? Briefly, a little while ago, at a press conference."

So, she did remember him, or at least had been reminded that she did. He smiled, but not in greeting.

"Please, call me Malcolm."

"Thank you, Malcolm."

He noticed she did not ask him to call her Patricia. He was silent and wondered if she would offer coffee and biscuits; she obviously had some as there were crumbs on her shirt. "You're probably wondering what all this is about."

He raised one eyebrow, as he had taught himself to do in the bathroom mirror.

"I'll get straight to the point. The hospital will be issuing a Press Release later today about one of our consultants and I wanted to give you the heads up about it before it goes public, as it were. I believe that the relationship between the hospital and the local media is so important, don't you?"

She did not wait for an answer.

"So many of our patients watch Midland Eye Television and listen to local radio we want to be sure that they get only the most up to date and accurate information about anything that might be of interest to them about their hospital."

She stressed the 'their'.

"We want only the very best for all our patients and the people we serve."

Cut the crap and get to the point he thought.

"And that is where I come in?" he offered.

"Well, yes."

She was taken aback. He was more astute than she had anticipated. The Communications Director had said that he was a pedestrian reporter - steady but uninspired. He had been passed over for promotion too often for his career to ever really take off so was now a provincial time server and could be regarded as a safe bet: feed him the info and he'll not stray far from the fold she had been told.

"Yes." she said, reassuring herself.

"I hope that, purely in the interests of the hospital you understand, we can work closely together on this. The Press Release will be available for the 1.00 pm regional news but I would like you to have sight of it before then and break the story on our behalf. It is essential to ensure that the public do not receive inaccurate or misleading information which might lead to misunderstanding and over reaction."

Malcolm was intrigued.

"What has happened?" he asked.

The hairs in his nostrils quivered with a percolating stench of scandal but his face was controlled. Important not to look too keen or she might not follow through and he wanted this story. Badly; he felt a thrill in his loins. Patricia sighed, but said nothing, then opened a drawer to her right and pulled out an A4 envelope.

"This is a hard copy of the Press Release. The hospital Communications Department have got an email for you with the same information that they will send if you are happy to break the story for us. However - "Always an 'however' - he thought. Never mind. He'd agree to any amount of howevers on this one and then do it the way he wanted. There'd be nothing in writing and this was only a conversation that both of them would, and could, deny if necessary. He raised the eyebrow again and she continued,

"I would like to think that the Hospital Trust and your good self could work together on this one to present the matter in the most, er, professional, acceptable light for the reputation of the MCH and the good of its patients and staff. The consultant concerned has been suspended and what he has alleged to have done has yet to be proved, of course, but there is absolutely no cause for public concern."

By now Malcolm could bear it no longer.

"What has he done? Who is it?"

Patricia went for the jugular.

"Alexander Whiteley. Head of the Liver Department. Accused of marking his initials on a donor organ during a transplant operation."

Malcolm's eyebrows raised themselves far up into his forehead. He reached for the envelope.

CHAPTER TWENTY-ONE

Tiger Lily screamed. Fern heard from the kitchen, dropped the newly filled teapot and hurtled into the cluttered stuffy living room.

"Tilly! What's the matter? Are you ill? Where does it hurt?"

Tiger Lily did not reply but pointed hysterically at the television screen. Fern looked, and gaped. Alex Whiteley's face filled the large flat screen as Malcom's voiceover reverberated around the room. Tilly was holding the remote in her hand and had turned the volume up, very loud; there could be no doubt about what was being said, but surely it could not be true?

"The initials A.W. were spotted by a colleague in follow up surgery. Experts say that the argon gas allegedly used by the surgeon to make the marks would leave superficial burns but cause no lasting damage. However, that is small consolation to all those who have been operated on by Alex Whiteley and now fear that they have been branded in the same way."

"Branded!" screeched Fern.

"I couldn't care less!"

Tiger Lily shouted at the screen.

"He could have written his life story on me for all I care! I'd be dead if it wasn't for him."

She was crying, hot with anger and pain and fear. Alex's face had vanished from the screen which now displayed Malcolm, looking conscientious and buttoned up, his clear-cut vowels mutilating Alex Whiteley's name, reputation and career.

"In a statement from the hospital, the patient, who cannot be named for legal reasons, is said to be profoundly distressed by the allegation. The hospital has promised a full inquiry and is keen to reassure all their patients of their very high standard of care. The Chief Executive Officer of the Midland Central Hospital Trust, Patricia Shelton, has said that there is no cause for alarm but that if any patients have concerns, they should contact the hospital directly."

In her office at MCH, Patricia Shelton was also screeching.

"He said branded! He said fucking branded! How dare he!"

She was incandescent.

"That's exactly what we wanted to avoid. Now all hell will break loose."

She slammed her hand onto the receiver of the landline on her desk, picked it up and screamed into it.

"Get me the Communications Director. Now."

Too late. The damage was done. The genie was out of the bottle and already halfway around the world.

CHAPTER TWENTY-TWO

Patricia wanted to preserve an air of normality in the hospital so Garth was immediately appointed Acting Head of Department. It did not work.

All the staff and many of the patients were absorbed with the scandal and speculation. Those who subscribed to the hospital TV had seen Malcolm's broadcast and the word had spread. It went around the wards on the lunch trays; whispered through the ventilation system; followed wheel chairs and trolleys; was injected, scanned and x-rayed, infiltrating even lead-lined cubicles and isolation units. It was prayed over in the chapel and even heard in the morgue. Nurses dispensed gossip with drugs and drips; auxiliaries served out speculation with every replenished water jug. Once visiting hour started the feeding frenzy was renewed and reinvigorated.

Only Carlos, cocooned in his side room was unaware of the commotion: the eye of the storm. Julia had a view about that and made it very clear to Garth almost as soon as his promotion had been announced. She had called him on his mobile to congratulate him but found herself tackling his weakness in Hari's office over the photograph. Delete it! What had he been thinking of? Doubts about him would not be ignored but they could be shelved, for the moment.

They would celebrate that evening, wouldn't they? Garth had agreed. His wife had been planning a family dinner but he would ask her to postpone it until the weekend, blaming pressure of work in his new-found role. Julia was talking about Carlos:

"He's the victim and has a right to know."

Garth had protested as vehemently as he dared,

"He isn't supposed to know until he's officially informed. No one is supposed to know. He has to be protected - from all the fuss. The media ... "

"Yes, yes. Of course. I know that. But there are ways round it. Get someone to turn his TV on so he can see for himself. Say it's a perk of a side room of something that he gets free TV. You'll think of something. You're Head of Department now, so what you say goes."

"Acting Head ..."

She did not listen.

"We'll meet this evening. 7.00pm. Don't be late."

So, the Ward Sister had been instructed to ensure that Mr Cardoso had access to complementary television viewing and when his lunch was being cleared, the TV was turned on. The remote was left slightly out of reach so Carlos, who still found it painful to walk and preferred to sit in his chair or propped up in bed, found himself eye to eye with the local news channel. It was only a matter of minutes before he was witnessing his suffering in technicolour surround sound. By teatime he would be able to see it on every channel and network, hear it on every radio wave band and read about it on the internet. Within 24 hours he would be able to follow his story in the local, national and international Press. He had become a global sensation. He had gone viral, but no one knew his name. The words "Alex" and "Whiteley" however, remained the same in every language across the globe and for that, Carlos would never forgive him.

Carlos was profoundly distressed the first time he watched the media coverage. That distress multiplied and grew with every subsequent newsreel. The onscreen depiction of what had happened to him articulated the horror, pain and outrage of the experience and it became tangible. Reality. He was the innocent victim of a malicious outrage. No wonder the first liver had failed! He could have died. It was attempted murder!

A crime had been committed and he, He, was the innocent victim. Helpless, unconscious, in the hands of a power crazed egomaniac wielding a knife. A surgeon! A doctor! Someone who was supposed to heal and cure, not mutilate and kill. He had been branded like an animal – had had the initials of a madman burned on his body. It was a miracle that he was alive. My God!

He was traumatised; how would he ever recover? He clasped his fringe and clutched at the bottle of Evian always kept within reach. As he sipped tragically from the bottle – he did not trust the hospital water and you never knew what might be on the ghastly plastic cups provided – he considered his position and the important question of how best to present himself in it? He had a huge potential audience, the role of a lifetime. He would not always be anonymous. As the coverage went round and round on the loop he watched, listened and watched again.

CHAPTER TWENTY-THREE

James sat alone at a small table in the canteen contemplating a cheese and pickle sandwich. He was hungry but was doubtful about the pickle. However the coffee should be okay. Hot enough to hide the taste. He bit off a small corner of the sandwich while he waited for coffee to cool a little.

"May I join you?"

It was Hari Shah. The Medical Director. Known to occasionally prowl public areas like the canteen, always with a motive. He had a coffee in his hand and was already sitting down. James could only nod with a mouth full of food and try not to look surprised.

"Busy day?"

James nodded again. There were empty tables elsewhere so why choose to sit here? He and Hari had met before, briefly, formally. James had no idea that the MD even knew who he was but no prizes for guessing why he had sought him out.

Hari wasted no time. Alex Whiteley's disciplinary hearing was coming up and it was important that James was prepared. Not that this little chat was in any way an attempt to influence what he might say – God forbid – but as the MD, Hari wanted to be sure that James was fully briefed about the proceedings. For his own sake. All he had to do was tell the truth.

James had abandoned his sandwich and was studying his coffee.

"I didn't see anything. I was sorting out the biopsy sample and didn't see anything. That's the truth." Now he looked up and looked the MD in the eye. Who wasn't impressed.

"You didn't see the initials on the liver?"

"No. We had to get him sealed and closed. There was a risk of bleeding so we had to get it done asap. We'd been operating for hours; all night. It was stressful. We were really tired."

"You were standing opposite. You closed."

"I didn't see a thing."

"There is photographic evidence."

"Then why do you want me to testify?"

It was obvious why – they wanted a witness to the action of Whiteley burning the initials onto the liver. It was Hari's responsibility, he had been informed by his erstwhile boss, to ensure that the hearing went without a hitch and Alex Whiteley was found guilty. James MacKenzie was the key. Cooperation would not be unrewarded. Surely an intelligent, ambitious young man would see that? Patricia did not doubt it.

Hari sipped his coffee and watched. James was thinking. How was he to reconcile his knowledge of a caring surgeon with the power crazed monster that his mentor now seemed to be? He liked Alex. Trusted him. He would never knowingly hurt a patient. Would he?

"I didn't see him do it. That's what I'll tell the hearing. And anyone else that asks."

Neither spoke. James took another bite of his sandwich,

wincing at the acidity of the pickle and Hari sipped at his coffee before he broke the silence.

"I admire surgeons, very much. Not just for their skill but the way they manage and lead teams. They inspire the loyalty and trust of the people they work with as well as their patients."

He took a sip of coffee, meditatively contemplating the table top.

"It's the kind of loyalty and trust that makes for a successful hospital – corporate teamwork working towards the greater good. We all do our best as individuals, of course, but it's the sum total of our efforts together that produces the most successful outcomes. Teamwork is everything."

He stopped and looked at James who avoided his gaze. The message was clear. Play the game; join the team – not Alex's but the one led by senior management.

"I am sure you'll do well working with Garth Mahendran. He's an excellent surgeon. As part of his team you'll be able to develop your surgical skills, and your career. We'd very much like to see you become a consultant here, in time."

But only If I say that I saw Alex Whiteley initial that liver James thought, tearing the rest of his sandwich in half.

"God, look at the time! I must go. Thanks for the chat." Hari was on his feet and moving off towards the exit. James watched him go. Furious. He was even more determined now to tell the truth. His contract would soon be up review so he could go to another hospital somewhere – anywhere else.

Being a long way from Birmingham was starting to look very appealing.

CHAPTER TWENTY-FOUR

Jason, Meghan and Jack were having a scratch lunch in their untidy kitchen when they saw the news broadcast. Jack was talking about football, as always, and Jason was trying to make sandwiches, critique the defensive tactics of Cardiff City and keep an eye on Meghan who had insisted on getting up and joining them downstairs. She was pale and yellow, bloated and listless, but he and Jack rejoiced in her determination to sit with them and share at least part of their day.

It was Meghan who heard Malcolm's voiceover through Jack's footie-babble and cried out, slapping her hands to her mouth as she gaped at the screen. They all focused on the TV.

"That's your hospital, Mam" Jack observed. Jason went further,

"Meggie, that's your surgeon. That's Alex Whiteley."

Meghan was aghast.

"What's he done?" she asked with incredulity. "I don't believe it. He wouldn't do that."

They watched as Malcolm continued to wield the knife and

amputate Alex's credibility,

"The hospital is a centre of excellence and has an international reputation for organ transplants. Mr Whiteley was unavailable for comment but we will keep you up to date with any developments. This is Malcolm Piggott reporting for Midland Eye Television, always first with the news about everything in your region and beyond."

Jason slowly turned his gaze from the screen and stared at his wife.

"Meghan. That could have been you."

She returned his gaze.

"I wish it was. At least I'd be alive."

Lisa had also been making herself a sandwich when she saw the broadcast. She didn't like having a TV in the kitchen, preferring to chat or listen to something on Audible but it was useful for keeping up with what was happening in the world. When she heard the headline of the local regional news she froze. Freeze framed. Suspended in time and place, knife poised motionless above segments of bleeding tomato.

It was obvious that something was wrong with Alex yesterday but was waiting for him to tell her. He was a lovely man but could be moody. Caught as he was between the need to confide his worries and the ludicrous macho belief that men should deal with their problems themselves, she had learned to be patient and to wait for him to come to her. All she usually had to do was listen while he found the answers himself by talking. It was always work that caused the problems but as he and his work were inseparable, she had learned to deal with them simultaneously.

Suspended! Her husband suspended pending further

enquiries? For burning his initials on a patient? Alex? Surely not? He wouldn't do such a thing. It was inconceivable.

She was suddenly consumed with an anger and fear that made her head float and her stomach heave. Still clutching the knife in her right hand, she grasped the work surface for support and leant over it, her head swathed in her hanging hair. The kettle on the Aga had come to the boil and beyond, but she did not hear the shriek of the whistle or notice the steam turning to rain on the ceramic wall tiles. Baldrick sat at her feet on food alert, tracking her every move, oblivious to her pain. And the news reporter was still talking, talking, talking, telling lies about her husband. They were lies, weren't they? They had to be?

The screen went blank and then the only noise was the hysterical kettle which began to subside into a protracted moan. The steam started to clear and the tiles eased their weeping. Alex had come unnoticed into the kitchen, quietly turned off the television and removed the kettle from the hotplate. An earthshattering silence filled the room. Nothing except the water crying down the tiles moved; not even Baldrick.

"Lisa".

She did not move. Had she heard him? Alex did not know what to do. Speak again? Touch her? Wait? For perhaps the first time in his life he was incapable of making a decision or taking action. He simply stood there and then she slowly, slowly, turned around to confront him.

She raised her head, her hair adrift around her bloodless face.

"Is it true?"

He did not have to reply; she had looked into his heart and knew the answer.

"Oh, Alex. What have you done?"

She was still holding the sharp knife in her right hand so he gently took it from her and laid it to rest beside the abandoned tomato. Baldrick sighed and gave up the quest for titbits as a lost cause but he did not go to Alex. He continued to sit and watch Lisa, intently. Everything depended on her.

The doorbell rang. Baldrick barked and flung himself out of the doorway into the hall, skidding and scrabbling on the wooden floor, yapping, claws clicking.

"Who can that be?" asked Lisa without breaking her gaze at her husband.

"I'll go" Alex volunteered, thankful for a reason to escape her penetrating scrutiny under which he felt small, naked, infantile. He followed Baldrick out into the hall, bent to hold onto the dog's collar to prevent him hurtling out into the garden, and opened the door. Malcolm Piggott stood on the doorstep, the central panel of a triptych of a cameraman and a sound recordist. The reporter was buttoned up the neck again and holding a microphone which he thrust into Alex's face.

"Anything to say about the allegations made against you, Mr Whiteley? Is it true? Why did you do it?"

Alex yanked Baldrick's collar and pulled him inside while he slammed the door. The questions continued.

"Did you do it, Alex? What's your side of the story? The public has a right to know!"

Alex locked the door and put the chain across the top. He drew the draught-excluding curtain across it in a futile attempt to block out Malcolm's verbal barrage and dragged the yapping dog with him back into the kitchen where he shut the door to the hall. Lisa was standing where he had left her but her face had changed. The gaze had been replaced with something new. Something frightening, that he had never seen before: doubt.

"We need to talk" she said.

Icily calm. Terrifying. Alex nodded, undid the top button of his shirt and loosened his tie. He took off his jacket to fling across the back of a chair when he caught Lisa's eye, folded it neatly over his arm and went to change out of his suit.

Outside Malcolm could still be heard. Inside, the phone began to ring.

"Don't answer it!" Alex shouted.

Upstairs in their bedroom he changed out of his suit and hung it on a coat hanger. As he opened the wardrobe door to put it away, he looked at the dark crease-free cloth and the trousers still warm from his body. Hs favourite work suit. He had no idea when he would next wear it. The enormity of what was happening was becoming horribly, closely alive.

Downstairs Lisa had made two mugs of tea, his with milk, hers without. She was sitting at the kitchen table waiting for him. He sat down. The phone was no longer ringing and he noticed that she had unplugged it from the wall.

"No mobile."

He broke the habit of a working lifetime and turned off his mobile phone.

"That was the Press at the door?"

He nodded miserably.

"There'll be more won't there?"

"Yes."

"So, this is just the start?"

They both knew the answer to that one too.

"It was that all-nighter with the intimal tear when you nearly lost the patient, wasn't it?"

He nodded.

"Tell me what happened, Alex. Everything, mind."

So, Alex told her. Neither of them drank their tea; he talked and she listened until he had finished and then there was a silence punctuated only by the wheezy snoring of a small dog. Malcolm Piggott had gone long since.

Then she started.

"Why on earth did you do it? What possessed you?"

"I don't know. A moment's madness? It was so tense in there; we nearly lost him. I just wanted to lighten the atmosphere."

He could hear how feeble it sounded.

"How could you be so bloody stupid? How could you?"

She was venomous. He did not know she could look like that. His throat tightened; his courage shrivelled.

"I don't know."

"Why, Alex? Why sign it for God's sake? A donor organ!"

"It' quite common for surgeons to sign things. Retinas for example. Especially if it's a job well done."

"Not livers when the patient is out cold under anaesthetic they don't. You're not Van bloody Gogh."

Alex removed his glasses and put them on the table. He pressed his hands to his face and viciously scrubbed at his eyes as if trying to rub them out, trying to change what he knew he could not deny.

"The marks didn't harm him or the liver in any way. I would never've done it if he could've been hurt or the liver damaged. You know that. He was my patient! I'd never hurt a patient. I never meant him any harm. It was stupid of me."

"It was more than stupid, Alex. Stupid doesn't even go near it. It was... it was ... oh you're such a fool."

He was profoundly shocked. Lisa, his wife, the woman he adored most in the world was calling him a fool. Him! A fool!

But she wasn't finished.

"Oh Alex, what have you done? It's not just about how you've mistreated a patient which God knows is bad enough, but you've ruined everything. Everything! Your career, prospects, reputation. Everything you've worked for over the last 30 years. What happens if you lose your job? What if you get struck off? Have you thought of that? What if the patient brings criminal charges and you end up in prison? What happens then, Alex?"

"The pressure that surgeons work under is crucifying, Lisa, but I haven't committed a crime. I know I've crossed a line but it'll never happen again."

Lisa could bear it no longer. The effort of controlling her fury and trying not to shout was too much and she erupted. Lisa, who never lost her temper, who always saw both sides of the argument, who calmed and listened and pacified and soothed. Lisa blew up and took Alex's world with her. Baldrick woke up, sat up, blinked and looked bewildered. She was screaming, gasping for breath, hating him.

"No, it won't happen again because you'll never be allowed near an operating theatre again. How could you? I'm so angry I could scream. It's all gone to your head. You've become an arrogant, conceited egomaniac and you've ruined everything. Everything! For you, for me, for your patients, for organ donors, for their families, for the hospital. Everyone. You've done so much that is good. You could have done so much more good and now? Now it's all gone. Gone, Alex! Gone! I hate you."

She leapt up from the table as she spoke the last three words and stood over him, beating his head and shoulders with her fists, slapping him, shaking him. He was devastated; immobile; he felt no physical pain from the onslaught but would never forget the paralysing inner agony and shame that he experienced for the first time in his life. Baldrick was cowering in his basket, shaking.

Eventually she was exhausted, slowed down and stopped. He stood up to face her and put his arms around her holding her upright, trying to shield her from her grief.

“I’m sorry, Lisa. I’m so sorry. I’m sorry for all the pain and suffering I’ve caused. I’ve let you down. I’ve let everyone down. I’m so sorry.”

“What are we going to do, Alex?”

I’ll make it alright, darling, somehow.”

Calmer now but crying she pulled away from him so that she could see his face. For all his qualifications and all his surgical skill, he was naïve and she was not.

“No, Alex, you won’t. It doesn’t work like that. There are some things that even the great Alex Whiteley can’t fix, especially if he’s broken them himself.”

He was crying.

“Oh my God, what have I done? Lisa, please. Don’t cry. Please don’t cry. Without you I’m nothing. I love you. Please. Help me.”

Not just crying now but howling, alone in the darkness, lost, blind, hopeless.

“I hate what you’ve done, Alex. I hate what you’ve become and I hate the arrogance that’s caused it. Lost somewhere under the strutting surgeon that I despise is the kind, generous, gentle man that I fell in love with. That’s the man I married. Where is he, Alex? What’s happened to him?”

Unable now to speak for crying, primal body-wrenching sobs and shudders, he can only beg her with flooded eyes not to leave him alone. Not to desert him. For a long moment - his eternity - she considered the grief ravaged face before her. A large man-baby, foolish, flawed, pathetic really, but not bad, not unkind, not to be abandoned. She took his sodden face in her hands and sluiced away the tears on his cheeks with her thumbs.

“You need to get a lawyer. The best we can find. We’ll see this through, together. We have to, Alex. There's no other choice."

"Oh, Lisa. My Lisa."

He can only gasp for breath and cling to her to stop from drowning.

CHAPTER TWENTY-FIVE

Two Days Later

"Isn't it time for him to go home yet? Surely we can get rid of him now?

Patricia was talking to Hari about Carlos.

"He's being discharged today. After Garth has made him a final visit on this morning's ward round. He was supposed to go yesterday but there was a delay because of the Warfarin."

"Warfarin? I thought that was rat poison?"

Considering she was the CEO of an NHS Trust, Hari was regularly appalled at Patricia's ignorance of medical matters.

"It's a routinely prescribed blood thinner to prevent clots which also happens to be used as rat poison, yes. We tend not to refer to the rat connection though. Patients on Warfarin have to carry cards with their medical details on and it takes time to get organised. Hence the delay."

Patricia had stopped listening after he had affirmed that she was right about the rats and had moved on to other things.

"Good. One less problem to worry about. Are the Press still

hanging around?"

"Yes, but not quite so many. I'm told they've switched their attention to Alex Whiteley – 'The Letterman' as he's becoming known."

"The Letterman. Hm. Rather a grand title for what he's done I'd have thought. Hospital staff have been told not to talk to anyone from the Press, haven't they?"

"Yes. Repeatedly. They know it's more than their jobs are worth."

Patricia relaxed, a little, but had not finished.

"They know that if they speak anonymously, we'll find out who they are?"

Hari did not reply. What could he say? He had no idea how they – not him – would find out, but did not doubt what she said. Patricia could be a ruthless bitch. She continued,

"I think it would be good if you personally supervise Mr Cardoso's departure. Looks good and also makes sure he leaves the premises. We need to keep him sweet, Hari. I'm going to talk to the hospital legal team about Whiteley today."

So now he was not Alex but just Whiteley thought Hari. Patricia had neither compassion nor capacity for transgressors. He knew he would receive exactly the same treatment if he deviated. He also recognised that his interview was over and got up to leave.

"I'll go up to Liver and Upper Gastro. and check out Mr Cardoso."

Literally. Patricia nodded and ignored him; she was already tapping the keyboard of her desktop, her mind on other urgent business.

In his solitary side room Carlos was preparing to go home. He sat in the chair beside the bed which had been stripped ready for wiping, disinfecting and the next occupant. A nurse was packing his meagre possessions into a carrier bag provided by the hospital. The room however, looked much the same as when Carlos had been in residence. No cards, bottles of squash, grapes, magazines, moisturising tissues or even just a box of ordinary tissues. Just the copy of *Cloud Atlas* that the nurse was now placing on the top of the clothes in a white plastic carrier with Property of MCH NHST written in green on the side.

There was none of the other baggage that patients accumulate and pile on their bed prior to departure. Just Carlos. No one had managed to locate his nephew so he had had no visitors except the hospital chaplain (C of E but happy to serve all denominations) and an elderly female Friend of the MCH. Both had been given a polite but curt reception and had not stayed long. Their offers to return and spend time with him had been graciously declined. He was perfectly happy, thank you, had everything he needed, was enjoying the peace and quiet and the opportunity to take time out from his hectic life to recover his strength.

He would have loved to tell them about the agony that he was suffering after the ordeal he had experienced at the hands of that crazed surgeon, but alas, he had to remain anonymous. For the moment. He could not wait for the time when he could speak of it and had spent hours mentally rehearsing his lines and how he would deliver them.

Someone had provided him with clothes in which to go home; insurance company or hospital, he did not know and did not much care. The clothes were acceptable, if a little middle class, but obviously he could not wear the outfit he had arrived in. He sat in his open necked shirt, chinos and light jacket and watched the middle-aged nurse as she gathered up the toiletries that the MCH had provided. He wanted to be able to chat to her, easily, informally, spontaneously, but did not know how. Other people were always such a puzzle. How did one interact with them without a script? How did one begin a conversation? Perhaps he could tell her something about himself and then she would want to know more so the conversation would evolve naturally that way? What should he say?

She beat him to it.

"There, chick. All done. Anything else I can do for you?"

"No, thank you."

He smiled. How soon can I get out of here? she was thinking, smiling back. He sipped from the bottle of Evian in his hand.

"I'm sure you have much more important things to do than look after me" he added.

"Goodness, no!"

Her response was too effusive for sincerity but Carlos did not notice. She really should be getting back to her ladies on surgical but the ward sister had made it clear that this was a special patient and had to be kept happy. An order from the very top - from the Medical Director himself, and what the MD wanted, the MD got. As the nurse went to the sink to wash her hands, wondering how to legitimately escape from the room, in walked the MD and began speaking to the patient, enabling her to slide out unnoticed.

"Ah Mr Cardoso. All ready to go?"

"More than ready."

The charm offensive continued.

"What arrangements have been made for you after you leave us?"

Carlos looked tragic and answered a little plaintively,

"The medical insurance company – the ones who nearly killed me in that aeroplane – are supposed to be taking care of things."

"You're going home to the West Country?" asked Hari, solicitous, interested, concerned.

"To Stroud, yes. Well, just outside. Stroud itself is a little shabby but the villages around it are charming."

Carlos lived in the less charming outskirts of the town on a busy main road.

"I shall have a private nurse to look after me for the first week or so, which I'll need. Then of course the district nurse will visit. My GP is a personal friend which helps."

I bet he is thought Hari, smiling. Carlos went on.

"This has been the most terrible ordeal for me. And it shows no sign of ending."

His words hung in the air like a stale fart. Hari replaced the smile with a serious, compassionate face and waited for a couple of seconds before giving a sympathetic, non-committal reply.

"Trying times, indeed. We are, as you know, doing everything we can to bring this unfortunate situation to a speedy conclusion. I'm sure that once you're in the comfort of your own home things will be so much better."

Hari hoped this would pacify Carlos but he had hopelessly underestimated the quality of his opponent. His words were the cue that Carlos needed; a good actor never misses a cue.

"I cannot get the image of my branded liver out of my mind. I shut my eyes and it's there. When I open them, it's still there. Will it ever go away?" he murmured, tragically, and sipped from the bottle of spring water. There was so much more emotional effect in a subdued voice than a raised one he mused as he was speaking. The audience has to concentrate in order to hear; the performer has their undivided attention.

Hari wallowed on,

"Rest assured that we are doing everything in our power to resolve this er, incident. Please, contact me directly – you have my private number? – if there is anything we can do to help.

Anything at all. Providing the very best in patient care is our absolute priority."

The look with which Carlos lanced Hari was one of utter disbelief and cynicism. His response was a sneer.

"That surgeon tried to kill me. My life will never be the same again."

Hari was saved by the arrival of the cavalry in the unlikely form of the ward sister appearing in the doorway, bearing Carlos' medication like a votive offering. Immediately behind her was a porter with a wheelchair into which Carlos, his plastic bag and the substantial paper bag of prescription drugs were loaded. He was swiftly steered out of the room by the porter into the corridor followed by Hari and the ward sister, his retinue, as he made his progress towards the lift and departure. Only when he was out of the main entrance, settled into the hospital taxi and *en route* to wherever – Hari did not care – would senior management be able sigh with temporary relief.

CHAPTER TWENTY-SIX

The Whiteleys were under siege. Malcolm Piggott's sortie on their doorstep was merely the advance party reconnoitring for battalions of mercenaries engaged in a remorseless onslaught. Wave after wave followed of fully armed sound recordists and cameramen providing support for the reporters on the front line, wielding pin-pulled microphones and questions primed for immediate detonation. The noise was constant and variable, sometimes muted but always escalating whenever any sign of movement was detected. Alex and Lisa had all but abandoned the front of their home; the curtains were closed, the front door locked, chained and bolted and they had even taken to sleeping in a smaller back bedroom in an attempt to diffuse the interest of the besieging army.

A police officer had been posted outside their closed gate, adding to the consternation of some of the neighbours and intrigue of the others who revelled in the attention. These were the ones who gave the interviews about a couple they had never met and seldom saw but had now known for years and about whom they could never have imagined such terrible news. This had always been such a quiet, pleasant street for professional people, who kept themselves to themselves. It had always been such an oasis. Wasn't it awful? What was the world coming to? And him a surgeon!

After they had spoken to bored reporters under pressure from their news editors for some sort of story, however meagre, they would rush inside to watch themselves on television, endlessly revisiting the moment on catch up and i-player. Some of the more stalwart interviewees took to providing refreshments for their chosen reporters and established quite a rapport with them. The home-made shortbread had been so well received; it wouldn't surprise them if one of the journos asked for the recipe and it appeared on the women's page. The Avenue hadn't had such excitement in years, not since the suspected gas leak when the road had had to be dug up and that was nothing compared to this!

Inside the dimly lit house Alex and Lisa felt like refugees.

"I can't even walk the dog. They've imprisoned us."

Lisa was angry. She was often angry at the moment.

"There's nothing we can do except wait until they lose interest."

Alex was aware of the inadequacy of his response and all too aware of what he knew would follow.

"When will that be?"

He dismally shrugged his shoulders in reply. Lisa was incensed.

"How long will this go on? Baldrick hasn't had a walk for days. We can't go out. We can't even look out of our own windows without someone taking pictures and people shouting at us."

Alex could only shake his head ruefully; he had no idea. Although their TVs and radio were switched off he had been on the internet and was aghast at the extent and vitriol of the media coverage across the world. Hell, it was everywhere, in every language and alphabet, across every time zone and latitude. He was notorious, vilified, a byword in black humour. Who knew there were so many jokes and puns to made about initials? He guessed that Lisa had seen it too but dared not ask.

"What does the solicitor say?" Lisa was speaking.

"That we have a fight on our hands."

"You don't need a law degree to work that one out."

"Well, I'm not going to let them win. Come on Baldrick."

Alex was began preparing to go out. Baldrick began dancing around on one paw with anticipation. Once the dog lead had been lifted from the hook in the hallway there would be no turning back.

"Baldrick. Sit!" Alex ordered. The dog took absolutely no notice and continued to prance and twist until Lisa fixed him with a look, pointed one finger and raised her eyebrows. He sat. Still. She bent down and clipped the lead onto his collar.

"How do you do that?" Alex asked, as he always did. She fixed her look on him, her eyebrows rose into her forehead and she shook her head despairingly as she always did in reply. Then she stood up, straightened his shirt collar and comforted him up as a mother does a nervous child setting off for their first day at a new school.

"Are you sure about this?"

"No. But I've got to do it."

"Ok. Deep breath, eyes ahead, walk straight through them. Don't stop, don't talk. Walk, don't run. Ready?"

Yes, he was ready.

"Pretend they're not there" she said.

He nodded and inhaled. She unfastened the front door and pulled it wide open in a swift, single movement. He stepped into the doorway and out into the line of fire. Light, noise, shouts, calls, clicking camera shutters, jostling bodies, waving arms, a wall of microphones and lenses as he crossed no man's land towards the gate and the war zone. The police officer had spotted him and was ready to manoeuvre the gate open and shut but after that Alex would be largely on his own. Benign and innocent Baldrick took no notice whatsoever of the myriad feet, shoes, boots, tripods, boxes and clamour but simply bludgeoned his way through towards the scent of woodland and squirrels, dragging Alex behind him at a pace that caught most of the foot soldiers by surprise. The volley of rapid-fire questions ricocheted around him in a hail of accents and tones,

"Alex! Alex! Over here! What have you got to say, Alex? What have you got to say to your patients, Alex? Have you branded others? How many? Are you sorry? Why did you do it?"

He put his head down, eyes fixed on the pitted pavement and pursued the panting dog straining and throttling on the far end of the lead. Baldrick was in heaven – for the first time ever he was being allowed to pull without someone repeatedly yanking him back and telling him to slow down, walk to heel, not to pull, to behave. As fast as he pulled, the big man followed. The smaller one never let him do that. The dog pulled even harder and still Alex kept up, saying nothing but gradually outpacing his assailants. Eventually they stopped following and returned to their vigil by the gate. They knew that Alex would have to return at some point and the attack would begin all over again.

Lisa shut the door behind Alex without letting anyone see her. She locked it but left it unbolted so that she could let him in quickly when he arrived back; they had agreed that he would knock loudly three times so that she would know it was him. She went to the kitchen doorway and surveyed the remnants of their breakfast on the table. Since Alex was confined to home their hours had become erratic. Neither of them was sleeping well. Each lay awake, motionless, open-eyed, trying not to disturb the other but at about 3.00 am every morning one of them cracked and got up at which point so did the other. They would sit and drink tea in the shadowy kitchen, saying little but thinking much. The television was never switched on, the phone was unplugged and the radio silent. Mercifully they could screen calls on their mobiles and emails but they both felt persecuted. Isolated. Home was now a prison, an asylum, an island marooned in a swell of baying newshounds.

Breakfast clearing could wait. There was something she had to do. She turned and went to the foot of the stairs, paused guiltily for no more than a second then ran up to Alex's study – the room where the AppleMac lived on which he wrote his academic papers, private practice reports and everything else outside the prying eyes of the MCH. She knew it would be switched on and what the password was; it had been her idea: BaldLisa1970. A combination of the 2 people (yes, Baldrick counted as a person) Alex loved best in the world and her birth year. She had tried to add her birthday so that he had no excuse to forget it but the machine had rejected it as too long.

She tapped the mouse hurriedly and sat down so quickly in the swivel chair that it tried to spin her anti-clockwise. She steadied it with her feet on the floor as she scattered the cursor over the screen. Not much time before he came back but she needed to know and it did not take long to confirm what she suspected. Alex had been sneaking up here to torture himself by following his international notoriety on the internet. His browsing history was a list of global media articles about branding and burning. Little wonder he was increasingly morose and depressed. Events themselves were bad enough but feeding them with onscreen vitriol and salacious outrage could only make it worse. What to do? Confront him? Ban the computer? He would only speculate and fester in his imagination. No. Better to be aware of exactly how things stood and try to deal with them, step by step, crisis by accumulating crisis. But could he cope?

She was distracted by the metallic snapping of the brass letter box flap at the front door and the crustle of post landing inside the box on the back of the door. Baldrick as a puppy had decided that a letter from the Inland Revenue was a rat, had shaken it to death then torn it limb from limb. He had displayed great innate canine good taste and discernment Alex had said, but they had attached the letter box anyway. Lifting herself heavily out of the now docile chair, she put the computer to sleep and went to collect the mail.

This had become a task she dreaded. Oh, for the days when all they had to complain about was junk mail, credit card offers and medical journals. But they were expecting written confirmation from the solicitor and the medical insurance company that Alex's legal expenses would be covered so she knew she had to go and look. She raised the lid, lifted out the pile of letters and began to sift through them. Alex, Alex, Alex, Mr and Mrs A. Whiteley, a takeaway pizza flyer, The Occupier, The Letterman.

The Letterman? Who was that? She held onto the letter as she put the others on the narrow hall table beneath the gilt framed mirror in which Alex used to check his tie on the way to work, a lifetime ago. An innocuous white envelope for a folded three-way A4 sheet of paper, self-sealing so no DNA trace from saliva, cheap paper, probably bought from a supermarket. First class stamp though, so it was meant to arrive quickly and, on the front, to her horror, The Letterman and their address was made up of uneven, mixed letters cut out from a magazine or newspaper.

It had been done with great care. The letters were roughly the same size although of different types but all were black with grammatically correct capital letters and even some punctuation. An erudite sender. The post mark was nothing but a smudge. Her breakfast toast rising in her gullet, Lisa held the letter a little away from her with the tips of her index finger and thumb, like a dressing from a suppurating wound, and steadied herself. She could not let Alex open it. She would have to do it. Now. Meticulously she prised open the back of the envelope, preserving intact the address, postmark, stamp and front. Disgusted as she was, she was mindful that a police investigation would want as much evidence as possible.

Perhaps she shouldn't open it? No. It had to be done and it had to be done by her.

The sheet of A4 was neatly folded three ways, a standard piece of white paper available everywhere, non-descript, clean, crisp and cruel. She unfolded the paper, slowly, fearfully, without breathing.

On it, in capital letters cut from a newspaper, she read the words

BURN IN HELL A W

CHAPTER TWENTY-SEVEN

"We have to do something."

Tiger Lily pushed her bowl of Fern's home-made soup, secret ingredient love, away from her towards the centre of the table. She and Fern were sitting in front of the TV watching the lunchtime news.

"That man really gets on my wick" she added, lifting her knife from the butter on her bread roll to point at Malcolm Piggott.

"Smug git. He's clearly enjoying every moment."

Fern too had abandoned her soup and was following the image of Alex on the screen in coverage from earlier that day. He was being pulled by a small dog through a posse of reporters shouting and calling to him. Then Malcom Piggott was centre screen again, revelling in the fact that Mr Whiteley had said nothing to explain his actions or to reassure his anxious patients. This resolute reporter would, however, continue his crusade for exclusive information and justice and they could be certain that they, the much-maligned public, would be the first to know whatever he uncovered. He would not move from his position outside the Whiteley residence until he had the answers they deserved.

Fern got up and switched the TV off at the set so that Tiger Lily could no longer work it with the remote. Her beloved Tilly had been through enough already, without the agony of lascivious media speculation about the man who had restored her life. Leaving Tiger Lily negligently stirring tears into her soup she quietly went into the kitchen and retrieved her mobile from the garish everlasting carrier bag that served as her handbag. Scrolling down through her contacts she found the number she wanted. Should she call? Would it be too intrusive? No. He had said to contact him direct if there was a problem and this was certainly that, although not quite the problem they could have envisaged. Yes. She would call.

She tapped the call option and waited. Maybe he would not answer; he had probably gone to ground. It was unexpected when the call was picked up and she heard his voice.

"Mr Whiteley? It's Fern. Fern Anderson, Tiger Lily Lacey's partner."

She stopped talking and almost smiled, briefly. Of course, he knew who she was, he always did. None of the other consultants ever remembered even such a bizarre name as Tiger Lily and once you had explained who you were, then you had to go through the whole medical thing over and over again until you could have the conversation you wanted. Not Mr W though. How did he do it? He had hundreds of patients.

"She's fine. Thriving, thanks to you. We just wanted to give our support. Are you OK?"

An unusual question to ask a surgeon she thought as she listened to the reply. And listened, with growing horror creasing her forehead and twisting her eyebrows.

"But that's horrible. Who'd do such a thing? Your poor wife. Who did you say it was addressed to?"

Her face contorted to that of someone who has suddenly been

exposed to a nostril-frilling foul smell.

"The Letterman?" she repeated in disbelief.

She listened carefully, only speaking at the end of the call.

"Be strong Mr W. You'll let us know if there's anything we can do to help, won't you?"

He would, but he didn't think there was anything anyone could do. Thank you anyway.

Fern. Scruffy, baggy, bleached and spiky. Thinking. Squeezing her silent mobile for inspiration. Staring at its screen, motionless, intense, then enlightened; idea-conceiving.

"Tilly!" she barked as she swung herself round in a blur of Doc Martens and loose trousers and launched herself into the living room.

"The power of social media!"

Tilly looked up from the salty soup.

"What?"

She had no idea what her partner was talking about. Fern could be so erratic sometimes which was very annoying when you felt as miserable as she did.

"We'll start a Facebook page!"

Tilly was a blank. Fern continued, masking her exasperation,

"For Mr W... Mr Whiteley. To show support. There must be others who feel the same way as we do. We can't be the only ones."

Really thought Fern, sometimes Tilly could be so obtuse. She cleared the bowls, cutlery, tissues, mugs and clutter accumulated throughout the morning from the low table and dumped them in the kitchen sink. Her lap top replaced them and she squeezed herself onto the sofa beside her lover, opened the computer, switched it on and realised the battery was low. No problem, plug in the charger, try not to trip over the flex on the way back to the sofa and sit down again. This time.

“D’you know what to do, Fern?”

“No. But we’ll find out. It can’t be that difficult; everyone does it.”

Her finger tips were already tapping the keys.

“What shall we call it?” Tilly asked.

The tapping stopped. Fern mused.

“Save The Letterman” she announced and the tapping resumed.

CHAPTER TWENTY-EIGHT

Early September. There is still sunshine and warmth but ice cream summer, lazy days and school holidays are over; reality and harvest festivals arrive together. Thoughts turn to winter television schedules, secondary school open days, heating bills, warmer clothes, shorter days and longer nights. Christmas cards appear in the charity shops, Summer sales fade into final clearance and die. Leaves on trees flame and fall.

Alex and Lisa were still at home. Although the doorstep siege was over, temporarily suspended in favour of a behind the lines war of attrition conducted through the media and at ground level by word of mouth, they were still under self-imposed house arrest. Screened but not safe.

There had been no more poisonous letters but there might as well have been; the fear of receiving one never left them. Alex could go nowhere without recognition and confrontation. Lisa had managed to keep herself hidden so could travel incognito and became their physical link with the outer world during daylight. Alex went out as the day began to die, walking

Baldrick in semi-darkness, grateful for the cooler evenings when he could legitimately wear a cap and oversized scarf across the lower half of his face as if binding toothache or shielding himself from pollution.

Outside the MCH main entrance, before the start of the official working day, Patricia and Hari were talking quietly. Noisily visible they made a point of greeting those arriving earlier than their shift demanded.

They felt it was strategic to be seen as well as heard. Only the most discreet of ivory corner offices for them, open door policy at all times, team players, drinking the same coffee to go as everyone else, at one with the staff and their clients. Patricia preferred to think of patients as clients: more business-like and better for successful economic appraisal. Her mind was always on the bottom line of the audit sheet but even she baulked from regarding patients as units of cost. She had read somewhere that Napoleon had made a point of learning the names and family histories of a very few of his ordinary soldiers so that when inspecting the troops, he could single them out and make personal enquiries about their children, wives, elderly parents, finances, sick cattle, hopes, fears and feelings. Such loud intimate conversations, designed to be overheard and to impress produced the desired effect: his men adored him, their little father and would willingly die for him. An excellent business model and she was working on it.

"Lovely morning" Hari commented, smilingly acknowledging the arrival of a cleaner but frowning slightly as he noticed yellow nicotine stains on her inner fingers when she waved hello. The quietness of the morning was comfortable, peaceful, a world away from the rest of the day and no doubt what was to come. They were meeting their team for a pre-hearing briefing. Patricia read his mind,

"Enjoy it while you can."

Hari had one brief shining moment before she began.

"When are they due?"

He sighed inaudibly and then replied.

"Helena Gresham, our barrister is due in about an hour. Jeff Balaak is coming from Manchester so he'll be here later this morning."

"Is he any good?"

That was Patricia, thought Hari, always straight to the point. He answered equally bluntly; subtlety was lost on their CEO but perhaps that was a strength in a job like hers. He wondered about that as he spoke.

"Jeff's very experienced. He's been the Medical Director at the Ribblesdale Hospital Trust for years as well as the case manager for things like this before."

"I don't think there's ever been anything quite like this before." Patricia was scathing.

"No. Well. True." Hari wasn't going to argue; time enough for that later. "Our legal team are way out of their depth over Alex, although they won't admit it. Apparently, there's no legal precedent so no one knows if he's committed a crime or not."

Patricia snorted disapproval.

"Crime or no crime, he's crossed a line."

Everything was so black and white for Patricia, Hari thought. If only it were that easy.

She went on,

"We have to be seen to do the right thing and protect our reputation."

"And our patients" he reminded her. She bristled.

"Of course."

The silence was awkward. Patricia resented any kind of criticism, implied or otherwise. Hari resignedly repaired the damage.

"Do you know who is on the panel yet?"

Patricia was mollified by being back in control. She alone had that information. The disciplinary hearing was high profile which meant that she was on display and she was a woman who never gave a poor performance.

"MCH Chief Nurse, Medical Director from the Ribblesdale Trust, Senior Doctor from Ribblesdale, our HR Director - he can be relied upon to toe the Trust line - and a Patient Representative."

"What about the General Medical Council?" Hari the doctor made the enquiry.

"We'll inform them of the outcome and then they'll decide what action to take. Typical GMC."

"Will he be struck off?"

Hari the doctor again, and fearful. There could be no worse outcome as far as he was concerned.

"No idea. Depends what happens at the hearing." Patricia could not care less.

"They've confirmed the date?"

"September the 16th. A week today."

One week away from what might be the end of a consultant's career Hari thought. Alex was a colleague and a friend, a fellow physician, not that he would have said as much to Patricia.

"Alex is an excellent surgeon" he said, innocuously.

"World class".

No response. He was silent. Patricia slid the subject sideways.

"Do you think Garth Mahendran is up to the job?"

"He's a good surgeon. Steady but not inspired. A safe pair of medical hands and very professional. We were at Med. School together. I'm not sure how good a leader he is though."

Patricia nodded.

“Hmm. My thoughts exactly.”

Hari did not know whether to be flattered or insulted. She looked at her watch.

“Time to go” she said, striding towards the revolving doors and flinging the rest of her coffee onto the grass. Hari followed.

They were arrayed around one end of the long table in the Meeting Room. Previously known as the Conference Room due to its size and expensive furnishings, Patricia had renamed it. Conference sounded extravagant and gave out the wrong message in times of austerity; meeting sounded so much more egalitarian.

She sat at the head of the table behind the biscuits with Hari on her left and Helena Gresham on her right. Next to Helena was Jeff Balaak, who had just arrived by taxi from the station. As slim and tanned as his leather briefcase his Nordic, blue-eyed blondeness was the polar opposite of Hari and made Patricia seem clumpy and fuzzy edged by comparison. She noticed and did not take another biscuit. Helena was, as always, the barrister: black clad, smart, androgynous. No one thought of her as anything but the lawyer and they liked her more for it. She had her lap top open in front of her and was tapping the keyboard as they spoke. The meeting was not being minuted, officially, but she never liked to leave room for doubt and could always delete the notes later.

Helena liked it when Patricia chaired meetings; they were invariably focused and pithy. No wasted time or spurious debate, just salient information and defined outcomes. She was summarising what had just been discussed.

“So, if we could get Mr Cardoso to accept a written apology from Alex Whiteley, that would considerably ease our situation?”

Helena replied.

"Yes. And his. Obviously, an apology acknowledges wrong doing but it also goes a long way to mitigating the role of the hospital as well as the surgeon."

Patricia did not hesitate.

"My concern is for the hospital, not Alex Whiteley" she snapped back and turned to Hari.

"Do you think Mr Cardoso is likely to accept an apology?" she asked.

Hari groaned inwardly. This was a question he had wanted to avoid; saying 'no' to Patricia was risky and she bore grudges like limbs.

"He's very angry and believes he's been victimised."

Patricia stared at him but Jeff Balaak intervened before she could speak. Medical Directors sticking together thought Hari.

"It's worth a try, don't you think?"

Then Balaak spoke to Helena before Patricia had time to intervene,

"Can you liaise with Whiteley's lawyer and make that happen?" Helena nodded yes and tapped herself another note on the keyboard.

Patricia did not like the way Balaak was hijacking her meeting. She over-loudly interjected and resumed control.

"Who's representing Whiteley?" she asked.

Helena raised her eyebrows as she responded.

"RedheadCohen&LeFevre. London based. They have an excellent reputation."

Patricia looked surprised and reluctantly impressed.

"Expensive?" she asked.

"Very".

"Who's paying?" Patricia probed.

"His insurance."

Helena appeared to consult her laptop but she already knew the answer, "Advanced Medical Insurance."

Patricia nodded. Alex would only be covered by the best. She moved the meeting on.

"What about compensation?"

It was no good; Patricia helped herself to another biscuit. This was the thing that she was most nervous about and she looked at Jeff intently as she asked the question. Everyone else looked too.

"Depends on the outcome of the hearing but, yes, the patient will almost certainly be entitled to something. His lawyer is bound to ask. Have you got funds available?"

Patricia broke her biscuit in two as if cracking Carlos apart and retorted,

"Of course not. We're an NHS Trust".

"Let's see what next week brings" Jeff offered by way of consolation but no one was convinced. Patricia ate both halves of the biscuit.

On the other side of the city another meeting was in progress. Fern and Tiger Lily were sitting at their kitchen table surrounded by a grubby chaos to which they were completely immune. The uneven bamboo blind had been pulled down over the window to prevent glare on the screen of the lap top which was now never switched off or unplugged. Framed by kitchen cupboards, cluttered work surfaces, fridge magnets, utensils and spice jars, the two women sat hunched side by side in front of the screen, their faces a flicker of shadows and light in the dim room. Alex was there, smiling, in scrubs, on the Facebook page and above him in bold, the words 'Save the

Letterman'. Tiger Lily's index finger was adeptly stroking the mouse to scroll down the page in front of her. They did this all day, every day and most of the night. The activity that the page was generating was astonishing. Tiger Lily said, as she had said several times already that morning,

"It's unbelievable. I had no idea that there would be so much support." She paused. "Or that it would take up so much time" she added rather ruefully. "It's worth it though. The response is amazing."

"How many likes now?" asked Fern stretching forward to see better. Tiger Lily shifted to one side to make room for her and squinted at the screen for the answer.

"Up to 600 already. And it's only been up a few days."

She was inordinately pleased with the Facebook page and herself for setting it up, which had actually much easier to do than she let on to her partner. Fern, who already knew that, grinned and then became more serious.

"The hit rate must be much higher than that" she analysed. "Think how many people may have seen it but not clicked the like button. I knew we couldn't be the only people who felt like this, Tilly."

"Facebook keep offering me financial incentives to boost the hit rate" Tiger Lily boasted, archly. Fern indulged her,

"No! How much?"

"Not going there." Tiger Lily stopped crowing.

"We're doing this for Mr Whiteley."

Fern agreed, vigorously. "And for people like us" she added. "Think how many lives he has saved."

Neither said a word but both had the same thought: how many others would die because he wasn't allowed to operate? Tiger Lily broke the silence,

"I don't care if he initialled me. I'm alive. He could've written his life story on my insides for all I care."

She tentatively fingered the livid dark red scar like a zip on her abdomen as she said it, and meant every word. Fern put her own stubby fingered hand over the fingers on the mouse and stroked them.

"He shouldn't have done it though. Tilly. It was stupid. And wrong."

"But no one got hurt, Fern. Stopping him saving lives is ridiculous. That patient is only able to make all this fuss because Mr W. kept him alive. That's what I find so difficult to understand about all this. If it was me, I just wouldn't care."

Fern understood, agreed, stroked the fingers again and changed tack. It was the here and now they had to deal with, not the what if.

"When's the disciplinary hearing?"

"Next week. The 16th. I'm going to ask everyone to email the hospital Chief Executive Officer, Patricia Shelton, to express their support for Mr W. before the hearing. There's a way of making her email a live link on the page so the messages will go straight through to her desk."

Fern laughed, a deep bellied raucous laugh, the first time she had laughed for weeks.

"Oh God! She's going to love you! Go for it, Tilly!"

Now they were both laughing as Tiger Lily rapped at the keys.

CHAPTER TWENTY-NINE

Jason was making breakfast and getting Jack ready for school. Meghan was still in bed and might be there for, well, it would depend on how she felt. Certainly, all the time it took to get Jack organised and his lunch box prepared. There would be the usual fuss about a piece of fruit instead of a biscuit and the white versus brown bread debate but Jason liked the predictability of the routine. It felt normal.

"Don't spill!" he admonished too late as Jack slopped milk down the clean school uniform sweatshirt.

"Slow down!" he added pointlessly as the bowl of cereal was noisily emptied. He soaked one corner of a tea towel in the bowl of tepid washing up water in the sink and was wiping the milk off his son's top when the landline rang. Jason glanced at the kitchen clock on the wall – 8.15 am. Too early for a social call. Maybe Latisha wanted him to collect her younger kids and walk them to school with Jack. Tea towel in hand he lifted the receiver as Jack jumped from his chair and ran upstairs to get his football.

"Don't forget to clean your teeth!" his father shouted to the receding footsteps.

“Jason Orchard” he said distractedly into the receiver.

“Sorry. Who did you say you were?”

His colour evaporated as he heard the reply.

“John Hardman? The Organ Recipient Coordinator at the Midland Hospital?”

The niceties first.

“We’re OK I s’pose. Well, me and Jack are.”

Then a silence as he listened, and an eternity before he answered.

“Is there? Is there really? It won’t be like last time, will it? We can’t go through that again. It would destroy her. And me. All of us.”

More silence, but his colour has changed and he is reddening with hope, excitement and fear. But he has to be certain.

“You’re absolutely sure? No last-minute cancellation? You give me your word?”

He held his breath. Exhaled. Shouted.

“Right. Straight away. We’ll meet you there.”

He flung down the receiver, hurled the water heavy tea towel towards the sink, missed and hit the box of cereal which fell, spilled into the butter, a mug of tea and pebble dashed the table. Euphoria.

“Meghan! Meghan! They’ve got a liver for you and this time it’s going to be alright. Jack, have you cleaned your teeth?”

They were already in the car on their way to the hospital. Jack and his football had been deposited at school and now Nev was driving them to the MCH. No one said much, Nev because he was tired having come straight from the night shift, Jason because he was nervous and Meghan? Meghan did not care anymore. It was too painful. There was too much to gain; she was frightened by the possibility of hope. One step at a time;

don't look ahead; focus on the now, not the maybe. And yet … what if there was a maybe?

Nev switched on the car radio which launched immediately into an effusive jingle and announced the presence of their local independent radio station:

"all things to all men oops, sorry, not p.c. enough, can't say that, all things to all persons ha ha ha." They were just in time for a morning phone in – "your chance to have your say and be heard, and today they were discussing the fascinating case of a local surgeon who had, allegedly, written his initials on a patient's liver during surgery. No need to go into details about the incident which was being reported everywhere and I mean, everywhere. You must have seen or heard about it unless you lived in a complete media blackspot with absolutely no access to the outside world, like the lost city of Atlantis for example, or Wales – no offence meant, ha ha ha, we love the Welsh. Surgeon Alex Whiteley, 'The Letterman'. Saint or sinner? Maniac or maverick? Call me, Ricky, on 0181969696 and tell the world what you think."

Another jingle, a blast of Ellie Goulding's 'Burn' and the irrepressible Ricky was back. Jason glanced at Meghan to see how she was reacting. Nothing. Her face was a blank, her eyes wide shut. She was in pain again.

"And our first caller is Rob, all the way from Bath. Hello Rob. Nice city. How's the weather there? What would you like to say about Alex Whiteley?"

"I think he's a brilliant. My wife would've died if it wasn't for him. Yes, if he did it, he shouldn't have, but we all make mistakes and do things we regret. I think he should be allowed to carry on doing operations and saving people's lives."

"So, you know him personally do you Rob?" Ricky scented a story; the personal angle was always popular. Probe this one.

"Yes, he's looked after my wife ever since she became ill and he's been wonderful. So kind and caring." Sincere Rob. Ricky needed something meatier.

"So, you don't think he could be capable of branding his name on an unconscious patient?"

Rob bridled and reacted. Ricky was pleased; this was more like it.

"I'm not saying that. We don't know the circumstances. All I know is that the Mr Whiteley I know wouldn't do a thing like that."

"But what if he did, Rob? What if he did? Is that what other listeners think? Call in now and tell us your views."

A challenge thrown out over the airwaves and Rob had had his moment.

"Thanks for that Rob" Ricky was saying, "and now we've got Ashanti on the line who feels rather differently, is that right Ashanti?"

"Yeah, Ricky. I do." A strong Midlands accent, more local, more pertinent, better listening. Ricky was starting to enjoy himself.

"Where you phoning from, Ashanti?

"Dudley, Ricky."

"And what would you like to say about Alex Whiteley? He's the local surgeon accused of burning his initials on a patient's liver for anyone who's just tuned in."

"It' disgraceful." Ashanti was vehement. "What kind of power trip was he on, like, to do something so terrible? Did he think he was God or something? It's sick. He should be locked up or better still, someone should write something on his liver and see how he likes it. But keep him conscious when they do it so he knows how it feels and..."

Nev had turned the radio off and was studying his passengers in the rear-view mirror. Jason was wide eyed but Meghan's head was bent downwards so he could not read her face. She still had that awful yellow look though, sort of thick and waxy like you could peel her skin off. Jason caught Nev's eye in the mirror and mouthed a "ta mate." He put his hand out to clasp Meghan's which was lying listlessly in her lap.

"It'll be alright, Meggie. Don't worry. You'll be fine."

She said nothing for a moment but raised her head to look at him, searching for the truth.

"Will it?" her eyes asked. Then she turned her head to gaze out of the side window, seeing nothing.

"I still wish he was doing my transplant" she murmured. "I trust him".

"Mr Mahendran is an excellent surgeon. John said so. You know, that recipient coordinator guy I don't like, John Hardman."

"It wasn't his fault I didn't get the transplant" she said to the window. "You care too much."

Jason squeezed her unresponsive hand.

"C'mon annwylyd. It'll be alright. You'll see."

They were pulling up into the drop off area outside the MCH main entrance. Nev parked the ageing Renault and plodded off to find a wheelchair while Jason opened Meg's side door and eased her out of the car. She looked so frail, Nev thought, as he steadied the chair while Jason settled her into it.

"Good luck, mate" he said to Jason as he began gently pushing his wife towards the revolving doors.

CHAPTER THIRTY

The Same Day.

Clutching his bottle of unopened Evian water Carlos was warming to his role. He was sitting in a shabby not chic office in a faded Georgian town house in Stroud. Once charming and occasionally elegant, the dimly lit, narrow, sash-windowed building now housed the Crown Prosecution Service.

Little had changed and nothing had improved since they had acquired it from a retiring septuagenarian solicitor who had long ago given up efficient practice but who had for too long continued in business to the dismay of local estate agents and unsuspecting clients. The CPS had inherited his furnishings and secretary, neither of which were up to date or in good condition, but there had not been the funds to replace them. Now his once book-lined office was occupied by Jayne Lavery LLB (Hons. hard won). The dark wooden bookcases reluctantly sported a few brightly coloured legal spines like a flashy tie on an old-fashioned suit and a great many files, stationery and empty space. Outside the dusty window panes trying to hide themselves behind yellowing lop-sided Venetian blinds, the intermittent traffic filtering into the one-way system could be heard and on the raised track above the road the trains slowly gathered speed out of the station onto the Victorian arched bridge. At least she did not have a top floor office right beside the railway track Jayne thought as she leant back in her creased leather chair that no longer swivelled. Opening a window would be completely impossible, even if you wanted to.

She regarded her client who seemed oblivious to her presence. He was immersed in his speech. It was undoubtably that. Rhetoric. Not discussion or information or description but a dramatic delivery. Jayne was annoyed and forced herself to listen beyond the words to the message beneath. Carlos was a paradox; this was their first meeting although they had spoken on the phone several times but unusually, she could not make him out. As well as being a diligent, principled lawyer she was astute and perceptive, believing that her role as a legal adviser was as much psychology as knowledge of the law. For her it was all about knowing how to handle the client and steering them towards the most appropriate legal outcomes. Justice mattered, of course, but justice and the legal system seemed so often to be at odds. Carlos puzzled her. He exuded confidence and self-assurance but was so obviously insecure and vulnerable; she had not yet worked out why. The dramatic delivery and contrived mien were all an act but she doubted if even Carlos knew where the acting ended and the person began.

He had his hand to his brow and was clutching the Evian water like a talisman. His tone was plaintive.

"I can't sleep. I can't concentrate. It's impossible for me to trust ... anyone". The final word was delivered as a *coup de grace* after a dramatic pause. Jayne let it roll around the room for a few seconds before replying, dead pan, calm, pragmatic.

"We need to document this."

Carlos ignored her.

"How am I supposed to work?"

Now the Evian was being held against his fevered brow.

"As I say, we need documentary evidence."

She wondered if the water bottle would leave a mark he was pressing it so hard against his forehead and was tempted to smile – the water was tepid and would not cool anything, let alone his imagination.

"Could you keep a diary to show how your life has been affected?"

"I have been violated. Raped."

"Mr Cardoso..."

"When I was unconscious, in hospital, on an operating table, that man, who had my life in his hands, branded me like an animal."

Carlos now opened the bottle of Evian and took a single delicate sip as if to soothe his troubled soul. Jayne seized her chance.

"Mr Cardoso! Please, listen."

It worked. Carlos looked at her as if hearing her voice for the first time. He took a second delicate sip of water as if to verify her presence then replaced the cap on the bottle, screwing it slowly and rhythmically into place as he fixed his eyes on her.

"Write all this down" she was saying, opting for a straightforward single syllable form of instruction that he could not misinterpret. "It will be valuable evidence if we have to go to court."

She was concerned that Carlos was the kind of client who heard only what he chose. KISS she decided – keep it simple, stupid. Not a bad man she thought, but self-obsessed. Difficult. Lonely. She almost felt sorry for him but if it went to court she did not want him on the witness stand.

"I want justice" he replied.

"That is what the Crown Prosecution Service is for."

Did she believe that? She was not sure but let it go.

"And compensation." Ah, here it comes she thought. The real reason he's here, or am I being unfair? She let that go too and stuck to safer ground.

"I've had a written notification from Alexander Whiteley's solicitor asking if you would you accept a written apology? I understand that he is genuinely sorry for the distress he has caused. I've got the letter here."

She indicated a sealed cream envelope on her scratched desk addressed by hand to Mr Carlos Cardoso.

Carlos was outraged. Insulted.

"Certainly not! An apology? It's going to take a great deal more than that to put this right. My whole life has been ruined."

Before she could respond he had reached over the desk in one fast lunge and picked up the envelope. Triumphant he stood up and with a flourish and surprising strength, tore it in half.

"That's what I think of his apology" he proclaimed with perfect diction, and threw the pieces on the desk. Jayne wondered if there was any difference between Carlos the actor and Carlos the person or whether they were in fact, one and the same. It did not matter; she did not much like either.

CHAPTER THIRTY-ONE

The corridors of the Midland Central Hospital were buzzing and flowing. It had started in the arterial passages and was now coursing through the smaller vein and pathways filling the entire concourse with excited furtive whispers, nudges and a battalion of fingers and thumbs enlarging images on smartphones. 'Save The Letterman' was everywhere and everyone was talking about it. Those who had not seen it, knew about it, and those who did not know about it were largely asleep, unconscious or dead.

In her office Patricia was livid. She had ordered her PA to block all emails of support about Alex bloody Whiteley and had opened a packet of chocolate biscuits. She did not even attempt to hide them. Her secretary did not block the emails but quietly diverted them to a large and flourishing file marked A.W. Testimonials. She quite liked Alex; he remembered her name and knew she preferred cats to dogs. It gave her a perverse thrill to use his initials in the title of the file and she knew her boss would never notice. Had she been offered at least even one biscuit she might have felt less insurrectionary, but no, not even at Christmas.

Julia Voss had been one of the first to log into the Facebook Page. She always followed Facebook anonymously – not stalking, just looking. It was a fascinating and useful source of information about her colleagues and hospital staff. Really, some of the things they posted! And the photos! Did they not realise how vulnerable they were making themselves; so much personal information to compromise and embarrass them.

Her own profile was empty, she used her mother's maiden name and had a profile picture only of Klimt's 'The Kiss'. She knew that Whiteley's own profile had been taken down as soon as the media circus about him had begun but this Letterman page was really gathering pace and she was astonished. Mostly patients, of course, but one or two colleagues from his past or other hospitals which even she felt was courageous. Senior management would be watching and noting, reading the comments, monitoring the likes, recording the names. She wondered what the hit rate was but had no way of knowing. And what the hell did this Tiger Lily woman think she would achieve with it? Yes, she had been very ill and Alex had operated successfully on her, but what these ridiculous over-emotional patients did not realise was that it was all about team work and without a team, without people like Her, Alex would be nothing.

In the wide central corridor between the lifts and the central concourse James was peering at his phone. His inbox was empty and he did not know why. Where were all his NHS Trust emails? He would have to contact IT and find out what had happened. In frustration he tapped on the Facebook icon. Someone in Radiology had mentioned something called Save the Letterman which was supposed to be about Mr Whiteley.

Yes. There was Alex, smiling out from the page beneath the bold heading 'Save the Letterman' and an explanation of the page from its founder, Tiger Lily Lacey. He wondered, fleetingly, if he should contact her. Then came to his senses. The statement he made for the disciplinary hearing had already caused enough trouble. No matter that he had told the truth. He hadn't seen anything. Not the initials, or him writing them, or anything else that shouldn't have happened.

Telling the truth was clearly not a good career move. Everyone who had been in theatre that day had been interviewed but he alone had said he had seen nothing.

CHAPTER THIRTY-TWO

While Carlos was in Stroud, Alex was in London. Both were visiting their lawyers but there the similarity ended. RedheadCohen&LeFevre was prestigious, expensive and confident. Their offices proclaimed it; they were the senior judges of their kind, bewigged, exclusive, revered. What they did not know about the law was not worth knowing and woe betide anyone who tried to tell them otherwise. A smart Victorian exterior testified to their solidity and maturity, the discreet black front door with understated brass furniture articulated their superior taste. Triple glazed sash windows and black wrought-iron work suggested a moral fortitude within and politely intimated absolute impregnability to any onslaught from without. Behind the edifice however it was a story of glass, chrome, AppleMacs and technology. Plush, affluent, efficient and driven; well lit, open, airy offices with glass walls, modern art, espresso machines and interns. Nothing Dickensian about their law except the Rule of Precedent and the antique clock in the foyer where Alex was waiting.

Derek Redhead himself, senior partner and principal shareholder came down to greet Alex and take him up to the meeting room.

"Mr Whiteley?"

He extended his hand and gripped Alex's briefly but firmly. "Derek Redhead. May I call you Alex?" Certainly. "This way. After you."

Pleasant, enviably slim, mid 50s, smartly suited, expensively shod with a gold crested signet ring on his little finger, Derek stood to one side to allow Alex lead the way and held open the lift door for him. They glided upward in a silent chrome and glass capsule, the floor beneath their feet clad in the same sound-absorbing grey Axminster as the rest of the building.

"Everyone is here" said Derek as he opened one of the double doors and Alex entered, feeling feted but knowing how much it was costing. Seated around the large round table were his team – another one - but now he was their patient and that felt wrong.

Alex knew only Margaret Wycliffe, the representative of Advanced Medical Insurance which was funding his case. They had spoken several times on the phone and met once when the hospital had suspended him. Then there had been a preliminary consultation in an outpost office of the insurance company in the Midlands where they had drunk instant coffee out of mugs sporting company logos. She was an accountant with sleek symmetrical shoulder length white hair. She wore dark skirt suits, platinum jewellery and Chanel No. 5. Alex liked her. What was more, he trusted her.

Charles Somerton was introduced as his barrister, assisted by Arash Fadaei, a junior barrister learning the trade. Charles was a floppy-haired blonde, slender, confident and sharp witted. He really ought to have been called Sebastian the way he repeatedly flicked his hair with long, pale fingers. Arash was tall, bespectacled and promising, but down trodden. He might have been good looking had he only believed it possible. His lot was always to carry the brief, not always successfully. He kept the documents in a suitcase on wheels which went with him everywhere like a loyal dog in a black coat with zipped pockets.

The introductions were made and Alex took the seat offered to him. Derek launched straight into the meeting; no time to waste. Time was money and Margaret was already looking at her watch.

"Unfortunately, Mr Cardoso has refused to accept your apology, Alex. Charles, what can we expect from the hearing?"

Derek passed the baton to the barrister who fingered his fringe.

"The hospital will try to prove malpractice. They'll find it difficult though, as no harm was done."

Alex appeared impassive but his stomach was churning and he wanted to gag. Malpractice! Of course, no harm was done! He wouldn't do that.

He focussed on the barrister as the conversation continued. Everything else in the room was a blur.

"What about psychological harm?"

Derek did not mess about. Charles' response showed he had anticipated the question.

"Tricky. The Act that encompasses Actual Bodily Harm leading to a recognised psychological illness is outdated and has never been successfully proved. What they certainly will claim is that the hospital has been brought into disrepute."

"Has it?"

Derek asked before Alex could react.

"We'll argue that the Press coverage and adverse criticism is focussed on Alex Whiteley, not the hospital. They will want to prove, however, that there has been a breach of contract by the defendant."

It's as if I don't exist anymore mused Alex as Charles unwrapped the legal defence without even acknowledging him. I'm just the defendant.

"However," Charles's voice rose slightly, "there has been an unexpected development."

Everyone perked up and studied the barrister who flicked his hair back like a thoroughbred.

"Yes" he continued, happy with the attention, "there has been a significant demonstration of support from many of the patients, their family and friends, and even some medical personnel which strengthens our case considerably. Arash?"

As if it was rehearsed double act, Arash took his cue and opened his lap top with a flourish. A click of the mouse and the screen immediately revealed the 'Save The Letterman' Facebook page. He turned the machine around with a single gesture for everyone to see and they leaned forward in a chain circle for a closer view. There was a surprised silence as they surveyed the screen which Arash surreptitiously scrolled down in time with their reading of it. Profile pictures, comments, likes, shares, more comments, emojis, more likes. The responses were coming in even as they watched. It was extraordinary. They were astonished. Arash felt like a conjuror who has just pulled a rabbit from a hat at a children's party.

Alex was the first to speak.

"Who's done this?"

"A lady called Tiger Lily Lacey." Arash answered, gleefully. He was enjoying a rare moment of power and it felt good. "Do you know her?"

"One of my patients." Alex replied in wonder. "I had no idea."

He looked up at the others who now regarded him with renewed interest. Even Margaret felt that this was becoming a more intriguing case. She liked Alex but had been deeply shocked by the allegations made against him and had begun to doubt her own judgement. It looked as if she had been right about him after all, but there was still a long way to go. And an expensive way she reflected.

"This could make all the difference" Charles said. "The hospital will find it difficult to prove that patients have lost confidence in you, Alex."

A person again, not just a defendant thought Alex as he regarded his barrister with gratitude. Margaret the accountant was thinking ahead.

"Are the Hospital Trust aware of this campaign?"

Arash jumped cue with undisguised enthusiasm.

"Ms Lacey has published the email address of the Chief Executive Officer, Patricia Shelton, and asked everyone to contact her direct with their messages of support for Mr Whiteley." He could not help but smile.

"And have they?"

Derek almost had his fingers crossed below the table.

"Disclosures to date suggest that she has been inundated."

Now Alex smiled.

"She won't like that", he said, grinning. Margaret, however, did not share the moment. There was a financial agenda.

"What about compensation?"

Alex's smile died and he felt his stomach twist.

"That is between the hospital and Mr Cardoso."

Margaret's face softened slightly and she pursed her lips *en route* to a smile but it did not arrive.

Now came the question that Alex had to ask. He was not afraid, but he had to know.

"Will he be present at the hearing? Mr Cardoso?"

"No." Charles was definite. "We have a robust defence, Alex, but there is one thing you should know. If the judgement of the hearing goes against you, it's a legal requirement that you're immediately escorted off the hospital premises. You will not be allowed to return. Until the outcome of the hearing you will remain suspended on full pay but must continue to have no contact with the hospital or anyone employed there. There is one more thing. The identity of the patient must remain anonymous. His privacy must be respected and preserved at all costs, especially in the media. He is to be known only as The Patient or Patient C."

Alex was aghast. He hoped that the hearing would clear him but was terrified that it would not. And if that happened, what then?

CHAPTER THIRTY-THREE

The Same Day

Fern had a present for Tiger Lily. Finding a time when she was not hunched over her computer screen was proving a challenge so she had resorted to drastic measures.

"Close your eyes, Tilly!" she ordered, slamming down the cover of the laptop. "Don't argue. Hold out your hands. Both of them together, I don't want you to drop it." She placed a parcel wrapped in brown recycled paper into Tiger Lily's hands. The package was about 25 cm square and 6 cm deep, the size of a small pizza box but heavier and not as greasy. Or warm.

"Open your eyes!" Fern's excitement was palpable and Tilly caught it.

"What is it?" she asked. Fern rolled her eyes,

"Open it and see, numpty."

Tilly shifted the laptop to one side and put the box down onto the table where she began carefully unpicking the Sellotape on the paper. Meticulous and painstaking, sticky millimetre by millimetre, Fern could not bear it.

"Tear it for God's sake!" she roared. Tiger Lily grinned and defied herself as she abandoned care and ripped the paper apart. Inside was a bubble wrapped glass fronted box: an unusually deep white picture frame containing a heart made of staples, some rusty, some twisted and some stained black with dried blood. It was set against a pale pink background and written below the heart was the word 'Love'. Tiger Lily looked up at her partner, puzzled, for explanation.

"They're yours" Fern said, "The staples from your surgery. You know, to hold the wound together."

Tiger Lily stared at her. Fern was enjoying the moment immensely.

"I kept them when the community nurse took them out" she elaborated. "You thought she'd thrown them away but I kept them all, every single one, and had them made up into a heart. Because I love you. And I nearly lost you, but I didn't and you're still here ... " her voice trailed off into nowhere. Tiger Lily shook her head in wonder and kissed away Fern's tears.

Meghan was lying, conscious, quiet and crumpled in her NHS gown on a trolley in anaesthetics. Jason was standing beside the trolley holding her one free hand with both of his own; he did not want to let go. Ever. On the end of her index finger was the plastic peg linking her to the pulse oximeter and the cardiac monitor. Her other hand was taped and stiff with a cannula in one of her lumpy veins, tied to a narrow tube which chained her like a docile puppy to whatever they chose to trickle into her system. The small room was full of people in green gowns, white gowns, aprons over gowns, sloppy rubber shoes and creased lower face masks that sucked in and out over their mouths as they talked. Hairless in hats, fleshless in protective gloves, only their eyes rendered them human as they padded about, hands and arms aloft to avoid contamination, cumbersome in their one size fits all theatre uniforms. One of them, petite and slender was wearing pearl stud earrings and seemed to be in charge. She did not say much but her eyes never stopped watching and the Anaesthetic Registrar – she had called him that when giving an order to what seemed to be an assistant – was clearly terrified of her.

Meghan saw everything but would remember nothing. She felt Jason's hands around her own and the cool cotton of the surgical gown warming against her skin as she lay on the trolley amidst a confusion of sheets, tubes, white and green arms. She wanted to see her feet and wiggle her toes to prove to herself that she was real but someone had covered them and all she could see when she moved them were small cloth valleys running down from low starched cotton hills. Suddenly she was a child again, in bed in the semi darkness of her bedroom in the terraced house in the Rhondda. She used to create worlds and lands with her limbs under sheets making mountains and valleys, earthquakes and then volcanic explosions that metamorphosed the landscape into new and wonderful shapes. Childhood. Oh, so long ago. So far away. Then she thought of Jack and felt the grip of Jason's hands, and she was lying on the trolley again, facing the double doors that led to the theatre. Jack was at school so that was alright and Jason would look after him.

Someone was talking to her. The woman with earrings. What was she saying? That she was the Consultant Anaesthetist and was going to give Meghan – she was Meghan, wasn't she? – a relaxant while the surgeon had a word. A word? What word? What could anyone say? A cold sensation in the back of her hand as something dripped through the cannula. There had been a tap that always dripped in their old bathroom in Wales and Jason had fixed it with a new washer. He was a good man. Resourceful. Kind. Jack would be alright.

Now a different man with dark eyes was talking and he was nice. Tall, reassuring, all white and green and covered up but he said he was the surgeon. Mr Whiteley? No, not him. Another one. Mr Ma, Ma, Drone, something. It did not matter. She focussed dreamily on the conversation she knew she was having with him. No, no last-minute questions. She was having a liver transplant, wasn't she? To make her better? Had she signed a consent form? A glance at Jason who said yes so obviously she had and then she remembered sitting in an office a lifetime ago and signing her name on a permission slip like Jack going off on a school trip and she knew she had said yes and she would gladly sign again, and yes, her name was Meghan Orchard, and she was born when they said she was, and her hospital number was the one on the weightless plastic wristband on her thin yellow arm. And everything was in order and the man was talking to the woman with the earrings, who said she was happy to proceed. Happy. What a strange word to use in the circumstances but never mind, only a word and Jason was bending down to her face and kissing her forehead, like a priest giving a blessing. He was crying. She smiled.

"Don't worry, love. I'll be fine. Look after Jack, won't you?"

Jason nodded his head vigorously and the tears spread over his cheeks.

"Love you, annlwyd. See you on ICU when it's all over."

She squeezed his hand and he vanished. The trolley began to move and the double doors opened. She looked up as she was being wheeled into the corridor leading to the theatre and saw an NHS strip light. Ugly, a stark white light in a yellowing plastic case littered with dead insects. Is this it? she thought. Is this my last view on this earth? An NHS strip light and I'm wearing nothing but an NHS gown. You really can't take it with you. And then there was nothing and she never saw the doors at the end of the corridor of destiny open out into the theatre.

Inside the theatre the surgical team were assembled and poised for action, waiting for curtain up, inwardly trembling with butterflies and pre-performance nerves. Since Alex's departure the teams had been reorganised and shuffled like a deck of cards. The game was the same but the hands and suits had changed; trumps had yet to be decided and some of the players were new to each other. It took time to get used to new partners and patterns of behaviour, to build up the tacit understanding and respect that underpinned efficient team work in their high-pressure environment. Garth followed the patient into the theatre, escorted by the three anaesthetists led by Julia. James was already in place, waiting at the table with the Scrub nurse at his side while the second surgical assistant stood opposite, waiting for the star turn to take his position centre stage. Julia smiled to herself behind her mask as she slipped into her seat beside Meghan's head. She liked the sensation she felt between her legs as she watched Garth assume his place as the head of the surgical table. In the wings stood the two runners, the theatre porter and the theatre sister while the backdrop was made up of assiduous students raised up on a viewing platform for a better view. A full house. At exactly 11.30 am by the clock on the wall, Garth opened Meghan and the performance began.

One o'clock and all was well. The theatre sister made a mental note of the time and disappeared into the office to update her records. The theatre porter followed, unnoticed, knowing that the sister would be preoccupied for at least a few minutes. At the table they were working together as a team with understanding and precision, led by Garth, who was in his element. Julia's smile beneath her mask did not quite reach her eyes but even the anaesthetic registrar noticed with relief that she was mellower than usual. Garth's performance was flawless and fluent; his promotion had made him more self-assured and he hardly stuttered at all.

"Suction ... Swab ... Swab ... Scissors. ...There!" He was tying off the hepatic artery and had adeptly carried out the shunt on the portal vein.

“Next step is to remove the liver.”

He turned his head slightly to make it clear that he was addressing his student audience.

“Make sure you can see. This is a difficult manoeuvre.”

His fingers were deep inside Meghan’s abdominal incision so only the fluttering of his wrists could be seen as he massaged a way forward with his hands under the left lobe of the liver to loosen it. Then he would lift it out.

“This requires skill and care and concentration” he was saying, head bent over the cavity, “to avoid damaging the hepatic veins.” No one spoke. The team held their breath and watched. The fingers dug a little deeper and then the wrists were still.

“She’s bleeding.”

Garth’s voice was small, surprised and unnecessary. They could see that she was bleeding. Profusely. Everywhere. Blood was pooling in the cavity, relentlessly rising then overflowing. Garth’s hands and wrists were hidden in the carmine depths and his arms stuck out of it like tree trunks in a flood. The covering sheets seeped red, became heavy and sank; the blood crept out onto the table then began to drip off it onto the floor in rivulets turning into streams, splashing their feet, soaking their shoes, creeping up their trouser legs. The room reeked of iron, metal and fear. Garth was frozen, arms immersed, sleeves absorbing the blood which was climbing up them - towards his shoulders. There were crimson splashes on his face when he lifted his head to stare disbelievingly first at the room and then at Julia.

“Blood for transfusion from the bank! Now!”

It was James, shouting to the runner.

Then Garth found his proper voice,

"Bloody hell, she's bleeding, er, everywhere."

Shouting now.

"Sucker … second sucker. Quickly!"

Voracious, noisy, slurping sucking.

"James. Retract. Retract I said."

Still the blood swelled up and up and out and over and down.

"You bloody fool! I can't see!" he screamed at James.

They were now stepping in it, treading it across the floor, slipping and sliding as runners tried to locate the blood supplies in the theatre and to contact the blood bank for more. It was pandemonium, biblical. The theatre sister had returned and skidded on her way into the room, landing heavily in the rising tide. She was streaked and smeared red and shouting for the porter, for blood supplies, for calm. At the table which now looked like a sacrificial altar to the black arts, James, Garth and the second assistant were desperately packing the wound. Frantic hands, fingers, fists pressing and pushing into the wound to try and stem the flow. They were all shouting but no one heard what was being said. Calls for the porter, blood, packs, transfusion, phones ringing, furiously loud demands and instructions to those on the other end, feet slopping and slapping on the sticky floor, the students mesmerised and appalled into silence and then, cutting through the chaos like an icy draught, the sound of the monitors alarming like frantic pinball machines signalling a change in Meghan's condition. Julia had been studying them with horror. The shrillness of her voice pierced the mayhem as she called to her assistants and anyone else who would listen,

"Calcium! Bicarbonate. Adrenaline. Get me adrenaline!"

Garth was still shouting at the hapless James to

"Suck. Suck. I said retract you idiot! I can't see a bloody thing!"

He looked up from the table, yelled "Get me someone who

knows how to bloody assist!" then screamed at the second assistant, "Pass me a clamp ... No, a bigger one."

Somehow the larger clamp found its way from the instrument trolley to the table and Garth slammed it into the bleeding hole where he threw his weight behind it to shut off the blood flow. For one wonderful instant it seemed to stop but then there was an explosion of liquid upwards, a jet of livid red that soared into the air and cascaded down in a flurry of mist and spatter and gore.

"Oh Christ. The clamp's gone through the IVC."

Garth had perforated the huge, fast flowing crimson river of the inferior vena cava delivering blood from the lower part of the body back to the heart for oxygenation.

"She's arresting!"

Julia was transfixed by the monitors charting every passing second of Meghan's life. Garth was galvanised into action and began immediate CPR, soaked in blood, sweating, oblivious to everything except the need to keep the heart pumping, the chest moving in and out, the patient alive. Both hands, palms down, one hand on top of the other he pressed and released, pressed and released. Again. Pressed. Released. And always the blood; so much of it.

"We're losing her. Garth, do something!" Julia pleaded.

"I can't control the bleeding. I can't..."

"You must! Think!" Julia was desperate.

"Er, packs! 2/0 Prolene. More packs...."

He tried to plug the abyss as James administered the Prolene but still the blood pulsated out and up and out.

"Suck!" ... "More suck!" Garth continued, frantically shovelling more packing into the already sodden pads that were doing no more than absorb the liquid.

It was Julia who assumed control and restored composure.

“Garth, we need to stop. Nothing is clotting. Look at her lines - they’re all bleeding.”

The noise in the room was fading with Meghan’s life. The monitor was erratic, infrequent, then silent - for a moment, before it started to emit a constant, high pitched monotone.

“I think she’s gone”.

Julia spoke quietly. The pinball was slowing to a stop. The only sounds to be heard were the flatlining monitor and the dripping of blood; the only movements the single moving stripe on the monitor screen and the silent snaking of the blood spreading across the floor.

James looked up at the clock. “Time of death 13.44” he said.

CHAPTER THIRTY-FOUR

Patricia was uneasy. She looked at her watch, then at the time on her computer screen, then back at her watch, suspiciously, as if it was a child caught hiding sweet wrappers. Surely the hearing must be over by now? It was after three. She got up from her desk and paced over to the one of the windows but not to look at the view. Hari was sitting in an uncomfortable easy chair watching her and wondering how she balanced in those spiky shoes. They had red soles which he knew meant something but couldn't remember what; his daughter would know. He'd ask her when he got home.

"Haven't they come to a decision yet?"

She had spun round and left vicious dents in the carpet from her vertiginous heels as she headed back to the chair behind her desk. "The actual hearing finished hours ago."

"They're being thorough" he replied serenely. She glared at him from under her portrait behind her on the wall. She looked better in oils he decided; less haggard, kinder. Silent.

"A surgeon burns his initials on a comatose patient. How long does it take to find him guilty of malpractice?" She was studying her watch again with disbelief.

"Marked, not burned." Hari was still serene, but unambiguous. "You know it's not that straightforward."

"I know that if I get one more bloody email from someone telling me what a marvellous surgeon he is, I'll brand him myself."

She really meant it; Hari took evasive action.

"I'm more concerned about the death of Mrs Orchard."

He had Patricia's attention now. Serious and focussed. Genuinely concerned. Meghan's death had shocked them all.

"Yes. What happened?"

"Catastrophic bleeding from the hepatic veins. She died of blood loss." He said it very quietly.

"She bled to death?" Patricia spoke much louder.

"Yes. She bled out."

"In my hospital?" He nodded and sighed together.

How?"

"A combination of poor surgical technique during the removal of the liver and an inherent problem with the patient herself. Her liver disease was very advanced because she had to wait so long for her transplant. She deteriorated significantly while on the waiting list. She was also very coagulopathic."

Hari caught Patricia's lack of understanding and elucidated.

"What I mean is that because of her advanced liver disease her own blood wouldn't clot as well as it should and the team were a little behind in correcting it."

He was paraphrasing but it was not so much the medical details she was interested in as the culpability.

"Garth?"

Hari considered carefully before he answered. He knew that his answer held a friend and colleague's career in the balance.

"Impossible to say. The anaesthetist may have played a part. The blood clotting issue" he added by way of answer to her raised eyebrows. "But there's no way of knowing how stress and pressure can affect even the most experienced surgeons and their teams."

His Chief Executive regarded him with extreme irritation and some distaste.

"Hell" she said. Hari sighed again then threw more fat onto the fire.

"There will have to be a SIRI of course – Serious Incident Requiring Investigation."

"Thank you, Hari, but I know exactly what a SIRI is."

Tetchy and riled. She rolled her eyes and put her manicured hands to her head which she held tight, as if to prevent it falling apart.

"My God!" she said, talking to the desk top. "And it's only Monday."

The landline on the desk shrilled, shattering her pity-me moment. Saved by the bell thought Hari wryly. Suffused with sudden energy she seized the receiver, put it to her ear and listened, galvanised.

"Decision time" she announced to Hari. "Let's go."

They slipped unnoticed through one of the double doors into the meeting room. The hearing was still in full session as the summing up and verdict were about to be delivered. Patricia had wanted to be present from the start but it had been deemed inappropriate for her or members of the senior management team to participate in or even witness the proceedings. A conflict of interest she had been told which had done nothing to improve her temper or modify her dislike of Alex. She could see him clearly, sitting with his legal team at the end of one side of the table. He was wearing his usual white shirt and dark suit with a very subdued tie indeed, she noticed.

It was the suit Alex had taken off the day he was suspended. When he had taken it out of the wardrobe that morning it had smelled of the MCH: hand sanitiser, hospital corridors, canteen coffee, ventilated air scented with the powerful aroma of death and dying. His ties were neatly arranged in lines on the inside of the wardrobe door but when he saw them, garish, cocky and loud, he wanted to weep. Was he really the kind of man who wore such things? Sitting forlornly at the long table he looked smaller somehow, Patricia mused, overshadowed by a rather foppish barrister who no doubt cost a fortune. Beside him sat a sharply suited solicitor (also outrageously expensive) and a white-haired woman with a hatchet face who must be from the insurance company that was paying for it all. On the other side of the table facing them was the MCH lawyer, Helena, looking intense, smart, capable but markedly less expensive. Patricia hoped it was not an omen.

The Disciplinary Panel were seated together at the other end of the long table. In the centre was the Chief Nurse of the Midland Central who was presiding over the meeting with the authority and presence of a cinematic Matron. Her slight frame and youth were misleading; she had the voice of a Drill Sergeant if she chose and a glance that could ossify wood. Sitting on her right was the Senior Doctor from the Ribblesdale Trust and next to him his colleague, Jeff Balaak, all blondeness and briefcase as he leaned back in his chair and studied Alex. On the other side of the Chief Nurse were the MCH Patient Representative and the MCH HR Director. No problem there, Patricia knew that the HR Director would toe the MCH line but she looked with curiosity at the Patient Representative who was unknown to her and had been selected without her input.

He looked reasonable enough. Middle aged, innocuous, healthy complexion. It was impossible to tell which way he would jump. For or against Alex? What if he had the decisive vote? Someone had to in a panel of five.

"Who's the Patient Representative?" she whispered to Hari.

"Don't know" he whispered back. "A member of the patient/hospital forum I think but I don't know his name."

The Chief Nurse was speaking, addressing Alex directly, clearly and calmly.

"This Disciplinary Hearing must decide whether or not you are a fit person to continue working at the Midland Central Hospital. We have heard in depth all the arguments and have finally, after much careful deliberation and, I may say, robust debate, come to a decision."

She paused and peered into the absolute silence. Alex had inhaled deeply on the word decision and was holding his breath. Beneath the table he was clenching his hands into tight fists which were punched into his thighs. Oh, if only Lisa was here, Alex thought, but she had been refused access and, in a way, he was relieved. What if it went against him? He would not be able to bear her pain.

The Chief Nurse resumed her judgement.

"Your behaviour has been totally unacceptable. You have abused your position of trust towards a patient in your care. No such behaviour must ever happen again."

Patricia silently screamed yes and mentally punched the air. Here it comes she thought. Alex held his breath. No one moved. Outside, even the traffic seemed to have stopped.

"On that condition it has been decided that you be allowed to continue in your current role."

Alex breathed out and released his fingers leaving white marks on his palms and narrow red arcs where his nails had dented the skin. Patricia was aware of a loud gasp and only realised she had made it when Hari turned to her in surprise. The Patient Representative was smiling at Alex as the Chief Nurse continued, stern and uncompromising.

"I may say that the support of your patients has influenced our decision to no small degree. Without their obvious confidence in you it is unlikely that you would have been reinstated. You will be issued with a final written warning."

The atmosphere softened, the traffic noise resumed and the panel made to move as the hearing drew to a close. Subdued conversations and whispered conferrals started up among the various factions. Alex looked stunned while his team stood and shook each other's hands with the relaxed smiles of the politely victorious. Helena looked as dark as her clothes as she packed her papers into a folder and got up to leave. Patricia nudged Hari and hissed,

"Find out who the Patient Representative is."

Poor sod thought Hari, I hope he's not going to be ill any time soon. He decided he would forget to find out the man's name.

Alex sat, motionless, eyes closed. Relieved, stunned, ashamed.

CHAPTER THIRTY-FIVE

"Try and eat something, Jack. Breakfast is the most important meal of the day."

Jason was doing his best.

"Look, I've made you eggy bread!"

Jack said nothing but pushed the plate away the full length of his short arm into the butter. Jason tried again.

"Is there anything you'd like instead? Cereal? Coco Pops to make chocolate milk?"

Jack made no response.

"Do you feel okay?" his father asked and then wanted to punch himself for such stupidity.

"You don't feel sick or headachy or anything like that?"

Jack shook his head and focussed on the tablecloth. Jason was helpless. Latisha had said that Jack was very quiet and had barely eaten since he had been told about his mother's death. It had been done gently and kindly and lovingly but it was the news that he would never see his Mam again and no one was quite sure how it would affect him, or when. Or if he had understood quite what it meant. The hospital had been very good and there was lots of support and advice from the welfare people and even Social Services but in the end, it was just him, Jason, on his own, without his beloved Meggie. And he did not know what to do.

"How about school today?" he ventured, brightly. It had been suggested that he should get a sense of routine and normality back into Jack's life as soon as possible but that frightened him. What if Jack forgot his Mam? What if the lad did not realise that she had gone for good; how would he explain it to him? How would he cope alone when his son was out of a house that was so full of Meghan but so achingly empty?

"We could go to the park and play football?"

Jack said nothing and continued to stare at the surface of the table.

Jason had an idea. He went out of the kitchen into the hall to the row of hooks on the wall behind the front door where they kept all the coats, jackets, scarves and hats in the winter. On the floor was a muddle of wellies, shoes, trainers and Jack's lucky football. As he bent down to pick it up his head brushed against the softness of a fleece which released a wholesome earthy aroma of warm sunshine, Welsh hills, coal dust, Palmolive soap. Meghan. He buried his head into the pale blue velvetiness, the colour of her eyes, her smile, the silkiness of her hair, her downy supple warm body before she became ill and he wanted to howl the world away.

"Dad!"

Who?

Him?

Him. Jason. Jack's only living parent.

And then he knew. Knew that he would have to clear the house of her clothes and her physical presence but that she would still be there. Would always be there - in Jack. Jason picked up the football and took it into the kitchen where he put it on the table in front of his son who finally looked up at him.

"The park?"

Jack nodded.

"School tomorrow?"

Jack pulled a face.

"School tomorrow then." said Jason.

CHAPTER THIRTY-SIX

In Stroud, Jayne Lavery had just delivered the news to her least favourite client that the surgeon who had left his initials on the transplant liver had been reinstated. She had predicted what the reaction would be but its vitriol had taken even her by surprise. It was an un-rehearsed performance; Carlos had never imagined for a moment that that monster would ever be allowed to set so much as a cloven hoof inside a hospital again, never mind operate.

"It is absolutely outrageous. Totally unacceptable. That, that..." he searched for the words, "that assassin, that black hearted-devil tried to kill me."

"Mr Cardoso..."

"He destroyed my liver and now he has destroyed my life. How can he be allowed to continue working?"

"Actually, Mr Cardoso, you no longer have that liver."

He ignored her. The eloquence had to be continued. There must be something in Macbeth or Hamlet that he could draw on for dramatic effect; he'd have to check. Meanwhile, the rhetorical question:

"What will he do next?"

Dramatic pause. Step forward, address the audience.

"No one is safe."

Second pause. Inhale.

"Mr Cardoso, this is not helping."

She might as well not have been in the room.

"What about me? What about my pain and suffering? How could a so-called disciplinary hearing disregard the agony to which I have been subjected? I am in torment and who cares? No one!"

"Mr Cardoso! Sit down! Please!"

Finally, he seemed to hear and responded by flinging himself into a hard-backed chair with an ancient horse hair seat that creaked as he landed on it. Furiously he twisted himself to one side and rested one arm on the back of the chair while he gripped the ubiquitous bottle of Evian in the other. Jayne wondered how long it would be before he opened it and took a sip. She gave him two minutes.

"He cannot be allowed to get away with it, Miss Lavery. He must pay for what he did."

Jayne knew that while he implied retribution he was actually referring to financial recompense and she did not blame him. What had happened to him was awful by any standard and she too had been astounded to hear that Mr Whiteley had been cleared of malpractice. She also knew that as a lawyer she should not be surprised at the way that justice sometimes worked; perhaps that was why it was so fascinating and she stuck with it, even when she had to deal with clients like this one.

"We are discussing compensation for you with the hospital, Mr Cardoso. They are currently offering a one-off payment of

£20,000 plus costs."

He did not hesitate for a moment before he came back at her,

"I deserve more. Much more."

"I'll see if I can talk them up, but what they are suggesting is fair" she answered in measured tones, then added slyly "considering no physical harm was done."

He eyed her cynically, unscrewed the top of the bottle of Evian with his free hand and took a slow, deliberate drink of water. She wanted to glance at her watch but resisted.

"It's not about the money of course." He was being chattier now, but she was not deceived for a moment.

"Alexander Whiteley is a criminal. He ought to be in prison for what he's done to me."

"Whether he has committed a crime or not would have to be proved. I think we should talk to the CPS – the Criminal Prosecution Service – about bringing a possible case. You may not get Legal Aid I'm afraid, but I can look into that for you if like?"

Yes, he would like, but if he did not qualify, he did not care.

"He mustn't be allowed to get away with it, Miss Lavery." Carlos was on a crusade. For the first time in his life, he had a mission and it gave him purpose; he was empowered.

"The public needs to be protected from people like him. It is my duty to bring him to justice and that is what I am going to do. Whatever it takes."

CHAPTER THIRTY-SEVEN

It was a perfect early Autumn afternoon. The rain had cleared leaving the dusty summer-bleached countryside washed and laundered, refreshed, smelling of wet grass, blackberries and fruit ripening. It was noisy with birds and trees adjusting their leaves against a teasing breeze that tweaked and tugged small branches as easily as the hairs on a baby's head. The tree trunks groaned slightly at the windy impertinence but did not move. Dressed in the fiery colours of the dying world they knew that soon they would lose their foliage so hung on to it as long as they could, defying the approaching winter with increasing depths of burnished bursting colour, a tenacious storm of reds, yellows, oranges and umbers. The wind would occasionally mount an attack, rushing into them and shouting wildly, weakening their resolve, picking off the vulnerable and weak, but in the main the trees stood firm, bending and flowing with the assailant but never succumbing. This maddened the wind that wailed with frustration and renewed its assault but then exhausted itself with crying and blowing and retired to lick its wounds.

Lisa and Alex were walking Baldrick away from the tarmac and the city, away from the hearing and the hospital but not the reality of what had happened. Holding her husband's arm, Lisa was a small figure beside him but they walked together, pace for pace into the belligerent wind under the crashing waves of the trees. Since the hearing had ended, he had said little. Having told her in detail what had happened, who said what, how they spoke, what it meant, he had been reticent and quiet and she had not pushed him. In his own time, she had thought.

He had got up in the night and gone downstairs to make tea and sit in the dim kitchen with Baldrick wheezing and snoring at his feet while he stared out into the darkness, sipping his tea without tasting it or noticing when it had gone cold. She had felt the duvet shift and heard the mattress sigh as he had crept out of bed, heard the muffled slap of his bare feet on the wooden floor as he retrieved his dressing gown from the back of the door and the flutter of the cloth as he put it on and tied the belt. And she had lain immobile so that he thought she was asleep and could pride himself on not having awoken her. Alex was fighting with himself and he had to do it alone.

They walked for some time without speaking except to call Baldrick back when he wandered too far or started to sniff something unsavoury. Off the lead, for once, he was making the most of the freedom, pushing boundaries and exploring excitingly unforeseen possibilities in every scent. The humans seemed preoccupied so he would make the most of it. When Alex had brought Lisa a cup of tea in bed that morning, as he always did when he was at home, he had said only one thing to her by way of explanation for his sleepless night.

She had not commented but merely said that he should think about it. Now it was time to talk.

"You've made up your mind?"

They were still walking but she was looking directly at him.

"I have no choice. My position is untenable. You lead by example. I can't possibly head up a department now."

"What about your patients?"

"They'll be taken care of. MCH will do that, with or without me."

He had clearly thought this through.

"But Alex, what will you do?"

"I don't know. Find another job somewhere else? Not as a head of department obviously, but maybe as a locum or something like that. Medicine is my life, Lisa. It's all I've ever done; all I've ever wanted to do. I don't know how to do anything else."

Lisa was quiet for a moment, trying to imagine what lay ahead.

"Have you heard from the General Medical Council yet?"

"Not a word. Any future I might have in medicine depends on them. You know that don't you?"

Yes, she knew. She knew only too well. After considering for a few minutes, assuming a contrived nonchalance she did not feel she threw the outlook wide open.

"Perhaps it's time to do something completely different?"

He froze mid step and looked at her. She met his surprised stare with equanimity and composure. In the near distance Baldrick also briefly came to a halt, eyed them briefly to ensure they were not changing direction and then enthusiastically resumed his explorations.

"Like what?"

It was a good question.

"I don't know." She paused then added,

"You do know that I'll go along with whatever happens?"

He was amazed and shook his head in awe as he marvelled at her.

"I love you" was all he could say.

"I know" she replied, then glanced ahead to check that

Baldrick was behaving himself. He wasn't. Having suddenly encountered a particularly attractive smelling decomposing small animal of indistinguishable origin he was just tucking into it with relish and alacrity when she spotted him.

"Baldrick! No! No! Drop it! Whatever it is. Drop!"

Now she was running towards him. No time to savour it, just eat. Baldrick gulped down as much as he could before she flung herself onto his collar and yanked him away.

"Baldrick! Bad dog! Spit it out! You're disgusting."

She was trying, unsuccessfully to wrestle the decaying flesh out of his mouth but he won and swallowed it with just a slight gag as it lodged, momentarily, in his gullet before it was beyond reach. Then for some reason the big one was laughing and the small one joined in and he wasn't in trouble so he wagged his stumpy tail. Humans were really very odd.

CHAPTER THIRTY-EIGHT

Patricia Shelton was not a happy Chief Executive Officer but she was always a professional one. She had dressed with especial care that morning in a navy fitted shift dress and collarless knee length coat. The dress was sleeveless so she would have to keep the coat on to conceal the sag of her crêpey upper arms but it made her feel streamlined and moved easily over her curves which gave her confidence. Waisted skirts were becoming uncomfortable and tight these days; blouses rode up out of them when she walked but she disliked the alternative - loose tops always looked so matronly.

On the day of the Hearing she had worn her Laboutins which was a mistake and she hoped no one had noticed their red soles. They gave out the wrong message about her status and she would stick to the High Street pencil heels in future, especially if she was to be seen in the public areas of the hospital. She always drove herself to work in a modest middle of the range eco-friendly Vauxhall of inane description and left the Range Rover at home. Really, she thought as she walked from the car park to the main entrance, some of her senior consultants would do well to follow her example.

In her office she walked over to her desk and put her briefcase on the floor by her chair as she sat down. In the middle of the desk was a hand-written envelope, addressed to The Chief Executive Officer of the Midland Central Hospital Trust, written out in full. Unusual. Formal, official. There was no stamp so it had obviously been delivered in person. The internal hospital post never arrived much before her mid-morning coffee and the general mail sometime after. She picked up the envelope, studied the front for a moment then turned it over. Clearly hand sealed and stuck down so meant to be private; for her eyes only. Normally her PA routinely opened all the post for her and sent it through in a creased but tidy pile so that all she had to do was read, sift and respond. This was intriguing and she was curious. She opened the envelope with one flourishing swipe of the decorative letter knife she kept in the bottom drawer for opening packets of biscuits.

The letter was word processed on a sheet of A4 paper, folded three ways; formal, neat, bland, hand-signed in ink. Ink, not biro. From an old-fashioned fountain pen. It took her no more than fifteen seconds to read the letter but her mouth opened slightly with surprise as she followed the sentences. As soon as she had finished, she jabbed her finger on the numbers of the phone on the desk and barked into the speaker.

"Hari. My office. Now."

Then she returned her attention to the letter which she re-read more slowly. This time her mouth was closed and had curved into a self-satisfied smile which nearly reached her nostrils. There was a knock at her door and Hari bowled straight in, unsummoned, looking anxious.

"What is it? What's happened!"?"

He was surprised to see her smiling and was by now utterly perplexed.

"Read this."

She handed him the letter and watched his face with anticipation and undisguised glee. At first Hari was too astonished to react with anything other than dilated eyes and flying eyebrows.

“He’s resigned” he said, his voice rising in pitch at the end of the second word. It was a statement and a question and he looked to Patricia as if for clarification.

“Yes!”

She was loud, grateful, relieved. Exultant.

“We’ve got rid of him.”

The initial euphoria soon wore off. Patricia was not one to dwell on the present but preferred to keep her sights on the future, although she never forgot the past.

The problem now was what to do about the Head of Department job. Whether or not Garth was capable was irrelevant as he was the subject of a Serious Incident Investigation and could not possibly be made substantive. He would have to continue as the acting Head of Department for the moment – but no longer than that - and they would have to appoint a replacement. Whatever he was, Alex had been a reliable leader who had introduced innovative procedures and established a cost-effective, well-run department. There were factions within it that occasionally clashed and bickered but that was normal: too many intelligent, ambitious people in the same place all pursuing the same goals. Like over-bred pedigree dogs, she thought and smiled to herself at the Crufts analogy. It was such a high-profile department and that froze her good humour. Hmm. High profile before Lettergate as she now thought of it for all the right reasons, and now, even more in the public domain since for all the wrong ones. Whoever took on the role would have to be not only medically impeccable but media savvy.

There was a patient knock at the door.

"Yes. Come in".

It was Hari.

"Ah. The very man I wanted to see. We need to discuss the Liver department and who's going to head it up. I think we need to make a new appointment. What about someone from outside the hospital? New blood."

Hari flinched. Was that her idea of a pun, a joke? In the light of the current Serious Incident Investigation, it was in exceedingly poor taste. But then he remembered that Patricia did not make jokes so ignored it.

"This is an opportunity to find somebody with skill and vision who can take the department forward in the right direction." Hari knew what that meant: someone who would do exactly what Patricia wanted and who would ultimately become the new Medical Director. Well, he hadn't gone yet so she was stuck with him for the time being. He put on his earnest 'I share your vision' face.

"I absolutely agree about the need for someone with fresh ideas and energy to take the department forward but I'm not sure about an external appointment. It would cause huge problems within the existing set up."

"Go on."

"They're an established team; they know each other, warts and all. It's expected that one of them will be the new clinical lead and there'll be a riot if they're all passed over for an outsider. It's the one thing that will unite them and they'll all work together against the newcomer. It'd be a disaster."

Patricia sighed. Bloody medics; prima donnas all.

"So, what do you suggest?"

Hari was relieved to have reached safer ground.

"An internal appointment. No doubt about it."

"Any suggestions?"

That was more difficult and no less fraught, but not insoluble.

"There are a number of options. There's Garth who can be made substantive."

Patricia shook her heard vigorously.

"No. Impossible. He's under Serious Incident Investigation. What kind of message would that send out? There's also the issue of photographing patients without their consent.

"Then it has to be one of the other senior consultants already in the department. They're not as experienced as Garth but are just as skilful and may even be more up to date in terms of training and research."

Patricia was listening intently.

"Anyone in mind?"

Yes. Laura Beechwood."

"A woman?" It was out of Patricia's mouth before she could check herself. Hari was shocked.

"Yes. A woman. Is that an issue?"

"No! Absolutely not. It's a great idea, Hari. Inspired. Someone with a completely different perspective on things. Forward thinking. Moving with the times. Equal opportunities. Is she up to it?"

"I believe so, yes. She is respected and liked by her colleagues and not just in the Liver Department. The patients love her, especially our ladies who often ask for her as they say she understands them better and they can talk to her. She's very capable, good with people and I think she got a distinction when she qualified but I'd have to check that."

Patricia was already convinced but erred on the side of considered caution as good form. Besides, she wanted to know more about the woman. Would she tow the line? Follow protocol? Do as she was told? It was a shame that Garth had fouled up so badly on the medical front; in other respects he would have been an ideal HoD: so pliant.

"I'd like to see her CV and then maybe have a chat with her, informally, over a coffee or something. A chance encounter, that sort of thing. Can you arrange it?"

"Of course."

"How would the others react to her promotion?"

She's already making up her mind, thought Hari. Well, it's a good decision and he wanted to smile because it had been his idea but Patricia would always think it was hers.

"There might be some initial jealousy and reaction but nothing insurmountable. She's one of them; they know her; they can put her promotion down to the fact that women are being positively discriminated against these days so it reflects more on the times than on them. Yes, I think it would work."

Patricia was already anticipating the positive public image that a female Head of Department would convey and feeling exhilarated. She was working ahead.

"Will she be the first female Head of a Liver Department?"

"Not sure; I'll find out, but certainly she'd be the first in a hospital of this size and importance. It would definitely be a high-profile appointment."

"I'd like to change the job title in keeping with the forward-looking nature of the appointment. A new title for a new era. How about Clinical Director of the Liver Transplant, Hepatology and HPB Surgery Department? It's a bit of a mouthful but it has gravitas and shows that we take the role of women in medicine very seriously. This will put MCH on the political map, Hari."

Hari had never seen Patricia so animated. However, he had to be realistic.

"Does Garth know?" he asked.

"About the resignation or the decision to make a new appointment?"

"Both."

"Neither, unless you've said something to him?"

Hari shook his head.

"No. Nothing."

"Good. But you'll have to, sooner rather than later. Today don't you think?"

Hari nodded without enthusiasm.

"What was it you wanted to see me about?" Patricia asked.

"Garth, actually." Hari replied. "But it looks like we've covered it."

"Excellent!" beamed Patricia. "I'll leave it to you then. Can you also put together a job description for the new appointment? Shall we say by the end of today? Excellent! Thank you, Hari."

As he walked away from her office down the corridor to his own, Hari felt depressed. This was not what he had come into medicine to do and he recalled the exuberance and ideals of his med. school days with Garth. So, it was with some trepidation and regret that he texted Garth, asking him to come to the Medical Director's office at his earliest convenience. A bit formal he thought, but he hoped that it would give his friend a hint that it was something serious.

It did. Garth was sitting in a meeting with other departmental heads and senior colleagues discussing the wording of the MCH Mission Statement. It was an annual event, considered utterly meaningless and a waste of valuable 'patient interface' time by everyone present but was an obligatory part of their 'leadership agenda' as laid down by the Chief Executive Officer so they were all there, in body if not in spirit. Julia was sitting close enough next to Garth to experience the vibration of his phone as the text arrived. Neither of them ever touched in public: too indiscreet, but Julia especially enjoyed the frisson of an illicit, covert physical magnetism between them hidden in plain sight. Surreptitiously Garth read the text, showed it to Julia and got up to leave. She would explain his sudden absence if necessary but it was not unusual for senior staff to be summoned from meetings – it was a hospital after all, and who knew what might be happening?

"Text me" Julia hissed as he was leaving. He nodded and headed for Hari's office.

"Come in!" Hari called and even he was surprised at the speed at which Garth had arrived.

"Garth! Thank you for coming so quickly. This won't take long but I wanted you as Acting Head of Department to be the first to know. You've heard that Alex has been reinstated?"

Oh Yes. Everyone in the hospital had heard. The outcome of the Disciplinary Hearing had reached as far as Podiatry, Maternity and Tropical Diseases on the perimeter of the hospital site even before the Panel had disbanded and the Minutes of the meeting been completed. Since the news had been posted on the Facebook page people had been talking of little else and it was perhaps the only single subject that had bridged the traditional patient-doctor divide.

Hari plunged on.

"Well, there has been a development. Alex has resigned."

Garth boggled.

"Resigned? When? Why?"

He was genuinely baffled. Who on earth would resign as a Head of Department? It was inconceivable.

"He feels that his position is untenable. That he has lost credibility and must therefore step down."

Hari paused for a moment for Garth to absorb this concept

before he continued, "It shows some integrity and courage I think, don't you?"

Garth could only nod in disbelief and wait. Who would replace Alex?

"You will of course continue as the Acting Head of Department for the time being."

Hari stopped and looked at his friend properly for the first time. This was not what Garth had wanted to hear. The ensuing silence was heavy and awkward, suffocating. Garth's face was reddening with resentment and anger. For the time being? Not permanently? He rose to leave; he had nothing else to say, at least not to Hari.

"Garth!"

Hari was calling after him as he stormed towards the door. He turned, hostile and humiliated.

"What?"

"The resignation is confidential for the moment, until an announcement is made. Please keep it to yourself."

Garth ignored him, wrenched open the door and was halfway down the corridor by the time the door slammed stridently behind him.

It was lucky that the meeting had finished when Julia picked up Garth's text or she would have caused consternation. He kept it simple: 'AW resigned. Say nothing' but that was more than enough to make her whoop loudly with triumph. Yes! Alex Whiteley had gone! At last! Garth would be confirmed as the Head of Department and they could all get on with lives as if the dreadful man had never existed. It was moments like these that made life inexpressibly sweet and she was an image of smiling beatitude as she prepared for routine surgery that afternoon, to the utter amazement of her colleagues and terror of her students. An antagonistic autocratic Ms Voss they had learned to cope with; a grinning benevolent one was unknown, deeply disconcerting and left them feeling vulnerable and insecure.

Garth had sent another text arranging to meet her in the early evening as he 'had things to discuss with her.' He did indeed she surmised and she could hardly wait. Hari had confidentially emailed Alex to inform him that his resignation had been confirmed but would not be announced until his successor had been appointed. This would be very soon so please could the news of the resignation be kept quiet until then? Alex had readily agreed, anxious to delay it long enough for he and Lisa to pack, put Baldrick in the back of the car and take off somewhere remote to be out of the way when the bomb went off. He had privately messaged Tiger Lily who had prepared a statement and would post it on the 'Save The Letterman' page the moment he gave her the go ahead to do so.

Patricia had decided to make a dual public announcement in the hope that one would cancel out the other.

"Damage limitation" she told Hari. "There's bound to be a reaction and everyone will be talking about it so we might as well get them both over together. With luck the news about Laura will offset Alex's departure, it'll be a five-day wonder and then it'll be business as usual."

Hari had his doubts, but kept them to himself. It was Garth he was worried about. Had he known about his friend's affair it would have been Julia who worried him more.

Garth meanwhile was in a state of barely suppressed agony which those who witnessed it put down to disappointment about not being made the substantive Head of Department now that Alex had been reinstated. Garth was sure he loved Julia; had never met anyone like her. He loved her intellect, her sensuality and the edge of danger he felt in her company but there were times, he had to admit it, when the depth of her passions and unpredictable volatility frightened him. He had no idea how she would react to the news that he had been passed over. And he was right to be apprehensive.

“What do you mean ‘for the time being’?” she screamed. “How dare he? And that Shelton bitch, I bet this was all her idea. She’s never liked you. You’re the next in line, the natural successor, the most senior, the most experienced; you’ve been there longer than any of the others. They can’t just appoint someone else, not when you’re in charge.”

She barely paused for breath.

“How dare they? Are you sure you heard correctly? What exactly did Hari say? I thought he was your friend? The bastard. I’ll never forgive him. Never.”

She was panting with fury and venom. Garth wondered about trying to appease her but elected to remain dumb. Let her rage it out then try to speak. He watched her chiselled features become sharp angles fused together by loathing and fury. Ugly. Thin lips in a tight line when not flanking white, precise teeth spitting out bile and wormwood, increasingly acidic and bitter, eyes small and mean.

“I blame Alex Whiteley for this” she screeched. “I bet he put them up to it. This was his idea. Anything to get back at you.”

Even Garth had to say something now.

“No. That’s not possible. This is nothing to do with him.”

“How do you know? There’s nothing he’d stop at to get revenge on you. He probably agreed to resign as long as you weren’t made Head of Department. I wouldn’t put anything past him. I hate him. None of this would have happened if it wasn’t for him. If he hadn’t branded that patient and been suspended you wouldn’t have had to operate on that patient who died and be investigated and you’d be Head of Department. Everything is all his fault. I hate him.”

She was crying hot ferocious tears, violently gasping for breath, shuddering. He timidly put his arms round her and began to rock her as she stood upright, gently, like a baby. She turned on him with fury, shoved him aside and slapped his face.

Fern was pushing the shopping trolley in the home baking, herbs and spices aisle when her phone burst into song. Easy to find for once as it was in a trouser pocket with the shopping list that Tiger Lily always made and she never read. Tilly hated shopping and always made such a fuss about the time it took. Fern listened to her phone in silence then simply walked out of the supermarket, abandoning her trolley, squeezing past the queue at the busy check out, marching out of the automatic doors to the car.

Tiger Lily was watching for her out of the front window. She waved then disappeared as she went to open the door and then they were sitting in the cluttered living room in front of the laptop.

"But Tilly, are you sure? How do you know?"

"He private messaged me on Facebook, on the Letterman page."

"What did he say?"

"Just that he was going to resign, with immediate effect and that he wanted me to know and that it'd be alright for me to post something about it at the appropriate moment."

"What did you say?"

"I didn't know what to say. But yes, of course I would post something but he'd have to let me know when. And that I was really, really sorry. Oh Fern! It's such a shame. All those patients who need him."

"But why? Why is he doing this?"

"He said that his position was untenable so he had no choice. He says he's lost credibility."

They looked at each other: Tiger Lily emotional and tearful, Fern more measured.

“In a way he’s right.”

“Oh Fern! Don’t say that! You don’t mean it, surely?”

Fern shook her head at Tiger Lily apologetically and put her arms around her.

“Don’t worry.” She was trying to console her. “We can still support him and do what we can to help. If that’s what he wants of course.”

CHAPTER THIRTY-NINE

As one storm passed another, far more tempestuous, cracked open. Like everyone else, Malcolm Piggott was completely blind-sided by the MCH Press Release stating that it was with regret that the resignation of Consultant Surgeon Alexander Whiteley had been accepted by the hospital but that they were delighted to announce that his successor would be Consultant Surgeon Ms Laura Beechwood, who would henceforth be known as the Clinical Director of the illustrious department of which she as assuming control. They thanked Mr Whiteley for his dedicated contribution to the hospital and wished him well for the future. Ms Beechwood's appointment would take place with immediate effect.

Patricia had made it very clear to the Communications Director that on no account was that dreadful Piggott Hack to be given any kind of preferential Press treatment after the outrageous way he had behaved. He could find out what was happening the same way as everybody else. Malcolm was livid but not surprised. He had no regrets about spicing up the presentation of the initialling incident. It had propelled him into international renown, the story had gone viral largely, he liked to think, because of his vivid coverage that had been televised across the world. What really irked him was the fact that Alex Whiteley had completely disappeared and no amount of stalking and staking out of his home or the hospital could make him reappear.

In the hospital reaction was mixed and very vocal. Laura's appointment was almost universally applauded. Even her male colleagues attempted to endorse the decision, in public at least. Good for the hospital, good for the department, great for female physicians everywhere. Time for a change, happy that she was one of them and of course they would all work together to take the department forward in new and exciting ways for the benefit of patients everywhere. Yes, of course she had their full support and one or two even managed to smile.

Garth joined in the general applause - was glad to have been able to keep things on an even keel for such a worthy successor but then kept a very low profile indeed. When he applied for a few days leave due to personal reasons, Hari agreed immediately. Julia was her usual taciturn, aggressive self so no one noticed anything different.

James was ambivalent. It had been made very clear to him that his decision not to testify against Alex had seriously upset senior management. Not only had he been asked to return his Trust phone but his emails had been suspended. He knew that he was being monitored and watched.

Tiger Lily had heard the announcement on local radio and posted the prepared statement on the Facebook page before she heard from Alex. The reaction was immediate, outraged and vociferous. Comments were being posted in an apparently endless procession of protest and disbelief that such an accomplished surgeon and kind man should have been forced to tender his resignation. Hadn't he been cleared by the Hearing? Why did he now feel he had to leave? Who would care for them in the same way? Who would save so many lives? What did the management of the MCH have to say about it?

Patricia, who was monitoring the page, was taken aback. From his former patients yes, it was to be expected, but she was astonished to see the names and images of hospital employees popping up. She might not know the names of all those who worked there but she recognised many of their profile pictures. Well, more fool them. Pressure could be brought to bear. Most were only nurses or admin. staff it was true, but occasionally she spotted a more senior name and there were a number of high-profile posts from other hospitals. Whiteley's secretary was threatening to resign in protest but no loss there, Patricia thought. Good riddance. However it was disconcerting that there had been such a ground swell reaction. People really did seem to have liked him. They seemed to be prepared to overlook and accept what he had done wrong and pass it off as an uncharacteristic act of stupidity which was outweighed by his other achievements. What confounded her was the fact that she found only two comments on the entire page to the contrary and even these were tempered by an acknowledgement of his surgical skills. She hoped that Laura Beechwood was as proficient as Hari claimed and that she had a Hippo-thick skin.

The organ transplant community were less sympathetic. Sally Crowther was more disappointed than angry but was, nevertheless, scathing as she responded to the bombardment of questions and comments from scandalised SNODS. They phoned, emailed and texted and the nature of her job meant that she could not avoid any of it. She became heartily sick of Alex Whiteley.

"Organs are so difficult to get hold of. We work so hard to persuade people to be donors, telling them how much we value their contribution and how important it is and then he goes and does something like this! And we want people to trust us! This could set us back years."

She was complaining to John Hardman in the canteen over its execrable coffee. She was cross about that too; why did she never remember how awful it was and have tea instead? John was more philosophical but no less exasperated.

"It'll pass" he said. "We just have to be honest and tell people it was the action of one man, on his own and in no way reflects on me or you or anyone else in the transplant system. No harm was done, remember and to be honest, most of the organ recipients I've talked to about it don't care. Some think it's quite funny actually."

"Funny?"

"Yeah. They even laughed. Said he could've written his life story or poetry on them for all they cared. They're alive when they would've been dead."

Her glare could have frozen fire.

"Only saying" he added. "Obviously I don't think he should've done it but now he's resigned we can just get on with our jobs. People'll forget and get over it. They always do, especially if they're really ill and someone offers them a lifeline. No-one's going to refuse a transplant because they think a surgeon is going to initial them."

He paused as she appeared to be mollified, but not convinced. "Come on Sally. He's not the first to do it, we both know that."

"He'll be the last though, that's for sure."

"Yeah." John nodded. "We're never going to have to deal with a problem like this again. There must be surgeons out there cacking themselves. There but for the grace of and all that." Sally pulled a face.

"You don't agree?" he asked.

"It's not that. It's the coffee."

John got up from the table.

"I'll get you a cup of tea and a scone if you promise to cheer up.

It's not the end of the world, Sally, just a setback. It'll soon be history. This time next year no one will even know his name."

She looked sceptical but liked the idea of a scone and tea even more.

"Go on then. A cheese one."

And where were Alex and Lisa when the volcano went up? Malcolm Piggott would dearly liked to know. They had headed north on an impulse and were staying on the island of Lindisfarne, cut off from the mainland twice a day by the tide, peaceful, cold and remote. They had read the papers and followed social media but avoided the spoken word. Anonymity meant that they could wander unmolested and ignored, Baldrick could wrestle with seaweed and waves and steer a clear berth of the seals while his humans sat on the desolate sandy beach and listened to the curlews crying in tune with the lamenting wind.

"Laura is an excellent choice" Alex replied to Lisa's question about his successor. "If Patricia made the appointment, I've seriously underestimated her. It shows insight and strategic thinking. Only Laura will be able to unite the others behind her and give cohesion to the department. It won't be easy but she's already had to fight hard to get where she is, so I know she can do it."

"It's never easy being a woman in a man's world" Lisa commented. Alex looked at her. Was that aimed at him? He let it go. She might have a point.

"What are we going to do, Alex?" she said, staring out at the grey sea as if the solution was somewhere to be found beyond the horizon. Perhaps it was he thought.

"I have to find another job. What about up here, in this part of the world? There are lots of hospitals in Newcastle. They always want locums."

Lisa said nothing but continued staring into the gunship grey and shifting white void.

"I'll only be able to get work as a locum, a general surgeon. You know that?"

She nodded abstractedly. "If the General Medical Council let me."

"Will they?"

"The solicitor says almost certainly as I was cleared by the Hospital Hearing. I'll probably get a warning or something but I won't be struck off."

Another nod. He wished she would look at him.

"What about up here?"

"Too cold."

"Somewhere warmer then?"

"What about the south west? Cornwall?"

"Yes!"

For the first time in weeks Alex glimpsed real hope. Cornwall. Yes. A new start in a new place where they would be unknown and ordinary. Anything for a mundane, unexceptional, quiet life. He reached for Lisa's hand and held it in his own as if the sky would fall off the edge of the world if he let it go.

CHAPTER FORTY

September was closing its eyes but Autumn was vigorous and embracing the chill and increasing darkness of October. One final exuberant colourful fling before gloomy November. October could be fun when the winds rattled the trees and boiled the sea but November was always so miserable, moaning that there was never anything to look forward to. October had Halloween and Harvest, some sunshine and all that ridiculous colour; December had Christmas and the New Year but November had nothing except Remembrance Day. Guy Fawkes and fireworks were a celebration about burning a man alive for goodness' sake. It wasn't fair. No wonder he was depressed. Short grey days and long black nights; it was the same every year.

In Stroud, Jayne Lavery was ruing the inefficiency of their antiquated central heating system and wondering if CPS funds would permit an upgrade. Or an overhaul. Anything. It was only going to get colder. Her office looked as if it should be an old-fashioned library in a country house, with a noisy fire throwing out heat over creaky chairs and dark wood. She should be dressed in rusty black warming her hands before a fulsome blaze. Instead, she was an underpaid CPS solicitor in dark blue reaching for yet another cardigan. She sighed.

“Sorry”. “It’s none too warm in here I’m afraid. Old heating system.”

The others had noticed but had refrained from comment. The barrister, Stephen Morris, discreetly warmed his hands between his thighs below the table and smiled. He had been with the Crown Prosecution Service all his legal career and well understood the privations of the system. Lawyers certainly did not come into it for the money but he had rarely lost sight of his ideals and sense of social justice, even when the heating broke down. He was an impeccably polite and well-mannered man by nature as well as by design. Too easy for the unwary to misjudge his benignity for weakness as many had expensively discovered in the courtroom. He quietly enjoyed dismantling the cases of his legal opponents with incisive logic, extensive legal knowledge and a twinkle in his eye. Clad in sheep’s clothing he said little, watched much and missed nothing.

Seated next to him was another man, younger, taller, sharper, less subtle, more aggressive. Kieran O’Connell had joined the CPS straight from university and had an agenda. He had rapidly been promoted into the Special Crimes Division and in it had found a world of legal exploration where he could break new ground, update Legal Precedent and make a name for himself.

They had assembled to discuss the case of Carlos Cardoso. Jayne had given them the details of the case, including the outcome of the MCH hearing and Alex’s resignation. Stephen wanted to know how their client felt.

“Mr Cardoso is angry. He feels victimised and persecuted. Being a man of feeling rather than reason, unfortunately listening is not his strong point.”

Jayne was apologetic – Kieran's response was not.

"Who can blame him? He has every right to be angry. He's been abused and degraded, subjected to an assault by a man who should have known better. Alexander Whiteley is a criminal."

"Is he?" Stephen enquired mildly. "I'm not sure. Has a crime actually been committed?"

Kieran was adamant.

"It has to have been. We need to find a charge that sticks and prosecute. This is about justice for the ordinary man; the helpless patient."

Jayne was not sure that Carlos would like being described as ordinary, or helpless, but she was certain he would comply if a prosecution was brought on his behalf.

"I'm not sure there's a case to answer, Kieran."

Stephen was, in the politest of terms, pressing his point. "Jayne, what would Mr Cardoso be like as a witness?"

"Unreliable. Emotional. Inclined to the kind of exaggeration and melodrama that would undermine any case we might bring. A witness statement would be better."

"Psychiatric reports?"

"I'll organise that. What are we looking for?"

"Post-Traumatic Stress Dis..."

Before Stephen could complete his sentence there was a full-bodied knock at the door which immediately swung open and Carlos strode in, unbidden and unabashed.

"Good morning" he announced, waving his Evian water by way of greeting.

"Mr Cardoso. Come in. Let me introduce you."

Jayne indicated a chair for her guest who sententiously sat himself down, centre stage.

"Crown Prosecution Barrister, Stephen Morris and his colleague, Kieran O'Connell from the Crown Prosecution Service Special Crimes Division. They're here to discuss the possibility of bringing a case against Alexander Whiteley."

"Possibility? I hope it is more than that. I am a wronged man."

"You are, Mr Cardoso, you are indeed."

Kieran was in like a shot.

"May I call you Carlos?"

Most certainly he could. Carlos liked this young man – his spirit and passion augured well.

"I want justice!"

It was a declaration of war by Carlos and Kieran answered the cry to arms.

"That is what we are here for. I work with the Special Crimes Division based in Manchester. We work with the CPS across the country and this is exactly the kind of case we specialise in. Crimes change with the times and it is our task to bring successful prosecutions that will update the law to keep pace with advances in technology, medical science, computer data protection, all that sort of thing. Yours is a most interesting case in view of the developments made in the field of organ transplants. I may say that my colleagues and I are very excited about it."

"Really?"

"Yes, Carlos. It is our intention to prove that Mr Whiteley has committed a crime and must be punished accordingly."

"And you will have to change the law to do that?"

"Update it rather than change. You know that English law is based on Precedent? What has gone before is used as an example for cases that might follow in the future."

Carlos did not, but nodded anyway.

"A successful prosecution will establish a precedent for any subsequent cases. In short, Carlos, we need to make an example of Mr Whiteley."

"And make him a criminal?"

"That too."

Stephen could be quiet no longer.

"There's no guarantee that a prosecution will be successful, Mr Cardoso. It's important to remember that."

"And I'm afraid you won't get Legal Aid towards the costs of bringing the prosecution."

Jayne hoped he was listening. She reinforced the point.

"Legal Aid is only available for the accused."

Carlos heard her.

"So that monster can get it and I won't? That's outrageous. How is that justice?"

Kieran glared at Jayne and smoothed troubled waters.

"How Mr Whiteley funds a defence is his problem and I'm quite sure that on his salary he won't qualify for financial help from the State. I just hope he's got insurance."

Carlos relaxed and decided that Kieran was a man after his own heart. This was more like it.

"We would apply to the court for costs in the event of a successful prosecution and these would be granted as a matter of course so we wouldn't end up out of pocket," Kieran reassured.

"If my case is so important, then I have no doubt that the CPS will support it. And if it's the legal landmark that you claim, then surely, they will be willing to pay for it?"

Carlos directly addressed Kieran who fidgeted and wondered if he had under estimated the actor. Jayne suppressed a smile and Stephen's eyes twinkled as Kieran hedged a reluctant response.

"It could certainly be discussed. There are funds available in exceptional cases. It will need looking into."

Carlos was mollified and enthused.

"We could call it Carlos' Law" he suggested.

Kieran allowed himself a smile. Jayne and Stephen said nothing. The room felt even colder.

CHAPTER FORTY-ONE

"What's on the agenda today?"

It was still dark outside so Alex could not yet walk Baldrick. He was awake but had nowhere to go. Lisa pretended not to hear him.

"When do the clocks go back?"

In the enclosed world of the hospital, it had not made much difference. Outside was more of a concept than reality. Now that he was at home Alex had begun to realise that there was a world elsewhere, not least in the activities of his wife. He had had no idea that she did so much. Was so busy. How did he not know? Every time the phone rang, which seemed to be all the time, it was for her. Someone else he didn't know enquiring whether they could speak to the Chair of Governors or the Secretary of the Friends of the Midland Museum and Art Gallery. Could she do an extra day in the charity shop to help out as they were so short staffed and would he remind her about their Finance Committee meeting in two days' time? He was astonished that she did so much and yet had said so little.

Alex wanted to be useful.

"I'll walk Baldrick as soon as it's light, I'll do the shopping and I'll make a list which I might even stick to. How about I cook something for tonight?"

He liked cooking and it kept his fingers supple.

"If you're in?"

It was new for him to be fitting in around Lisa and he was not sure yet how he felt about it. Not that he minded or a chauvinist, but for the first time in his life he was unemployed. It was unnerving. He seemed to have lost his place.

"That'd be lovely. Yes." Lisa would be happy not to have to cook.

"Good. I'll have a look in *Jamie Oliver*. Something a bit different maybe. I've got the time."

"Where will you go?"

He pondered. This was always an issue. They both now avoided local shops and supermarkets because of Alex's notoriety. He had taken to walking Baldrick in the early morning or at dusk: a man of the shadows. In daylight someone always seemed to recognise him and reactions varied from supportive to downright abusive. He had tried wearing sunglasses but that had been even more noticeable. He could not see without his glasses, contact lenses were not an option, so it was a cap, scarf and thick skin that had to suffice.

"Out of town. Mid-morning, when it's quieter."

She nodded.

"Yes. What else will you do today?"

Important to keep him occupied.

"Job hunting. I've updated my CV but just need to check it through again. Once the GMC have made a decision then I can start applying. The sooner the better. I've got a list of potential placements and the applications are ready to go. We need an income."

Another nod.

"When will you hear? They're taking their time."

"Soon. Derek is surprised they haven't been in touch already. That's the GMC for you."

They did not have to wait long. The letter from the GMC arrived that morning while Alex was out shopping. He had scuttled from the car to the front door as fast as several large, heavy, badly-packed bags of shopping would allow, trying not to bump the bags too much. Lisa despaired about his inability to pack groceries.

"Soft things and eggs on the top, not the bottom. Tins and heavy stuff go in first and remember to keep the washing powder separate from the fresh food".

How was it that a man could unpack someone's intestines, dismantle their vital organs, put everything back in working order with replacement parts but couldn't pack shopping without causing carnage?

Alex balanced the bags upright with his feet while he unlocked the door, pushed it open with one elbow and placed himself, armed with the shopping, across the gap to prevent Baldrick rushing out. It worked; Baldrick launched himself from the inside door mat but was blocked by Alex brandishing a carrier bag of nibbles and white wine. Together they fell into the hallway and Alex used his foot to slam the door behind him. Victory! Then he saw that the letterbox contained one white envelope which clearly displayed the official GMC logo. Everything seemed to immobilise; the world had flatlined. He took a very deep breath and kick-started reality.

Oblivious to Baldrick's investigations into the bags at his feet, Alex reached over and extracted the letter from the wire box. He handled it gently, carefully, apprehensively. So much at stake. One letter for his whole life.

Should he wait for Lisa to come home and they'd open it together? No. She'd suffered enough. This was his mess so he would deal with it. Standing exactly as he was when he picked up the letter, he slid one neatly cut finger nail under the very corner of the envelope flap and began to ease it open, prising it apart without tearing or splitting. The self-adhesive seal separated without protest and he was able to remove the letter precisely and neatly. Putting the envelope under his armpit where he clamped it steady with his upper arm, he unfolded the sheets of A4 paper and began to read. It took less than a minute for him to get the gist of the ruling.

CHAPTER FORTY-TWO

When Lisa saw that the call was from Alex, she picked up immediately but did not speak.

"It's arrived."

"And?"

"It's a warning. There won't be an MPTS hearing."

Lisa wanted to cry.

"Oh, thank God" she breathed. Then, "MPTS?"

"Medical Practitioners Tribunal Service."

"Read me the letter."

"Dear Mr Whiteley..."

"Not all of it; just the important bits."

"Okay. Sorry."

He was obviously scanning the letter and she could hear the

crackle of the paper as he searched.

"Right. Got it. ... *and the independent doctor appointed as the case examiner has studied the evidence submitted by you under Rule Eight of the General Medical Council Code of Practice.* That's when I can submit evidence to support why I can keep on working" he explained.

"Yes. Go on."

" Blah, blah, ... *The extensive file of evidence submitted on your behalf has convinced the ruling body of the General Medical Council that they do not believe that an MPTS hearing would come to any other conclusion than a warning, hence their decision."*

"So it's just a warning?"

"Yes. Written. But it's going to be alright, Lisa. It's going to be alright."

When he came off the phone Alex was euphoric but before he reached for the cookbook to prepare something really, really special for the evening meal, there was something he knew had to be done. At once. He rushed from the kitchen and headed up the stairs to his study.

Baldrick was amazed. All the shopping was still in the bags, on the floor, within reach, unprotected. He surveyed the kitchen. Yep. Alone. He'd go for it. But which one first? Overcoming option paralysis, he headed for the cheese.

Upstairs Alex was sitting at his desk, feet planted on the floor to stop the chair from spinning and had woken up the computer. On the screen was the 'Save The Letterman' Facebook page – it had hardly been off it – and Alex was stroking the mouse to take the cursor up to the top right corner where he could private message Tiger Lily.

She was online – as always – and her response was immediate. "Wonderful! Thank God for the right decision" she wrote. "Send me what you want to say and I'll post it straight away."

Hardly stopping to think he began writing, stopped, amended, deleted, rewrote, deleted again. So much feeling to be conveyed in so few words. He had written hundreds of reports, academic papers, at least two dissertations, reviews, articles, assessments, everything medical, analytical, authoritative. Now he wanted to write a pithy heartfelt thank you to all those who had supported, encouraged and believed in him even when he had begun to doubt himself but he could not find the words. Why was it so difficult?

As Baldrick systematically worked his way through the shopping Alex sat at the desk staring at the message box on the screen, the cursor blinking patiently in the vacant space. Occasionally it stopped and became a static line so he stroked the mouse, reactivated the black line and waited for inspiration. His finger tapped the desk in time with the cursor, a pulse, beating time with his heart. ... From the heart. ... Honesty. That was it! Just say it. Apologise for your stupidity; thank those who have stood by you. He began to write as his heart felt and the words formed themselves.

As soon as she received it, Tiger Lily copied and pasted the statement onto the page and it went viral. She knew as the page manager, that the views and hits on the page far exceeded the comments and posts that actually appeared. Thousands and thousands of views met every post she made but Alex's apology and thanks took the response to another level. She could only speculate about the identity of all those voyeurs and wonder what they would make of the humility of Alex's gratitude.

Patricia snorted when she read it but Hari was touched by the simplicity of the statement. Alex's secretary burst into tears and handed in her notice. Sally Crowther was mollified, a little, but John Hardman was genuinely gratified. He means it, he thought. Every word. It's a shame; he's a loss to the transplant world but we'll soon move on. I wonder if he will?

Julia texted Garth a bitter 'He'll have to do better than that' but received no reply. Her sentiment was shared by Carlos who had heard about the campaign on Facebook from Jayne; he did not have a computer of his own but curiosity had propelled him repeatedly into the local library where a charming young lady showed him how to turn on the machine and then find the sight? site? he wanted. She even showed him how to roll the page down with the mouse thing so that he could see what all those people had to say. Extraordinary. Were they all out of their minds? What was wrong with them? And who on earth invented such bizarre computer language? Hardly the Bard.

Derek in his London office read the comments with satisfaction and suggested to Arash, needlessly, that they were all recorded. As well as taking screen shots Arash had been in touch with Tiger Lily and she was forwarding to him all the managerial data about the page. The file of evidence submitted to the GMC had been substantial but it was now becoming enormous.

"Should we shelve it?" Arash had asked but Derek, who knew enough about the vagaries of the legal system, had shaken his head and told him to keep accumulating everything he could find in favour of Alex.

"You never know. We might yet need it."

In Manchester, Kieran had read the comments with cynicism and written them off as the emotional knee jerk reactions of little people without substance and significance. Jayne however had notified Stephen who had studied them with unease and some admiration.

"Social media shouldn't be underestimated" he told the solicitor; "this kind of evidence carries weight in court." The case manager at the GMC shared the same view and reported back to the ruling council that they had made absolutely the right decision by issuing only a written warning to Alexander Whiteley.

Jason had been following the page religiously, partly because he was curious but mainly because it somehow brought him closer to Meghan and he had nothing else to do except worry about Jack. What would his beloved Meggie have thought? It tormented him to know that if she had been the patient whose liver had been initialled, she would have been here with him now and none of this would have happened. Life was so bloody unfair and he hated it. If it wasn't for Jack there would be no point to it.

James MacKenzie also followed the Facebook page daily and closely, even when rushed off his feet. Away from patients the hospital staff talked freely about The Letterman and views varied hugely from the staunch loyalty of those who had worked with him like James, to the disgusted, shocked and appalled. There was general consensus that what he had done was wrong, but what was that exactly? Mischief? Black humour? Assault? Betrayal of the sacred patient doctor bond of trust at the very least, egomaniacal attempted murder at the most lurid. And why? What had possessed him? Was he possessed? The theories were rife and became daily more salacious and less informed.

One thing was certain though. He was not going away. Patricia Shelton would gladly have eliminated him from the face of the medical earth. And the outcome of the Serious Incident Requiring Investigation had yet to arrive. She reached for another packet of biscuits.

CHAPTER FORTY-THREE

October

Julia's bedroom gave her much more pleasure than any activity that took place within it. White, grey, pale, soft, cool. Icy Egyptian cotton sheets which offset Garth's tawny skin when he lay in them, his eyes darker than anything except the night sky outside. Blinds - horizontal hexagonal tubes pleated together into weightless bodices fitted over the glass panes to be moved up and down to fit any part. Julia chose to leave the upper halves exposed, preserving her privacy to all but the sky from which she had nothing to hide and everything to prove. And she liked to prove things. Besides, she had a great body.

She studied her lover's face as he lay in the bed. Shadowed on one side his finely chiselled features were highlighted into handsome by the chilly light. Really, he was wasted on that dumpy wife. Julia thought with pleasure of her own body and slowly stroked herself from shoulder to thigh with an elegant hand. In that way, she and Garth were well suited. As he slept, his breathing was soft and almost soundless, thank God. She hated men who breathed noisily almost as much as people who made a noise when they ate.

She reached out to press the button on her digital clock and the ugly green letters read 2.40 a.m. Their momentary luminosity tainted the purity of the monochrome room before she let them lapse back into darkness. Time was kept out of her bedroom: her world, her rules.

She lay for a moment, thinking. Her mouth tightened, revealing deepening lines that creased her upper lip and frilled the lower one Her cheeks hollowed; her eyes vanished into the clutches of her eyebrows. Almost imperceptibly she levered herself out of the bed and stole over to a chair at the side of the room where a small pile of clothes was neatly folded, patiently sitting as if waiting for an appointment. Picking them up in one movement with a pair of trainers on the floor close by, she crept not to the *en suite* bathroom but to the door to the hallway on the other side of the room. Silently she turned the handle, opened it just enough to slide through then pulled it seamlessly shut behind her. Garth did not stir.

In the moonlit kitchen downstairs, she dressed. Black trainers, tracksuit trousers and a hoodie – cheap - discreetly purchased from Primark a few days before. Nondescript, mass produced, unremarkable, untraceable. An outfit she would not normally be seen dead in or a shop that she would go near, but needs must. No underwear – no time – but black short socks to prevent the new trainers from rubbing. She carefully picked her way across the room, avoiding the marble topped central isle and headed for the sheen of the steel sink gleaming in the moonlight. There she picked up and put on a pair of neutral coloured latex gloves like those used in an operating theatre. With her reskinned hands she opened the fridge. Light flooded into the room in a torrent, lancing the obscurity. Holding the door with one rubberised hand she reached right to the back and pulled out a small moist package, wrapped in cling film. Then she left the room by the back door and disappeared into the night.

Garth stirred briefly and was then immediately awake. Was he On Call? A quick survey of the room and a touch of the bedlinen assured him that he was not. He was in Julia's bedroom but where was she? Fully awake now he glanced at the digital clock which showed nothing. Damn. He recalled, with irritation, that she always blanked out the digits because she did not like their colour. Did not suit the ambience of the room or some such guff. Sliding out of the bed and finding his way by moonlight to the door of the *en suite* he peered into the cold, white porcelain room and shivered. No Julia. And so cold, a place where even the hottest water seemed to lose heart and go wintry without even trying to stay warm. Silver tawny in the spectral light he padded across the bedroom floor to the other door, opened it and fumbled out into the dark hall.

"Julia?"

He padded along the hallway to the top of the stairs and then carefully placing his feet on each stair he edged his way down. She was probably in the kitchen drinking a glass of water or tea. He did not know exactly what time it was but it had to be the early hours of the morning; he had done enough night shifts to know that. It was something about the way the body was simultaneously alert and sluggish. He had occasionally wondered if nocturnal creatures felt the same way during daylight.

Julia did not like the taste of water straight from the tap so if she was thirsty would have gone to the kitchen for filtered water; until bottled water arrived in white china bottles, she would never have them in the bedroom.

"Julia?" he murmured as he pushed the kitchen door fully open and looked around. His eyes began to accustom themselves to the gloom and as he surveyed the room he was confounded. Where was she?

Jogging, towards the other side of the sleeping city. On a route she had planned and rehearsed regularly over the preceding weeks although she had never actually made it as far as her final destination. On those occasions it had been busy and daylight. She was just another fitness freak weaving between pedestrians, avoiding cyclists and trotting on the spot as she waited for crossing lights to change. She had been wearing ear phones so that anyone watching would assume that she was listening to music as she ran so no eye contact or communication were required. Only she knew that the there was no music and that the wire from the earphones simply hung, unattached, against her chest, enabling her to ignore everyone as she familiarised herself with the route.

It was exhilarating to run through the night, liberating, empowering, trotting through red lights, crossing the dual carriageway, breaking all the rules. She patted the sloppy plastic package in her hoodie pocket with satisfaction and never broke her stride.

Away from the garishly illuminated city centre the des. res. suburbs were less well lit. Intermittent streetlights cast desultory smudges over the wide empty roads; less parked cars here, most of them tucked neatly onto drives or into double garages. Julia passed unnoticed through the orange patches from the lampposts through the overarching white moonlight. The only sounds were the desolate, distant cry of an owl, the soft thud of her running feet and the controlled breathing of the seasoned jogger; it was not for nothing that she paid her gym membership and worked out on the cross trainer whenever possible between the hours spent putting people under and bringing them round again. As she rounded the corner into a leafy avenue she came to a temporary halt and looked carefully around to check that she was alone and unseen. She glanced up at the lamppost beside her. No CCTV. Good. One of the benefits of living in an expensive area: no ASBOs, winos, dealers, knife crime and social unrest here. Everything safe behind walls and remote-controlled gates, or so they thought. Smugness made her smile as she tightened the hood around her face and tucked a stray strand of blonde hair behind her ear.

At a slower but consistent pace she set off down the pavement until she found the house. White walls glowing in the moonlight, it slumbered behind the garden wall. She was tempted to sneer with disdain at the middle-class mediocrity of it all but knew that speed and silence were more important. As she approached, she pulled the squelchy package from her pocket. It had leaked a little into her hoodie but no matter, that would be going straight into either someone else's wheelie bin or the MCH contaminated waste disposal system. Without stopping and after furtively glancing all round, she removed the cling film and flung the sloppy contents into garden.

When Julia arrived home, her kitchen was in darkness. She had taken her trainers off before she gently squeezed the door handle down and clasping them in one hand she eased her way into the room, carefully shutting the door behind her. The plastic bag and latex gloves had long since been dropped into a large bin outside a restaurant kitchen in the city along with the other detritus of a busy night in the catering business. She would have deposited her clothes and shoes if she had not had to jog home. No matter, they would find their way into the MCH incinerator via a contaminated waste bin when she went into work that morning. She sidled into the kitchen, sliding slightly on the hard floor in her socks, noticing that central isle looked twice its size in the shadow of the moonlight

"Where have you been?"

Had she been anyone else she would have screamed with fright. As it was, she dropped the trainers and gasped, but only for a moment.

"Garth! What the hell are you doing here?"

"I could ask you the same question. What's going on? Where have you been?"

She switched on the lights. Garth was revealed, sitting on a high stool at the breakfast bar on the other side of the room. He looked ludicrous and she wanted to laugh.

"You look ridiculous! Why are you wearing my dressing gown?"

"Where've you been?"

"You could have got dressed. It's far too small for you. I hope it isn't stretched out of shape; it cost a fortune."

"I've been sitting waiting for hours. I didn't know what had happened. You might have been hurt. Much longer and I'd've called the police. What's going on, Julia?" He sounded genuinely concerned.

"You didn't?"

"What, call the police?"

"Yes."

"No. Should I? Are you OK? Has someone hurt you?"

Now he was really concerned.

"Tell me what's going on for God's sake."

"Justice."

"Justice?"

Garth was stunned. He pulled his wits together.

"What do you mean? What are you talking about?"

"He's guilty. He stopped my funding. He's not going to get away with it."

Garth was frightened. She was alabaster; headstone cold.

"What have you done?"

She said nothing but stared at him, hostile and unblinking. He wanted to waver, but stood his ground.

"Julia, what the hell have you done?"

CHAPTER FORTY-FOUR

Alex and Lisa had found themselves sleeping later these days. Baldrick, ever a creature of routine, was now awake before them, disgruntled, hungry and bewildered by the unfamiliarity. This had never happened before. Always the big one got up first, sometimes in the middle of the long sleeping time when the smaller one did not move but always, always when the alarm lit up and rang. Then the big one went downstairs and after playing with the whistley thing opened the door to the outside and went to the corner cupboard to prepare the canine breakfast. Baldrick knew while he was pottering in the garden seeing off intruders, surreptitiously relieving himself over the herbs that when he returned his bowl would be full and all he had to do was eat. That was the routine. Safe and comfortable. A dog knew where he was; what was what.

But not now. He snuffled around the foot of the bed making as much noise as he knew how without actually barking then threw caution to the cats and leapt onto the big one.

It worked. Big one lumbered out of bed, thudded to the door where he took the soft nestly thing from a hook and grumbled down the stairs followed by his faithful friend. At the bottom of the stairs in the hallway Baldrick propelled himself with grim determination towards the front door; needs must. Big one took the hint.

"Alright, alright. Hold on. Just a minute."

Alex shuffled over to the door which he unbolted and unlocked. As he pulled it open Baldrick shot out with undignified haste and made for the front lawn.

As he squatted over the grass Baldrick took the opportunity to sniff the lightening air. Like a smoker inhaling the first cigarette of the day he imbibed the scents and flavours of the chill morning, noted the dew on his paws, detected the aroma of next door's cat from the wall on which it had walked but not descended, traced echoes of ... a fox? Definitely from the other side of the wall though. And then, something else. Unexpected. Different and yet familiar. He stood up and stretched. Every sinew poised for exploration and discovery he followed the tantalising smell.

In the kitchen Alex had switched on the kettle and put Baldrick's bowl on the floor in its usual place. He was surprised when he turned back from making tea not to find the dog deep in his food. God, he hadn't left the gate open last night, had he? He strode out of the kitchen down the hall to the front door which had been left slightly ajar. A rapid survey of the garden revealed the truant eating something unidentifiable on the drive. Alex hurtled over to the miscreant, primed to haul him off the offending article and extract what he could from the dog's jaws. He arrested the dog mid gulp and grabbed hold of the bloody mess in his mouth. It felt cold and slippery and it stank. Foul. Metallic. Rank and acidic, like the chemical smell in an operating theatre. What in God's name was it? As he tugged it split and disintegrated. Baldrick swallowed the contents of his mouth with a single voluble gulp.

"What's going on?"

Lisa was calling from the doorstep clutching her dressing gown around her against the early morning air. She was drowsy, barefoot, tousled.

"Baldrick's eaten something."

"What?"

"I don't know."

Alex was sniffing the mess in his hand. His face corrupted with concern.

"Lisa."

"Yes."

"Call the vet."

"What?"

"Call the vet. Now. Tell him we're on our way."

"What is it? What's he eaten?"

"Liver. And I think it's poisoned."

CHAPTER FORTY-FIVE

Garth arrived exceptionally early at work that morning, having dressed and come straight from Julia's. Mariyah, his wife, had no idea that he had been anywhere but the hospital all night. When he rang her, she was surprised.

"I know you love me, Garth" she replied. "I love you too. You're tired; try to get home a bit earlier today."

He had been moved down the corridor away from the Clinical Director's office. It was a demotion and everyone knew it. He also now shared a secretary with another more junior consultant. It felt as if he had been put on a naughty step for something he had not done and then been forgotten. So, when the summons came from Patricia that she wanted to see him in her office at his earliest convenience he dropped everything and was there within ten minutes. It could only be the result of the SIRI and there was nothing he could do about the future until he knew where he stood. Time for the sword to fall, or for him to throw himself onto it. His mouth was dry as he knocked on the heavy door to Patricia's office.

"Come in."

Licking lips as arid as dried coconut Garth entered the room and set off on the long walk from door to desk. Patricia was, as always, sitting behind it, supported by its solidity. Sitting down she actually seemed quite small, but was definitely getting heavier. Hari was also there, sitting to one side of her, observing, a watchful raven.

"Garth. Have a seat. I'll get straight to the point. The SIRI report has arrived and we wanted to share its findings with you as you were the lead surgeon, although we're also going to talk to Julia Voss."

At the thought of Julia being in trouble Garth felt a little better.

"The finding is that a more judicious note of the advanced nature of the patient's liver disease should have been made by the surgical and anaesthetic team, as well as a more careful assessment of the patient's clotting factors, with better preparation and preloading of replacement clotting factors."

Patricia was reading from the final page of the multiple page document. She turned back to the first page and looked up at Garth.

"In short, you've been found partially at fault but not directly culpable. Bear in mind that a Serious Incident Requiring Investigation rarely apportions blame but rather hints and make recommendations. To be blunt, Garth, you are to all intents and purposes in the clear. Your professional integrity has not been compromised nor is it in doubt. However …" Cue Hari.

"This has been an unfortunate incident which will have to be noted on your file, although it should not affect your career or reputation."

Garth stared at his friend. Should not? Or would not? Hari averted his gaze to Patricia who had placed the document on her desk and assumed a more comfortable expression.

"Of course," she said, "we have always had complete confidence in you, but events such as these have to be thoroughly investigated. We have a duty of care to our patients. I am happy to say that now we can put all this behind us and move on. Quite a relief for everyone concerned, don't you agree?"

Hari's eyes widened in surprise. Had she completely forgotten about Meghan Orchard?

"What does it say about Julia Voss?" Garth wanted to know.

"I'd prefer to talk to Julia about that before discussing it with anyone else but I think it's safe to say that the finding is more or less the same."

What she did not mention was that Julia had been commended for displaying calm qualities of leadership and decision-making when Garth had lost control of the situation. Time enough for Garth to see for himself when he received his copy of the report.

"Is the report made public?"

"No. It's an internal investigation and even then, just the findings, not the full report, will be made known."

Patricia took pity on him.

"There's nothing to worry about, Garth. It's not as if you've done an Alex Whiteley!"

Patricia was still smiling after Garth had left the room. Moving the SIRI report to one side and reaching for the next item on her substantial to do pile, she noticed Hari's grim expression as he went to follow him and shook her head. Really, there were times when she did not understand Hari at all. As she began work on more pressing matters, she anticipated with pleasure the time when Laura Beechwood would be the new Medical Director.

CHAPTER FORTY-SIX

"How is he?"

"Okay. Drooling a bit and sleepy."

"Twitching? Convulsions?"

"No. Well, a bit of twitching. Alex! Red light!"

Alex stamped his foot down onto the brake as if crushing a cockroach. The heavy car bowled to a brusque halt, pausing, panting just over the white line at the traffic lights, poised for a rapid getaway. Lisa, with Baldrick cocooned in a towel on her lap lunged forward slightly. She clutched onto the inert bundle and turned anxiously to her husband.

"The vet's expecting us?"

"Yes. You've got the rest of the meat? And the vomit?"

She looked at the two clear plastic food bags on the dashboard, one containing the remnants of the torn, black liver and the other the rest of it, partially ingested, that Baldrick had thrown up on the hall floor within minutes of swallowing the offending substance.

"Is he going to be alright, Alex?"

"I hope so. He's still conscious?"

Lisa peeled back a corner of the towel and stroked the dog's ear. Baldrick blinked and drooled.

"Yes."

"That's good. He vomited quickly so whatever it is may not have been fully ingested."

"Should we have made him drink water? To flush it through?"

"No. We don't know what it is. The vet'll find out what the poison is and take it from there. He might have to pump his stomach, Lisa."

He looked at her, knowing what the procedure involved.

"We'll stay with him if he does."

"If they let us."

Alex glimpsed Baldrick's languid head grotesquely turbaned in the downstairs toilet towel, the nearest thing to hand when they wrapped him up for the journey and his heart clattered. He pressed the ball of his foot onto the accelerator and tried to push it through the metal floor of the vehicle, which surged forward.

Although he had not been in an operating theatre for weeks now, the familiar feelings of controlled stress, urgency and rapid decision making when everyone else was looking for guidance and composure had flooded back; he was the lead surgeon again, taking the responsibility for life and recovery. Except this was different. This was not someone else's loved one on a table. This was Baldrick.

Alex fought the panic levitating in his stomach and swung the car deftly round the final bend. The journey had taken less than ten minutes, even in the morning traffic. He had new respect for ambulance drivers.

He opened the front passenger door and Lisa gently edged out of the car holding her bundle of joy, except they were entering the hospital not leaving it and the vet, who was watching for them, had opened the door and was leading them straight through to the consulting room. Alex grabbed the squishy plastic bags from the dashboard and followed, slamming the door behind him, not bothering to lock it. Even one second spent pressing the remote-control key fob would be time wasted. He sprinted into the surgery and the door silently, hermetically, sealed itself behind him.

CHAPTER FORTY-SEVEN

In Stroud, Carlos was receiving the news with satisfaction. Jayne had asked him to come into the office so that they could discuss the development of his potential case against Alexander Whiteley. Carlos was now sitting on one of the scratchy old chairs opposite Jayne's desk in the chilly room. Remembering his previous visit, he was dressed for the occasion in layers, topped off by a bottle green huntin' shootin' and fishin' gilet with suede insets on shoulder (to protect against gun rub) and elbows (protection against leaning on rough ground while aiming aforementioned gun). He had wound a long, jauntily striped scarf around his neck like an upmarket Doctor Who. Peering from above it he noted that Jayne had acquired an oil filled electric radiator which was valiantly attempting to repel the invading cold air. Perhaps he would consider loosening the coloured bands around his neck later if it was sufficiently warm.

"So, the case is going ahead?"

As Jayne had already explained this she merely nodded.

"Excellent. But surely it was never in doubt?"

Carlos did not wait for a reply but answered himself, far better than he knew she ever could.

"Justice has to be done and has to be seen to be done. The Crown Prosecution Service", he did enjoy saying the word crown, "has a duty to the public it serves, does it not?"

If Jayne wanted to reply she did not have the chance.

"The public must be protected. Nothing like this must ever be allowed to happen again. It is a monstrous crime, a crime against decency. I don't think it is an exaggeration to say that the medical profession itself is on trial."

Having reached the pinnacle of his eloquence he stopped and leant back in the chair to witness his audience's response.

"You've been in touch with Kieran O'Connell?"

"We've talked over the phone on several occasions."

Yes, Jayne thought so. She moved the conversation on.

"Did he mention that there are certain preliminary investigations that need to be completed before a case such as this can be put together?"

"He said something about it but told me that you'd explain it in detail."

I bet he did, Jayne thought. Thanks Kieran.

"Well, it's important that we have a full medical and psychological evaluation of the effects and outcomes of your unfortunate experience. Are you happy for me to arrange this?"

"Of course! No problem at all. Anything to ensure that justice is done. I've nothing to hide and in fact," he leant forward in the chair confidingly, "talking to someone about it might be a very good thing. Therapeutic. Cathartic. I assume it will be a professional of the very highest calibre?"

"The CPS works with excellent medical and psychiatric

specialists."

There. She had said it. Psychiatric. She watched Carlos closely for a reaction. He was entirely sanguine.

"It'll be interesting to talk to someone like that. Do I need to do anything to prepare? Write down my feelings, symptoms, that sort of thing?"

"The psychiatrist will tell you what he wants when you meet him, or her. I'll arrange that as soon as I can. But you could keep a diary of what you experience on a day-to-day basis, how your life has changed, the impact the incident has had on you, that sort of thing. We discussed it before if you remember? How it might be useful to write it all down?"

No, he did not. No one had ever mentioned such a thing but it seemed like a good idea and had he known about it, he would have been keeping one since the beginning. Jayne swallowed her indignation and continued,

"It could be useful later if you have to write a victim statement for the court."

She did not tell him that he would on no account be appearing in the witness box. Why disappoint him?

"The psychiatrist would be interested in those things I'm sure, particularly for an evaluation of Post-Traumatic Stress Disorder."

"PTSD? Like veterans? Soldiers blown up in Afghanistan?" Carlos was thrilled.

"I'm not a medical expert so couldn't say but I understand from Kieran that this is the approach the Special Crimes Office would like to investigate. So, I can go ahead and arrange a preliminary appointment for you?"

"Yes. Absolutely. As soon as you like." Carlos could hardly wait. "I'll start the diary today."

In the Midlands, it was raining and murky; the sky was huddled over the land trying to keep warm, wrapped around tall buildings and hills like a grimy shroud. Inside the Whiteley's kitchen the Aga was pumping out heat like an over-enthusiastic body builder. Lisa was sitting in an old-fashioned modern Windsor Carver chair, clasped in its high curved back and narrow arms. On her lap lay Baldrick, in a blanket, immobile. Alex was standing beside them and with him were two police officers. Their black uniforms resonated sadly with the grey sky visible through the kitchen window. The female officer was taller than her male colleague and it was she who was asking questions and making notes, while her partner leaned over Baldrick and began stroking his soft ears.

"When did you say this happened?"

"Yesterday morning, about 7.00 a.m. or thereabouts I'd say. It was still pretty dark."

She nodded. "And the liver was already in the garden?"

"Yes. On the drive. Baldrick was eating it when I found him."

"Did you know what it was?"

"Not at first but when I touched it – I tried to pull it out his mouth – I knew then."

She looked at him. "How did you know? Are you a butcher?"

"A surgeon."

Lisa interrupted. "Liver transplants. At MCH."

"Oh!" The police officer looked at Alex more closely as if he was vaguely familiar. Had they met before? Where?

Lisa clarified.

"The Letterman."

"Oh!" No further explanation required. Suddenly the police officer was taking the situation much more seriously. Her questions became more pertinent.

"You didn't see or hear anything during the night?"

Alex and Lisa both shook their heads.

"Nothing." Alex spoke. "Nothing at all."

"CCTV cameras on the property?"

"No. Not in this neighbourhood. We've never felt the need."

The male police officer who had been caressing Baldrick's ears suddenly looked up.

"Poor little fella. How is he?"

"Rather upset at having so many emetics but the vet says he'll pull through. Thank God."

Lisa cradled the dog as she spoke and Alex put one hand on her shoulder. Baldrick did not move.

"Have you got any of the substance he was eating? For testing and evidence?" The policewoman addressed Alex.

"The vet took some for testing but left the rest in case of a police investigation."

"What did the vet say?"

That it's almost certainly lamb's liver and is obviously contaminated, probably with some sort of household detergent. It's impossible to say what without the lab results."

"We're going to need contact details for the vet and a full statement from you both but …" she hesitated and for the first time her efficient demeanour slipped slightly and she looked uncomfortable. "I have to ask. Can you think of anyone who might bear you a grudge or want to get back at you for any reason?"

Alex and Lisa exchanged glances. No one smiled.

"I'll put the kettle on."

Alex sighed as he spoke.

"Tea or coffee?"

Back in Stroud, where the weather was just the same but it seemed even darker as the afternoon aged into evening, Jayne was on the phone to Kieran in Manchester. She had called to let him know that Carlos was more than happy about the proposed psychiatric evaluation; seemed positively enthusiastic. However, what had started as an upbeat, very relieved conversation on Jayne's part had taken a turn for the worse.

"What do you mean the CPS can't afford a psychiatrist?"

Jayne was appalled. "What are you saying, Kieran?"

"It's quite simple. The budget doesn't run to a specialist psychiatrist in PTSD. It'll have to be a psychologist who does the evaluation and report, which is just as good and it won't make any difference to the outcome of the case. PTSD is PTSD, whoever assesses it."

Jayne was livid.

"Then perhaps you'd like to explain that to Cardoso? You know what he's like. If he thinks he's getting anything but the best there'll be a rebellion and he won't co-operate."

"Of course he will. He's got everything to gain and he knows it. But okay, I'll call him and explain - if you insist."

"I do."

"Leave it with me. It doesn't matter whether it's a psychologist or a psychiatrist. He won't know the difference."

Jayne had her doubts but knew one thing for certain.

"As long as he's the centre of attention it will be alright. Let me know when you've spoken to him and give me the details of the evaluation so I can arrange an appointment. By letter."

Kieran sneered to himself as he put the phone down. Provincial solicitors! He scrolled down his contacts to find

Carlos' number.

It was almost dark but the MCH car park was well lit. Julia glanced at her watch as she emerged from the main doors and headed towards her white Mercedes and home. A glass of wine, something light and nutritious to eat, perhaps some grilled fish with a quinoa salad. Important to get plenty of protein and cut down the carbs. No one had any idea how hard she worked to preserve her enviable figure. It did no harm to let people think she was effortlessly svelte and toned.

It had been another busy day but it was better that way. She had not seen Garth since the kitchen incident and could not say that she missed him, but he had certainly filled her limited spare time. She was just reaching for the key fob when she became aware of a man standing in a pocket of shadow on her right, close to her car. It was Garth.

"Oh, it's you."

Cold, self-assured, detached Julia addressing a stranger. Garth was seeing more and more of a Julia he did not know, or had he just not noticed?

"The police are here. Someone has tried to kill Alex Whiteley's dog with poisoned liver."

"So?"

"Where were you?"

"When?"

"You know perfectly well 'when'. The night before last. Don't play games."

"Who's playing games, Garth? I have no idea what you're talking about. Go away. It's been a long day and I want to go home."

Garth moved forward towards her, half hidden in the shadow

but exposed enough to be afraid.

"Julia. Was it you?"

She waited a moment before answering.

"He deserved it. A liver for a liver."

Garth stared at her.

"But his dog? The family pet?"

Julia shrugged her elegant, slim shoulders. Then with a vindictive passion that detonated her petite frame, she erupted.

"I hate him with his silly ties and smug face, lording it over us like he owned the whole bloody hospital. He's had it coming for a long time. If it wasn't me, it would've been someone else - except that you're all too pathetic and feeble to do anything."

Garth had never witnessed such vitriol. Julia had never looked so ugly.

"I thought I knew you".

"Garth. You're a fool. I thought I could make something of you but you're too weak. Parochial. Spineless. You'll never amount to anything."

She surveyed him as if examining a pair of shoes, deciding whether or not the colour would match her outfit.

"You won't go to the police" she added, as if it were an afterthought and she had rejected the shoes for being the wrong shade.

"Why not?"

"Because if you do, I'll tell your tedious little wife – what's she called? Mariyah? – all about us. And she wouldn't like that, would she? And nor would your bratty little offspring." She was smiling sweetly. Garth shuddered.

"You bitch" he hissed.

"You think this is a game do you, Garth? Well. I'm the one making the rules. Now, if you'll excuse me, I'd like to go home."

She had found the key fob and aimed it the car; a ping and a click, the car was unlocked and she was striding towards the driver's door which she jerked fully open. As stylishly as a departing Hollywood diva she sat down on the driver's seat and pressed her legs together as she swung them gracefully into the footwell. The door was shut firmly, not slammed, and the engine vibrated into life. Just as Garth expected to see the car glide away, the window silently descended and Julia turned her lovely face towards him.

"By the way. I carved your initials on the liver" she said.

Then the car pulled away.

CHAPTER FORTY-EIGHT

The clocks had gone back and the mornings were more cheerful. Alex and Lisa were sitting at the kitchen table drinking coffee, watching Baldrick begging at their feet with all the pride of new parents marvelling at their child's first attempt to use a spoon.

"I think he's feeling better."

Lisa gazed adoringly at her dog.

"Ah, bless him" Alex oozed. "Can he have a biscuit?"

"No! His stomach is still sensitive; you heard what the vet said. Honestly, Alex. You of all people should know better. He's still at the 'try a bit of ice cream and jelly and see how it goes' stage."

"Yes, yes. I know. But he just seems so much better, doesn't he?"

"Well let's keep it that way, shall we?"

As it was her 'don't argue with me because you know I'm right' voice he opted for a dignified retreat and was saved by the bell as the letter box flap was heard to clatter on the front door. Combat-ready Baldrick leapt, as far as was possible for a bandy-legged Jack Russell, into the fray and was almost immediately scuttling and slipping on the hall floor as he jumped up at the letter box to see the intruder off. Alex followed him with delight, ignoring the yapping, rejoicing in the energy of his hooliganism and retrieved the letter from the wire mesh. Mission accomplished, Baldrick trotted triumphantly back to the kitchen and the possibility of something to eat. He was sitting hopefully at Lisa's feet when Alex returned to the table, ashen faced.

"What is it?"

Fear in Lisa's voice.

"It's from my solicitor."

"And?"

"They're taking me to court."

Time, daylight, hope collided. Foundered. It seemed to have gone dark. Alex swayed.

Lisa leant over and pulled the chair out for her husband who slumped into it. He heard her voice speaking to him from somewhere faraway and returned to the letter, struggling to focus on the black characters warping on the paper.

"What for?"

"Psychological harm amounting to ABH."

"ABH?"

"Actual Bodily Harm."

"But you were cleared by the hospital. They said no harm was done."

Alex's body seemed to deflate.

"It's the CPS. If they can prosecute, they will."

Then, in a voice as small as his body seemed to have become,

"What am I going to do?"

This time it was she who took his hand and held on to it, balance in his distorted world.

The Facebook lady was in her kitchen waiting for the kettle to boil when she heard the ping of an email. Tiger Lily drank tea all day, every day and well into the night. Fern could never understand how her petite partner could consume such copious amounts of tannin, always strong, preferably Yorkshire and tempered only with unsweetened soya milk. An execrable brew which neither seemed to bore Tiger Lily nor keep her awake; she could sleep anywhere. Fern had only to have a sip of coffee or caffeine in the evening and she would be awake for hours.

Tiger Lily put the kettle down and went to check her lap top. She tapped the mouse and the sleeping 'Save The Letterman' page woke up and filled the screen. There was Mr W. endlessly grinning out at her, dressed in scrubs, a ghastly echo of what he once was but impossible to change as the image had assumed an iconic notoriety and guaranteed instant recognition. A private message had come in so she skimmed the mouse on its mat until the arrow landed on the access button and the boxed words appeared, slicing off half of Alex's face leaving him with a monocle and lopsided grin. It took less than ten seconds for her to read what it said and who it was from.

"Fern! Fern!" She was shrieking.

"They're taking him to court!"

"Who's being taken to court?"

"Alex Whiteley. Look!"

She looked. Read the short message, bald and anodyne.

"That's ridiculous!" she said. "They can't do that."

Tiger Lily was shaking her head in disbelief, denial and fear.

"I've got a really bad feeling about this, Fern. You know what the CPS are like. Look at the problems we had trying to get a case together for the drug trials. In the end we had to pay for the Avastin ourselves because they wouldn't have anything to do with it. Said it wasn't in the public interest, remember? They simply wouldn't listen to us no matter what we said or did."

She was thoughtful.

"You know what worries me most? The way they are influenced by the press. Forget justice. Whichever paper shout the loudest is the one the CPS listens to."

"Nothing to stop us trying though. We can do it through Facebook. ... I know! Get the lawyer's contact details and we'll get everyone to email him with testimonials! Like the hospital! It worked then so why not now?"

"Brilliant! I'll do

it now!"

CHAPTER FORTY-NINE

Lisa accompanied Alex to London for the meeting with his legal team. They had debated whether or not Baldrick was well enough to be left but Lisa was adamant that she wanted to know where they stood legally and besides, there were questions she might want to ask. The most recent consultation with the vet had pronounced Baldrick almost, miraculously, recovered, although long term damage to his kidneys could not be ruled out.

"He must have a cast iron digestive system" the vet had said, admiringly. "Possibly an inherent characteristic of the breed. Genetically designed rat catchers y'know and rats carry all sorts of nasties."

"Or years of practice" added Lisa, less impressed. "He eats anything. The more disgusting the better."

"Well, as long as he lays off the poison he should be absolutely fine" the vet pronounced "and certainly safe to be left for a day while you go to London. Just make sure he has plenty of clean drinking water."

So Baldrick had been left with great reluctance on Alex's part, an enormous serving dish full of clean water and access to the holy of holies, the master bedroom where there was no doubt he would avail himself of the duvet, pillows and cushions for a long, comfortable sleep. Lisa shook her head at her husband's ministrations.

"He could float on an airbed in that amount of water" she muttered "and you do know what state the bed will be in when we get back don't you?"

"Ah, poor puppy" Alex simpered. "He's been ill. He needs to take it easy."

Lisa rolled her eyes. "Come on or we'll miss the train."

Alex was clearly fretting about his beloved Best Boy throughout the journey to the lawyers but better that than his legal predicament thought Lisa, so she let him get on with it. When they arrived they were shown straight up to the meeting room with the large table where they took their places alongside Charles, Derek, Arash and Margaret. Lisa recognised them all immediately from Alex's descriptions. As Derek was outlining the CPS investigation and proposed prosecution, she had time to study them closely, particularly Charles Somerton.

Our future depends on these people she thought, especially him. It might all come down to his performance in court. She noted his sleek hair and smooth demeanour and harboured doubt. But I must be wrong her internal dialogue reasoned. He's a top barrister and charges a fortune which he couldn't do if he wasn't the best. We've just got to trust him.

Derek had finished talking and Lisa had a question.

"What I don't understand is how he can be cleared by the hospital and yet the CPS are taking him to court. The patient wasn't harmed. Everyone agrees on that, even the CPS."

It was succinct and pertinent and she was regarded with interest: more than just a supportive wife then, but someone with a clear grasp of the complexity of the situation. Alex was relieved she had raised the point because he also wanted to know the answer. Derek replied.

"The patient is claiming psychological harm in the form of Post-Traumatic Stress Disorder – PTSD. We're waiting for the psychiatric assessment but this is certainly the line the CPS will take. It's all about the definition of 'harm' in legal terms."

Lisa was puzzled.

"PTSD? How? I thought the sufferer had to directly experience or witness the trauma in order to get stress disorder. Surely Mr Cardoso was under anaesthetic at the time?"

"He was" Alex affirmed.

Charles, who had been quietly observing Lisa and following the conversation then spoke directly to her. She was not a woman to be messed with he had decided, or patronised. He spoke as a barrister.

"Psychological harm amounting to ABH - Actual Bodily Harm, is going to be difficult for the CPS to prove unless the psychiatric report unequivocally finds for PTSD, which, in my experience, is very unlikely."

Lisa locked looks with him.

"The CPS are bringing a charge of Actual Bodily Harm, aren't they? Even though the basis of their case is not assured?"

He nodded assent. She was quick. Would have made a good lawyer. However, she had not finished.

"Is it true that Crown Courts and Magistrate's Courts can both try cases of ABH - Actual Bodily Harm?"

Charles nodded yes but did not speak, not wanting to interfere with the logic of her thought development.

"So why are we going to trial by jury at the Crown Court and not a prosecution in a lesser court? I don't understand."

Nor did Alex, Margaret and possibly even Arash. They all waited for the answer. Derek chimed in,

"It's a question of possible sentencing and the level of punishment. The maximum prison sentence for an ABH conviction is five years but this can only be handed out in the Crown Court. The lesser court, the Magistrate's, can hear ABH cases but can only impose a maximum of twelve months imprisonment."

The air was filled with an icy stunned silence.

Alex gasped and stared at Lisa who had frozen. Prison? Five years?

"Five years?" Lisa was barely audible. Alex grasped her hand, desperately, as he pleaded.

"What happens if it isn't PTSD? What happens then?"

Inwardly he was praying for positive news; anything to relieve Lisa's anguish.

"That is up to the CPS. They might reduce the charge to Common Assault which is less serious and is tried in a Magistrate's Court" Derek responded and Alex felt mildly encouraged until Charles added,

"Or they might press for a jury in the Crown Court to reach a verdict of physical harm amounting to Actual Bodily Harm. The difficulty is that this is uncharted legal territory. We just don't know."

"The one thing that we do know is that the CPS are out to get me" said Alex quietly. Then more angrily, "I didn't do any harm! He wasn't hurt! We have the reports to prove it. The first liver would have failed anyway!"

His hand was squeezing Lisa's so hard as he spoke that she winced and grimaced but he did not let go.

"A jury can decide the level of harm" Charles said, almost regretfully. Lisa was appalled.

"How? They're not experts."

"That, Mrs Whiteley, is our problem" Charles answered. "And in the absence of any previous case and precedent to guide them, we don't know what might happen."

"When will the court case be?" Alex spoke, not daring to look at Lisa. Charles shrugged his shoulders.

"It's impossible to say. It all depends on how long the CPS spend on getting their psychiatric evaluations and evidence together. But there is a time limit of six months so they have to bring the case by April next year at the latest. They'll inform us of the exact date but we'll be ready for them, won't we Derek?"

"We're hard at work on it already, Alex."

Both Charles and Derek were watching their client with concern. He appeared self-controlled and calm but they were mesmerised by the rapid, involuntary blinking behind the spectacles as he repressed swelling tears, squeezing them to death. Derek noticed that Alex was still clutching his wife's hand; his knuckles were white and Derek could only speculate about the pain that Lisa was experiencing.

It seemed hopeless. No one spoke until Arash, looking round at the solemn faces marooned at one end of the vast table interrupted the despondency like an unexpected breeze stirring the sails of a becalmed yacht.

"On the brighter side ..."

Alex snapped,

"Is there one?".

Arash pressed on,

"Your friend, Tiger Lily, has put up a post on the 'Save The Letterman' page. Well, several actually, asking everyone to write letters of support and testimonials for you. They're being emailed to me and I'll include them in the bundle."

"The bundle?" Alex asked more graciously, regretting his

waspish retort.

"The documents we present to the judge before the trial."

"Are there many?" Derek glanced at Charles, both thinking that it might be of consequence.

Arash beamed. "Hundreds. Never seen anything like it. I wish we had that kind of support for all our cases; it would make my life so much easier."

Even Lisa managed a hint of a smile.

On the train home Alex was quiet. He sat back in his seat and turned his head away from Lisa towards the window. It was almost dark; she could see his face in the reflected light as his expressions were bounced back into the carriage from the obscurity outside. He was apparently transfixed by the passage of moving lights and artificial colours as the train headed north away from the city through the thinning suburbs. He had barely spoken since they had left the offices of RedheadCohen&LeFevre and had insisted on getting a taxi to the station, citing the need to get home to Baldrick but in reality, she knew it was because he did not trust himself to hold it together emotionally on public transport.

"Do you want a coffee?" she asked. Alex turned to her and shook his head.

"No, thanks. What about you?"

"I'm fine." Silence. He returned to his vigil at the window. Should she speak or wait for him to come to her?

"Alex. There's something bothering me."

Now he looked at her, moving himself closer, concerned.

"What?"

"The GMC. What happens if, when, there's a court case? Will they change their decision about giving you a written warning? Or will they do something ... more serious?"

He stared at her.

"They can't do that. They've made their decision. Haven't they?" He slumped back into his seat. "I don't know. Christ, I hope not. I'll ask Derek." Alex was already reaching into his jacket pocket for his phone.

But Lisa had not finished.

"There's something else."

Her husband gazed at her, too frightened even to ask what.

"Have you decided whether or not to give up medicine?"

To her utter astonishment, he smiled.

"Why are you smiling?"

"You're amazing. Because I've been thinking about it. Over and over. I was thinking about it just now."

"And?"

"And the answer is no. Not yet. Not unless I have to. I've really thought about it, Lisa, and I know I don't want to give up medicine. I don't know how to do or be anything except a doctor. Do you mind? I mean, it's not just about me and what I want. Would you like me to call it a day? Hang up my white coat and stethoscope?"

"As long as it's not like it was before, no."

Laser-eyed, piercing; did she have to say more or had he understood?

"It won't be. I promise." He was like a small boy promising eternal good behaviour in return for a much longed for puppy. "I'm not like I was when ... when I did it."

Not yet able to articulate what he had done to Carlos Cardoso she realised, but at least he now had insight. Early days though, she conceded. He'll get there.

"Let's see what happens with the CPS and deal with the GMC if we have to. You still need to look for a job; Baldrick's vets' bills need paying. Anyway, I can't imagine what else you could do apart from medicine. It's in your DNA."

He was smiling at her and shaking his head.

"What?" she asked.

"How do you always know what I'm thinking?"

She drove home from the station while Alex read the reply from Derek, who said that he thought it was unlikely that the GMC could change their ruling but that he would look into it and get back to them. Meanwhile Alex was to keep a low profile and get on with his life. Ha! If only! Lisa had not spoken for the rest of their journey and her husband knew enough to leave her alone; she would talk when she was ready. She parked up the Discovery on the drive while he leapt out and strode up to the front door.

"Baldrick! We're home! He shouted as the key turned and the door opened into the dark hallway. He stepped in and geared himself up, feet planted sturdily on the mat in readiness for the onslaught of irrepressible Jack Russell. Nothing happened.

"Baldrick! Where are you?"

Darkness. Silence. Utter stillness. Alex's stomach writhed; his body prickled; sweat and heat engulfed him; the hallway warped and distorted and he never knew how he managed to climb the stairs up to the master bedroom. Baldrick was couched on their bed, nesting in their pillows which had been rearranged to form a downy bubble in which he was enveloped, cossetted, insulated. His eyes were closed, one soft ear perched upright against his silky-smooth Egyptian cotton shell. He was stone cold.

The vet said that Baldrick had died of a heart attack in his sleep. A painless and instant death, he would have felt nothing but simply closed his eyes, dozed off and never woken up. And yes, there was little doubt in his professional opinion that the poisoning and subsequent treatment had been too much for his heart which had quite simply, given up. There was nothing anyone could have done.

"At least he was warm and comfortable" Lisa said. "You know how he hated to be cold and how much he loved to sleep on our bed, especially as he wasn't supposed to."

Alex, however, was inconsolable. He blamed himself.

"We weren't here. We weren't with him. He went on his own, Lisa. I can't bear it. He was all on his own and it's my fault, Lisa. My fault."

"How?"

"Because if I hadn't written my initials on that man's liver then none of this would have happened. Someone wants revenge for what I did and they poisoned Baldrick and now he's dead and I'm to blame."

She had no words but could only hold him as tightly as she could, her arms encasing his body and a mind so fragile she feared it was fragmenting.

The days were short, the darkness everywhere.

Lisa no longer knew what to say. Alex was a man suffused with anger. Grief and shame had made him rigid and harsh.

Finally, she tried to find words.

"Alex. You can't go on like this."

"Like what?"

Did he really not know?

"I'm grieving too."

"And coping with it so much better than me, is that what you're saying?"

"Alex!"

"I'm just weak and pathetic, a failed surgeon, unemployed and can't get a job, can't cope and almost certain to be found a criminal. That's what you're saying, isn't it?"

"No."

She turned and left the room. He heard the front door being shut carefully, as quietly as possible and the house was silent. It was what he most feared. He was on his own.

CHAPTER FIFTY

One Month Later

It had taken all Kieran's considerable powers of persuasion to convince Carlos that a psychologist was just as good as a psychiatrist when it came to assessing Post-Traumatic Stress Disorder. The consultation had taken place, the assessment made and the report itself was now in Kieran's briefcase although copies had already been emailed to the other members of the legal team. As it was central to their case he had arranged to meet with Jayne, Stephen and, reluctantly, Carlos, to discuss the findings before they were submitted to other side.

The train journey from Manchester to Stroud was indirect, tedious and long. Kieran had contemplated travelling down the night before and staying over, but where? Not in Stroud; there was not a single decent hotel in the town and certainly nothing to do or see. No, better to make an early start and arrive betimes in order to make a swift getaway. At least he could work on the train and if he reserved a seat in the quiet carriage, he could legitimately ignore his phone. So if he did not want to respond to a text or email he could argue that there was no signal. Always a silver lining.

When he arrived at the once quaint but now incongruous Victorian station blighted with incompatible twentieth century add-ons, it was late morning. A ten-minute walk to Jayne's office and he was seated once more on an uncomfortable chair listening to Carlos Cardoso. Did the man ever shut up? It seemed he had been on his feet in full spate before Kieran arrived and if Jayne and Stephen hoped that their colleague's appearance would make him stop, they were sadly mistaken.

"Naturally I was very unsure about seeing a psychologist not a psychiatrist but Kieran," a gracious nod in his direction, "convinced me that it was of no material consequence to the outcome of the case, and I must say that the young lady was most sympathetic and helpful. She knew how to listen – such a rare quality these days – and I really felt that she understood my pain. It was, in hindsight, a most beneficial exercise for me to be able to talk properly about the experience and describe how I felt. It was therapeutic. Just what I needed and once that monster is behind bars and I've been properly compensated for my pain and suffering, I really believe I'll be able to get on with the healing process and the rest of my life."

He sat down and reached for his bottle of mineral water from which he took a long, life-affirming drink.

Kieran could almost feel the torsion of Jayne and Stephen's screwdriver eyes as they glowered in his direction. It was not his fault if the man over-reacted. He ignored them and focussed on his client.

"We'll get you the justice you deserve, Carlos."

"We need a conviction first." Stephen's voice was mild; his gaze was intense. "Has the hospital already awarded you £25,000, Mr Cardoso?"

"But now we are looking not just at my appalling pain and suffering but also my loss of earnings. I can't possibly work at the moment and what about the future? And there are all the possible rehabilitation expenses, not to mention any costs incurred by the legal process. The payment from the hospital is derisory. It doesn't even begin to reflect what I've been through - and have yet to endure. God alone knows how I'll cope with the court case when I have to relive the whole thing, in front of other people, with that potential murderer sitting in front of me, watching and gloating as I stand in the witness box."

"That might not be necessary Mr Cardoso. A witness statement can be read out on your behalf by Stephen and you'll be spared the difficulty of testifying in court." Jayne had interjected and having seized the initiative, was not letting it go without a skirmish. "In fact, that is almost certainly the best option. It gives you the opportunity to write down exactly what you feel without stress and pressure and it also preserves your anonymity so that you're not exposed to public scrutiny of any description, in court or out of it."

Stephen spoke now, quickly, before Carolos could respond.

"Yes, Mr Cardoso. Protecting your privacy is essential, now and in the future and especially in the media. In terms of compensation we will, of course, apply to the Judge on the day of the trial after a ruling is given. Any level of compensation will depend on the judgement made but we'll be prepared for all eventualities. What needs to be decided today is whether or not we opt for trial by jury in the Crown Court or whether the case should be heard in a lesser court. Kieran?"

"Trial by jury. No question. Sentencing, public censure, levels of compensation; everything. This is a legal landmark case. It has to be done properly. There's also a principle – let the public decide, for the public, against a man who has betrayed a profession that is supposed to serve the public."

Stephen was not impressed but Carlos was nodding his head

vigorously and memorising every word. It had been a sizeable blow to hear that he might not be able to testify in person but time enough to address that problem and, by God, he could write a powerful witness statement. He would start with the diary he had been keeping.

Jayne was more cautious. “The Magistrate’s Court offers a more certain outcome.”

“But a lower sentence.” Kieran had no doubts. “Only twelve months.”

“All I want is justice!” Carlos declared. Kieran smirked, Jayne sighed and Stephen reached for his copy of the psychologist’s report.

“We’d better have a careful look at this then” he said, wearily. “Before we disclose it to Alexander Whiteley’s legal team and a date is set for the trial. ... By jury” he added in response to Carlos’ unspoken question.

CHAPTER FIFTY-ONE

It felt strange to be in the corridors of the MCH after so many months but at least she was walking, upright, brisk and energetic along the noisy, crowded, tiled central corridor. No wheelchair this time, just Fern's hand as they checked in at one of the touch screens on the central pillars and took their seats in front of the forever scrolling red loop of televised information on the wall outside the Liver and Upper Gastro department. After her name appeared and she trekked off down the white tube-like passage to the consulting rooms for her three-month post-operative follow up, Tiger Lily, still holding Fern's hand, wondered who would be conducting her examination. Not Alex, obviously, and not Mr Mahendran who was now on a two year sabbatical, in India, but there were plenty of others although they were strangers to her. She handed over her appointment letter to the receptionist who read it carefully, looked up at her even more carefully, and put it to one side.

"Just take a seat please and a consultant will be with you soon."

They sat down, backs to the large plate glass window

overlooking a sad little courtyard containing a single tree, spindly, lanky and tall, growing upwards towards the sky as fast as it could in an attempt to escape. The waiting room was busy, the orange plastic chairs full, the queue for the toilet methodically relentless. It was noisy in a subdued way; people talked in hushed tones as if in a library, some nervous, others too ill to speak but content to listen. At least it was a Thursday follow up and not a Tuesday cancer clinic.

Having come through the system Tiger Lily now knew its subtleties and implications – details that were never broadcast but became a familiar language to those unlucky enough to need them. She felt her phone vibrate in her bag but ignored it. No mobile phones allowed inside the hospital; it would have to wait. As did she. And so they sat, bod-watching, listening, wondering how much longer 'soon' could be. People who had arrived after her were being called, disappeared with a consultant, reappeared, then departed, but still they sat. Thirty minutes after her appointed time, Tiger Lily cracked, got up and spoke to the receptionist behind the desk. There was a polite exchange, a flushed face and a brief consultation with a male nurse in a short white coat also working behind the desk before the receptionist profusely apologised and Tiger Lily returned to her still warm seat. Exactly one minute later a casual young man in chinos and a check shirt with sleeves rolled up to the elbows appeared beside the desk and called out her name. Tiger Lily was surprised: he seemed to recognise her but she had no idea in the world who he was.

"Sorry to keep you waiting Ms Lacey. I'm one of the consultants here. Please, come this way."

"Doesn't seem to have a name though!" whispered Fern as they followed him into the hallowed ground of the consulting rooms. As they walked past a surprising number of open doors Tiger Lily could have sworn she heard someone hiss "It's the Facebook Lady" but surely she was mistaken?

Her follow-up consultation was succinct. No actual examination necessary, Ms Lacey, just a routine check up to see how you are getting on. No problems? Good. Eating well? No aches and pains? Excellent. Yes, of course you can do yoga – anything you want as long as you feel comfortable with it. Don't overdo it at first but you know your own body; you'll know what's right for you. Had she any questions? No? Even better. There'd be another follow up appointment in, oh, six months or so but he was confident that all would be well and they would not need to see her before then. For any reason.

You want to get rid of me thought Tiger Lily and glanced at Fern who clearly thought the same. The young man seemed ... nervous? Over anxious to please... Good God! Was he frightened? Of her? No, not her, but of her Facebook page.

Outside the hospital, when they had mocked and laughed at the hapless consultant's discomfort, Tiger Lily retrieved her phone from the recesses of her untidy capacious handbag, wiped crumbs and fluff off the screen and checked her missed call.

"Arash Fadaei! What does he want?

Fern did not recognise the name.

"Sidekick of Alex Whiteley's solicitor; the one who does all the donkey work."

"Call him. It might be urgent."

She tapped the call back button and Arash picked up at once.

"Hi Tiger Lily. I'm sorry to bother you but I thought you'd like to know."

"Know what?"

"We've got a date for Alex Whiteley's court case. Tuesday 11th February. Midland Central Crown Court, trial by jury."

"Trial by jury?"

"Yes. So the written testimonials you've asked for on Facebook really matter. It would be really helpful to keep up that momentum if we can."

"We can and we will."

Elsewhere in the MCH, support for Alex, albeit begrudging, was to be found in a very unlikely quarter. Patricia and Hari were sitting in her corner office ruminating over the recommendations of the investigation into the death of Meghan Orchard.

"Following our initial findings highlighting the shortcomings of the surgical and anaesthetic teams it has now been deemed necessary to take further action" Patricia read aloud.

Hari was in a state of shock.

"Further action? They never take further action! What further action?"

Patricia did not reply at first. She heaved a sigh of such depth that Hari wondered if she was going to deflate. He had never seen her so demoralised; disheartened. To his astonishment he felt sorry for her.

"The Liver and Upper Gastro-Intestinal Department has been put into Special Measures as a result of lack of effective leadership and unsatisfactory surgical outcomes."

Patricia had partially slumped over her statement desk, slack-limbed, head in hands as she spoke. Hari too, was mystified.

"But why?" Why now? We've put in a new Clinical Director. Garth has gone. Surely, it's not to do with the Alex incident?"

"No, Hari, it's not. I don't know why. I just don't know. I can't believe I'm saying this but I almost wish Alex was back; whatever else he was, he led a successful department. This would never have happened if he was still in charge."

"But what about Laura? She hasn't had time to make a difference yet; she's only just been appointed. This just isn't fair."

Another whole-body sigh and Patricia responded. "No, it's not fair. Presumably the SIRI has to focus on what was, so at least we can say we're already in the process of meeting their recommendations. We could argue that the Special Measures should be lifted as we're already addressing the problems but we'll have to give evidence of quantifiable change and that takes time." She had lifted her head by now and resumed her upright posture. "How is Laura getting on? Are the others cooperating?"

"Honestly?"

"Honestly."

"She's having a hell of a time. Not in the hospital but just the department. Being a woman doesn't help ... Sorry." As if it was his fault. "There's absolutely no question about her ability and skills but that makes it worse because they doubly resent her."

"They?"

Now it was Hari's turn to sigh. "The old guard consultants she's been promoted over."

"The men?" He nodded. "Then you have to do something about it, Hari."

"The problem is, what? If we intervene it will be seen as weakness and that'll only make things worse for her. There's nothing tangible to address, it's all passive aggressive polite non-cooperation. They agree to one thing but either do nothing or something else. It's infuriating."

"It's ridiculous. Unprofessional. Petty. Immature. What is the matter with these people?"

"Ambition. They all want to be at the top and will do anything to get there."

"Sod their ambition. I want a working department that doesn't discredit my hospital. It's got to stop, Hari. As of now. Do whatever it takes. We'll fire the whole bloody lot of them if we have to."

Indomitable Patricia the Chief Executive Officer had returned; she seemed taller and her desk to have shrunk. Hari responded in kind.

"What we need to do is break down the old alliances. Put some grit in the wheels. That'll upset their complacency and make them look to their own laurels instead of ganging up on Laura."

"How?"

"Bring in someone new – a man – academic, with gravitas and impeccable credentials. Promote within the department so that the younger ones remain on side and the older ones have to up their game to preserve their senior roles."

Patricia was almost smiling; she loved strategic intrigue and Hari was good at it. She listened with unforeseen enjoyment as he continued.

"Let's immediately offer a research registrar post to James MacKenzie leading to a PhD. Good for him, good for the hospital, good for our staff retention figures and very good for our reputation for in-house medical research. Then there's a Colombian Professor of Transplantation, Eduardo Moreno-Dias. He's just published a paper on Norothermic Liver Perfusion – improved organ preservation for transplant - and is in the UK at the moment to speak at the University of Southampton. I've known him for a while; we met at a conference about four years ago and I know for a fact that he would be interested in working here ... two years initially while Garth is on sabbatical and take it from there?"

"Yes, promote Mackenzie, and then someone else to fill his space. Shuffle them about; unsettle them. Why is this professor so keen to come here?"

"Our international reputation, facilities, research record - all the things that will enhance his already established reputation so that when, if, he returns to Colombia, he will have an extremely lucrative private practice. Or anywhere he chooses to open a clinic."

It all made complete sense to Patricia; Hari was talking her language and she felt a great deal better. They would implement the changes; she would be able to minimise any damage caused by the SIRI outcome with her exciting, innovative plans designed to take the hospital forward into an even more successful phase. Criticism was good: kept them on their toes; Special Measures were regrettable but valuable; as an astute Hospital Trust they had recognised what needed to be done even before the result of the Serious Investigation and were, as ever, ahead of the game. What mattered most was providing the best patient care possible; this was their vision and this their mission. Yes. Patricia's day had improved; she quite looked forward to the rest of it.

CHAPTER FIFTY-TWO

"Isn't it time you got up?"

"What for?"

"Alex. Get up. It's gone ten, the morning is half over and you haven't even got out of bed. I've brought you a cup of coffee. Now, get up."

Alex turned over to face Lisa and looked at her. He was unshaven but not sleepy, just exhausted.

"You need a shave. And a hair-cut. Get up. You've got fifteen minutes to get washed and dressed. No, don't argue. Just do it. I'll take your coffee downstairs. You can drink it there."

Recognising the futility of both argument and resistance, Alex heaved himself out of bed and stumped furiously to the bathroom, a stroppy middle-aged teenager. Bloody woman. He stood over the toilet and toyed with the idea of deliberately missing the bowl so that she would have to clear up the piss on the floor but decided against it; she'd only make him do it so it wasn't worth the effort.

As he was ferociously cleaning his teeth then washing his face, avoiding the mirror over the sink until it was no longer possible when he had to shave, his fury began to subside. What was the point? Might as well get up as not. Nothing to get up for but nothing to stay in bed for either.

"Just do as you're told" he said to his damp reflection in the mirror as he began hacking at the side of his face. He studied the razor scraping against his skin but did not see himself. Lisa had asked why he was not using his electric razor and he had mumbled something about it not doing a proper job. What he had omitted to say was that it reminded him of the days when there was time only for a quick, mechanical skim over the face because he was important, indispensable, revered. Necessary. Now he had all the time in the world and did not want any of it.

He was about to put on yesterday's tracksuit but decided to wear jeans; at least they were clean, with a shirt and jumper. Otherwise, she would only make him change and he really could not be bothered. Twenty minutes later he was downstairs in the kitchen.

Lisa was sitting at the table behind a cup of milkless tea facing the doorway, waiting for him. His coffee was also waiting. Both were going cold.

"Sit down. I've got something to tell you."

Now a small boy. Frightened. He sat.

"I've got a job."

"What?"

"I've got a job, Alex."

"You? Doing what?"

She chose not to feel insulted.

"Events Planner for the Midland Museum and Art Gallery. I've been the voluntary secretary of the Friends of the Museum for ages and now the Trustees have asked me to work for them full time doing promotions and publicity, organising events, that sort of thing. The salary's not great but that's something else

I want to talk to you about. We need to sort out our finances. Do you want another coffee? This is going to take a while and you're not leaving the table until it's done."

Now he noticed the pile of papers, bills, a couple of files, a pen, calculator and blank note pad beside her mug of tea. Clearly no point in fighting it but he could at least be annoying.

"Am I allowed to leave the table to put the kettle on?"

Lisa ignored him and began shuffling the papers.

"We'll start with the mortgage."

Over two hours and as many cups of coffee later, neither of which he had drunk, Alex found that he had agreed to a complete reorganisation of their finances and would follow daily guidelines set down by Lisa to 'structure his life'. He was not quite sure at what point he had acquiesced but anything was better than his present inertia.

"When I've gone to work you can sort out the house, do the shopping, take some exercise. Ironing. Clean the windows. Cooking you do already, brilliantly, so lots more of that. Then I want you to sit down for at least an hour every day and keep a diary."

"A diary? About what?"

"How you feel. What you want to do. Anything that comes into your head. Anger. Resentment. Carlos Cardoso. Baldrick. Grief."

"But I can't write. I'm a doctor."

"So? It's not great literature, just a diary. No one will read it but you ..." here she paused. "Alex. You need to do this. For yourself. You've got to work through this. I know you won't ask anyone for help but I'm your wife and I love you. Please, do it for me, if nothing else."

Damn the woman. He knew if he agreed, he would have to do it. One last stand.

"Do you really think I need to?"

"Yes. For your own sake. You can't go on like this."

Alex sighed.

"Alright. For you."

Lisa looked relieved. Time picked up its pace and moved on.

"I have been looking for a job."

"Alex, I know that. And I know how hard it is but with this court case coming up and the GMC warning and all the publicity it's no wonder people are wary about employing you. I'm not blaming you. Just being practical. Did the Somerset Levels Trust get back to you about the locum job?"

"Yeah. Another rejection. As soon as they realise who I am they say no."

Nothing said; nothing to say.

"Lisa."

"Yes?"

"What happens if I don't get another job?"

"We'll downsize, house and cars. Pay off the mortgage, use the equity to buy somewhere smaller, mortgage free and take it from there. We'll manage."

"Just my car. Yours is more economical."

Her heart melted. She knew what that car meant to him.

"I've got another suggestion" she ventured, less dictator, more diplomat. There was only so much she knew she could push through before he totally rebelled.

"I think we should get another dog."

CHAPTER FIFTY-THREE

Tiger Lily and Fern's front room was now a campaign office. Still home and hearth, it had assumed the appearance of an unkempt carpeted stationery cupboard with three piece suite, television and sticky coffee table, upon which Tiger Lily's laptop was a permanent fixture. An ancient angle-poise lamp that Fern had picked up in a junk shop was perched on a tall kitchen stool adjacent to the laptop for extra light. Weighted down with a bag of couscous, the lamp base was braceleted with dirty mugs and crumbs as it shone like the Nativity star over an unlikely birthplace for redemption. If the Facebook page was an improbable saviour then Fern and Tiger Lily were even more incongruous parents.

Tiger Lily now spent most of her time crouched over the keyboard. Her typing was getting faster but was still full of errors and her spelling more enthusiastic than accurate. The Facebook edit facility had become her new best friend. Fern kept up a ready supply of tea and meals which were usually eaten on the floor or perched on the edge of the sagging sofa in front of the screen. Tiger Lily was on a mission.

"We need to keep up the momentum. The court date will be here before we know it; I don't want Christmas to get in the way."

"I don't think that's likely" Fern replied, glancing round at their unrecognisable living room and starting to collect up some of the detritus. "More tea?"

"Look at this! It's from yesterday's *Guardian*. It's been written by another consultant and posted by one of Mr W's patients. '*The Law's an* Ass'. I could've told them that!"

"Tilly, shut up. I'm reading. This is really important. It means that serious people are taking notice and coming out in support of Mr W. Obviously there's criticism of him; bound to be, but the case itself is now on trial. Look, here, at the conclusion - Alexander Whiteley has been an idiot but he's not a criminal."

"I just hope the CPS read *The Guardian.* We need to keep an eye on the papers, medical journals, all that sort of thing. I'll put up a post and ask everyone to look out for things that might be relevant."

"And I suppose you want me to trawl the internet as well? Bugger."

Fern had just spotted a trail of spilled tea on the floor roaming winsomely across the carpet into an open packet of printer paper which was swelling happily in one corner and turning a muddy brown.

"Don't step back, Tilly. You'll get wet. We're going to have to clean in here soon y'know."

"Tomorrow."

CHAPTER FIFTY-FOUR

"Dr. Voss?"

Not a voice Julia recognised. The buzzer to her flat had sounded, a little too long she felt for politeness, and she was now listening to the internal intercom in her sterile hallway. She was not expecting visitors, commercial or social, of any description and resented the intrusion into her space and time. Who was it? Cold caller? She hoped not, for his sake. Cold callers were a speciality of hers; no one ever called twice. The buzzer sounded again.

"Dr Voss? Dr Julia Voss?"

"Yes."

Someone who knew both her professional title and first name. Well spoken. Who?

"My name's Mark Clulow. I'm an RSPCA inspector. I wonder if I can come in and have a chat with you." Not so much a question as an assumption.

"What about?"

"I'd prefer to discuss that in private."

"You have identification?"

"Of course."

"Are you sure you've got the correct person? Address?"

"Certain."

"Will it take long? I'm extremely busy."

"I hope not."

"You'd better come in then."

She pressed the button to unlock the main door just long enough for him to enter and waited for him to locate her front door. What did he want? It couldn't be anything to do with that dog of Alex Whiteley; no-one could possibly know about that and Garth would never say a word. Wouldn't dare. Mark Clulow was probably after money. She could make a donation and see him off. Charitable donations were subject to tax relief and it would look good on her hospital public profile. Julia the animal lover!

There was an abrupt single knuckle rap on the door; she slowly counted to ten then opened the door to reveal an unexpectedly smart, good looking, youngish man, slim and tall. He was holding out a photographic identity card for inspection which she took, leisurely, studied minutely, returned without a word then stood back to allow him access. As he stepped onto the plush white rug on the pale floor she ostentatiously stared at his feet. He removed his shoes and placed them neatly to one side then, and only then, she led him, in his silent socks, to the kitchen.

"How can I help you?" she asked as he stood beside the marble topped central isle and began preparing a non-existent meal by reaching for a sharp knife and chopping board. "I hope this won't take long" she lobbed at him over her shoulder as she opened the fridge door and helped herself to a lone tomato.

"Thank you for your time. I'd just like to ask you a few questions about an incident involving the poisoning of one of your colleague's pets."

"I'm sorry. I have no idea what you're talking about."

The tomato was in pieces on the board, seeds spilling out amidst wet flesh. Julia continued cutting.

"Someone tried to poison an animal belonging to ..." here he consulted a piece of paper in an open file he had removed from his briefcase, "Mr Alexander Whiteley, consultant surgeon at the Midland Central Hospital."

"You're mistaken. Mr Whiteley no longer works there. He is most certainly not one of my colleagues and I am at a loss to understand why you are here."

"You do not know Mr Whiteley?"

"I know of him and I've sometimes worked with him in a purely professional capacity at the hospital but he was a general surgeon and I am a senior consultant anaesthetist. Other than that, I've had no connection with him, then or now."

"You don't know him socially?"

"Absolutely not. We move in very different circles." She tried to repress a shudder and made sure he noticed.

"You have no reason to resent Mr Whiteley in any way?"

"Of course not! I hardly know him. What a ridiculous idea. And impertinent. Why, may I ask, are you here? There are a great many other people with far more reason to resent Mr Whiteley than me."

"I am aware of the events surrounding Mr Whiteley and the allegations made against him."

"Then you know that you should be focussing your enquiries elsewhere. I do not understand what you are doing here, wasting my time like this."

She was poised over the decimated tomato, knife in raised hand. "Perhaps you could explain why I am being questioned about poisoning a dog that has eaten contaminated meat, and what's more, an animal belonging to someone I hardly know?"

He looked at her for just a moment, then replaced the paper in the file which he closed.

"Your name was supplied to us anonymously" he said as he bent down to pick up his briefcase. To her intense annoyance he placed it beside the chopping board on the marble work surface and opened the lid in order to put away the file.

"There must be hundreds of people who want revenge on Alexander Whiteley. Did your anonymous caller tell you that?"

"It was a reliable source of information, Dr Voss. Thank you for your time. I'll see myself out."

He turned to leave and was in the kitchen doorway when he halted unexpectedly and turned to face her.

"Just one thing. How did you know that the dog was poisoned with meat?"

Then he was gone and she heard the front door shut behind him as he left, still in his socks with his shoes in his hand.

***

"Baldrick's irreplaceable."

Alex had been horrified at Lisa's suggestion. Another dog! Impossible. He could never love another dog the same way as Baldrick; it was inconceivable. Disloyal even. But Lisa had known that if she kept quiet and let her husband work it through, he would eventually come around to her way of thinking. He always did. The real measure of success was when he believed that her idea had originally been his.

"It's not replacing Baldrick, just moving on. No dog in the world can ever take his place, Alex, but it'll be different. Different type of dog, different character, different everything.

There are so many dogs that a need a good home. The shelters are full of them."

"I'd prefer a puppy."

"Yes. Why not? You're at home - at the moment - so training isn't a problem. If you're strict?"

Lisa smiled, the first in a long time.

"It's possible." Almost a smile from Alex, his first in even longer. "What sort of puppy?"

"What about those dogs of that Organ Donation Nurse - I can't remember her name - you were always telling me about? Labradoodles or something?"

"Sally Crowther! Yes. Something like that, what do you think? Couldn't be more different to Baldrick and they're lovely dogs. They don't shed hair and are very good natured. Larger than a Jack Russell, but probably not as feisty. Not many breeds are. I could make some enquiries if you like, especially if you're busy?"

"Good idea. I'll leave it to you. As long as we go and choose together?"

"I'll find out more about the breed then do some research about puppies. And other breeds too, for comparison; we have to do this properly. It's changed since we got Baldrick, d'you remember? We saw an advert in the vet's surgery so we rang and went to look and couldn't resist him. He was the chubby one with the wrinkled face sitting in the middle of the food bowl like a sumo wrestler while the rest of the litter were doing their best to escape."

Faces softened with grief and remembrance but Alex's now had animation; purpose.

"I'll get on to it straight away. What d'you think?"

"I think that's a good idea. The sooner the better."

"We need to check out the mother and provenance. I don't

want to take any risks."

"Alex! It's a dog!"

"We might not be able to get our puppy much before Christmas or the New Year. Would you mind?"

She smiled when he referred to 'our puppy', witnessing the rekindling of the embers of the real Alex, her husband, not everyone else's surgeon, The Letterman or the defendant in a court case.

"Not a bit. But Alex, what about the big question? I chose the name Baldrick so now it's your turn. What's it going to be?"

"Dave."

"Dave?"

"Why not?"

"Well, it answers the question whether it'll be a boy or a girl. But why Dave? It's a bit random."

"After my grandfather."

"Definitely different. I won't ask why! If that's what you want, then that's what it'll be. You'd better go and find him."

Dave arrived in a flurry of sleet and freezing temperatures like a mushroom-coloured snowball. Already at two months he was larger than Baldrick ever was. His size had taken them by surprise – well, Lisa anyway, especially as she knew he would only get bigger. Having met his mother, a gentle Golden Retriever of Shetland Pony proportions, Lisa wondered whether it had been the right thing to do to entrust the project to Alex.

"It's the breed" Alex had enthused. "Goldendoodles do grow quite a lot and are quite large. His father was a Standard Poodle."

Lisa merely looked at him. Extensive internet searches

followed up by on-the-ground enquiries had failed to locate a single Labradoodle so Alex had extended the search to include somethingdoodles of all descriptions. A litter of Goldendoodles had been located in Cheltenham so they had set off one Saturday when Lisa was at home, 'just to have a look'. She should have known what would happen, of course, and was not even mildly surprised when, after having been at the breeder's less than twenty minutes, she found that they were signed up for one of the two male pups which would be ready on New Year's Eve.

"What a great way to start the new year!" Alex had beamed as they were buying high protein puppy food, vitamins, expandable collar, training lead, low calorie training treats, puppy grooming kit, water bowls, food bowls and a dog tag engraved with Dave on one side and their telephone number on the other.

"Dave?" the engraver in the cobbler/keys cut booth outside the supermarket had asked. "Nothing else?" He had looked at Lisa for confirmation rather than Alex; experience had taught him always to refer to the woman for the final decision on anything retail.

"No. Just Dave. Thank you."

"Bone-shaped, round or oval?"

"Pardon?"

"The tag. You can have gold or silver, not real of course, bone-shaped, round or oval."

"Bone-shaped!" Alex announced as if he had discovered the secret of eternal life. "In gold! Because he's a Goldendoodle!" Lisa began to wonder whether she had strayed into a parallel universe.

They also bought a large cage with a high-tog, single duvet and cheerful 100% cotton cover for bedding so that Dave could sleep downstairs in it at night. They conceded that Baldrick wasn't the best trained dog in the world - by virtue of his size he could be lifted out of trouble and bodily removed if required. Clearly this was not going to be possible with Dave; even now he was almost too heavy to lift. Cage training was recommended by the breeder and all 'the experts' so having printed off several sheets of instructions from the internet, they erected the cage in a warm corner of the kitchen, put down the bedding and prepared for the night to come. Dave was repeatedly enticed into the cage with tasty morsels, toys and 'lots of positive encouragement' as per the instructions. Alex sat inside it himself for a while with, and without, the dog so that there would be 'no sense of fear or punishment associated with the confined space.' Dave seemed a little perplexed by the activities but was more than happy to participate: anything to oblige. It was only when the cage door was shut and the humans disappeared out of another door that you couldn't see through, did he realise that he was on his own and he did not like it. At all.

Alex and Lisa spent New Year's Eve sitting on their kitchen floor beside an open dog cage sharing a bottle of wine. Every time they tried to leave Dave wailed himself into heartbreak. Eventually Lisa went to bed in the early hours of the morning and Alex slept on the duvet with Dave, outside the cage.

"Do we really want to keep him in a cage at night, Alex? Why are we doing this?"

"I don't know. Dave's ours; he stays with us. It was a ridiculous idea."

They sold the cage – perfect condition, used only once – on Gumtree and bought two large dog beds, one for upstairs, one for down. Dave followed them everywhere.

CHAPTER FIFTY-FIVE

Christmas was long gone and the New Year was just learning to crawl. Schools had reopened, post-festive excess diets had been abandoned and resolutions broken. Patricia was already back on the Hobnobs.

Carlos was feeling extremely sanguine and confident. Always relieved when the Christmas season was over and he was no longer forced to confront the reality of his loneliness, this new year heralded the promise of fame, victory and substantial cash. He did not know exactly how much compensation he would receive but his hopes were as high as the amount he envisaged. Many contented hours had been spent in a solitary reverie of imagined expenditure and largesse; so many gestures to be made in his name for the benefit of others. He wouldn't be greedy – invest enough for his own modest comfort and the occasional luxury, but he would be munificent. What price Justice? It In some ways it was not really his money at all, although he deserved generous remuneration for all his suffering. No, in a sense it belonged to

The Public for the abuse suffered at the hands of the medical profession. He was merely the instrument of justice; he had performed a public service by sacrifice and suffering.

Ah, so many pleasant hours spent contemplating his future. Just one week to go before he would be vindicated, recognised, rewarded. Writing down his thoughts and feelings in the diary had been an excellent idea. He could not recall if it had been his idea or the solicitor's but no matter. As the basis of a witness statement, it was shaping up well but perhaps there was more to be done with it? Novel? Screenplay perhaps?

Such were his thoughts as he waited in the reception area at the CPS offices in Stroud. Ms Lavery would be with him in a second or two the secretary had said, rather brusquely he felt, then returned to her computer screen and he had been left to take a seat on one of the imitation leather chairs. Not even offered a coffee. Thank heavens he had a bottle of Evian. The wall clock, a hangover from the metallic, decorative space age style of the 60s and now elevated from tasteless to vintage, was clunking its way towards the 11.15 mark and Carlos felt disgruntled. His appointment was for 11.00 and being kept waiting like this was not only rude but unprofessional. He would have to say something. He was formulating a courteous but firm admonishment when Jayne appeared, somewhat flustered, apologising effusively.

"I'm so sorry, Mr Cardoso, to keep you waiting. Most unprofessional I know and I can only apologise but it really was unavoidable."

What she did not say that there had been an almighty row between Stephen and Kieran who were even now sitting in her room, indignant, defensive and angry. She had been caught in the crossfire although it was not fair to say that Stephen had been aggressive; he was much more subtle than that which only seemed to infuriate Kieran even more. The argument had arisen over the report about Carlos' PTSD. Kieran was determined to base the entire court case around it but Stephen had objected on the grounds that in itself, this was insufficient substantial evidence. Jayne badly needed a coffee, not Carlos Cardoso.

Nevertheless, she escorted him up the stairs to her not quite so chilly office, warmed by the oil-filled radiator and the exchange between the male lawyers. They greeted the diversion of Carlos with unexpected cordiality. It did not last.

"What do you mean there might not be enough substantial evidence of PTSD? I can't sleep, I can't eat. I can't concentrate - on anything. Every time I close my eyes, I re-live the horror. If that surgeon hadn't branded my liver, it wouldn't have failed and I wouldn't have had to have a second transplant. Two transplants! Can you imagine what that is like? One is traumatic enough, but two! That butcher could have killed me! My acting career is ruined – how can I ever have the stamina for a West End run after all this? I am dependant on medication for the rest of my life, which will never be the same again. I am a marked man. My whole life has been destroyed."

"Mr Cardoso!" Jayne could bear it no longer. "All successful transplant patients are required to take medication; that is normal procedure."

"How do you know? Are you a doctor?"

Jayne flushed, mortified.

"Mr Cardoso, this is not helpful."

Stephen's voice was measured but he was annoyed. He might get angry but would never be rude, especially to a lady. Carlos had crossed a line, but took no notice.

"You don't seem to understand what I've been through. What I'm still going through."

"Carlos, Carlos, we do understand. Believe me. And we share your pain."

Jayne and Stephen were embarrassed; Kieran might but they certainly did not. They stared at him as he continued placating their client,

"We will get justice for you, Carlos. A jury is bound to understand your point of view and to recognise your suffering so that is why we are going to the Crown Court for trial by jury. 'Twelve good men and true' will almost certainly find in your favour and Alex Whiteley will be punished. We even have the Press on our side. A week today and you'll be able to put this all behind you."

Carlos smiled, sadly, sweetly, beatifically. Stephen and Jayne glared at Kieran.

CHAPTER FIFTY-SIX

The arrival of Professor Eduardo Moreno-Dias at the MCH was more dignified than that of Dave but the weather no less kind. Flurries of sleety snow had given way to an endless freezing rain which made the towers glow like beacons of light and warmth in the colourless, cloud-wrapped cityscape. Expensive overtime was even allocated to the cleaners for the removal of mud, footprints and potentially lethal rain seeking asylum on the shiny floors.

“Sod the expense” Patricia had decreed one morning on entering the reception forum through the main doors and nearly breaking an ankle as she skidded on her pencil heels. “It’s cheaper than being sued. ‘Visitor breaks leg in hospital.’ Think of the headlines. We’d be a laughing stock.”

Over-sensitive thought Hari, to whom she was talking at the time, but she’s got a point. The Press would have a field day at which he repressed a smile, subversively imagining the tabloid puns.

“Besides” she was continuing, “It’s not good for our image.

People want to walk into a clean, professional medical environment, not a midden and I don't want Professor Moreno-Dias to get the wrong impression. He's an illustrious addition to our staff. Is Laura ready for him? What time does he arrive?"

"Any time now."

"Wait for him here and greet him personally, Hari. Then bring him to me."

She was gone, pencil heels subdued as she stepped cautiously on the floor until she reached the safer carpeted terrain of her office.

Hari took a hard seat in the large, open conclave to await his new colleague. He had just reached forward to one of the low tables to pick up a copy of the glossy Midland Central Hospital bi-annual brochure when his pager burst into sound. It was Laura.

"You're in theatre? What is it? ... Right. Who's with you? ... Yes, of course I'll look after him. Patricia wants to see him first anyway. Keep me posted."

Five minutes later he was shaking hands with the Professor. Eduardo was not much taller than Hari but a good deal wider due more to carefully cultivated muscle than fat. There was nothing soft or malleable about him except his hair which was gloriously abundant and not his own. His expensive suit flowed with his body as he strode along the corridors with Hari whose suit, by comparison, seemed to fight with his legs as he moved. Eduardo's idiomatic English was perfect, with just enough of an American cadence to suggest glamour, sophistication and money. Women found him irresistible to the utter astonishment of men who saw only a short, heavy-bodied man with too much hair.

"Professor Beechwood sends her apologies but she's in theatre with an emergency. A routine laparoscopic cholecystectomy cock-up elsewhere and now we have to sort it out."

Eduardo was intrigued.

"How does that happen? A simple removal of the gallbladder and the surgeon manages to cut through the common bile duct. It's nothing short of negligent."

"And happens far too often. The problem now, as you know, is repairing the damage. It's so technically challenging and there aren't many surgeons who can do it successfully."

"Professor Beechwood?"

"Yes, I hope so. In theory. She was being mentored by Alex Whiteley in the procedure but he's no longer with us. So, she's on her own although she's working with another of Alex's protegees so let's hope they can work it out together."

"Perhaps I can assist?"

"Meet our Chief Executive Officer first."

In theatre number three Laura Beechwood was leading the surgery assisted by James. Both had been called in from home even though neither were on call because no one else had felt confident enough to tackle the procedure. The patient had been blue-lighted from a hospital some 30 miles away and was now unconscious on the table, out of pain but not out of danger. Laura was relieved that the on-call anaesthetist had been Julia Voss; her experience, infamous calm and considerable expertise were reassuring and she provided a sense of stability as she sat beside the patient's head. Although she and Laura could not be more different as people, as female consultants in a male-dominated profession they were allies, united by their determination, resilience and sometimes, sheer bloody mindedness. Laura was very tall and skinny to the point of boniness with pale skin and nondescript eyes that assumed the colour of whatever she was wearing. Today, in her scrubs, they looked green and later, when she changed into her practical rather than smart navy trouser suit, would look blue.

She never wore red. Something of a paradox – impenetrably reticent about her private life yet friendly and open on the ward, she was always honest, occasionally to the point of bluntness, especially with female patients who refused to follow instructions and complained of pain. Her patience was almost as thin as her body and a lot less flexible.

Her characteristic

"Well, what do you expect? You've just had surgery so it's bound to hurt" endeared her to the nursing staff but not so much the occupants of Ladies Surgical. 'So much for bedside manner', 'men are more sympathetic', 'you'd think a woman would understand' and 'mean cow' were just a few of the responses her remark elicited but if she heard them, Laura was entirely unphased. She might have been brusque, but she knew she was right.

James was standing opposite her over the table and they were working in tandem.

"You don't need me to tell you that this is a tricky procedure, James" she had said before they began. "Alex was mentor for both of us so let's work closely together. I'll lead but I expect you to assist with initiative. Neither of us has repaired a bile duct injury on our own before so it's new territory and I don't mind admitting that I wish Alex was here to lead. However, he's not, so I've accessed his paper on it and asked the IT guys to fix up some sort of screen for us in theatre so that we can refer to it if necessary. I know we've both already studied it but in the heat of the moment it might be useful to have written guidance."

James could only agree. If she was half as apprehensive as he was there wouldn't be a straight incision between them.

"We won't rush anything" she said. "It'll take as long as it takes. We know the theory. We've seen it done; now we've just got to do it ourselves."

In the sterile capsule deep within the heart of the hospital, the abdomen of the patient on the table was finally open and pinned apart for easier access. He was a large, heavy man; his abundant body had made entry and discovery extremely difficult. Both Laura and James were sweating even before they had located the small bile duct – only 5 mm in diameter - which had been divided high up close to the liver and was leaking. If uncorrected, the greeny-yellow bile, essential for breaking down fats for digestion, would leak into the abdomen and cause severe pain, inflammation and ultimately a fatal infection There was also damage to the right hepatic artery. Key hole surgery was a wonderful innovation but if it went wrong, it went horribly wrong.

"The first thing to do is repair the small artery" Laura diagnosed. "Otherwise, the bile duct may well be starved of blood and I don't need tell you how dangerous that would be."

Easier said than done, and time consuming. It was difficult enough to deal with the vessels which were taut and under great tension, but the restricted visibility of such a tiny organ, no longer than a single grain of rice, made the task well-nigh impossible. Laura was as patient in theatre as she was impatient with uncooperative patients, but even she found herself feeling thwarted.

"More retraction please, as we're both wearing loops for magnification. Can you perform the anastomosis, James? As strong and secure a connection as possible."

"I think so."

Absolute silence. Concentration hung around them like fog. Julia's mascara rimmed eyes narrowed and focused on James' hands making the tiniest of movements within the huge hill of flesh; butterfly flutterings and twitchings. The young man was less easily distracted than she remembered, probably because he was working with Laura, who was so much more inspiring than her predecessor. Pity she had so little dress sense. They would never be friends but Julia would have liked to be able to take Laura shopping and revamp her wardrobe. Was there a man in her life? She would find out.

A large sigh of satisfaction and James' hands re-emerged from the bloody depths.

"Well done!" The creases in her face mask outlined Laura's smile. "Okay. Now let's get the bile duct spatulated into the left hepatic duct. We'll use 50 cm Roux loop to fashion an alternative route through the window from behind the colon. If we thought the small artery was difficult to see this is going to be far worse. Sorry!"

Her voice was cheerful but both she and James knew that this was the most intricate, challenging part of the procedure. They had seen it performed by Alex on only one previous occasion. Alex's academic paper on the subject glowed out from the flat wall screen but seemed chillingly distant and impersonal; they were on their own.

"Scroll it down a bit further please, Sister."

Laura was peering at the writing on the wall; James followed suit, hoping it was not prophetic. Neither of them noticed the door of the theatre open and the appearance of Hari and Eduardo, dressed in scrubs.

"Is this a good moment?"

Julia gave an involuntary, rapidly suppressed snort of derision. Laura and James were transfixed by the screen on the wall but everyone else turned towards the doorway in amazement and stared at their Medical Director. Eduardo was embarrassed.

"Obviously not."

Hearing a deep, unknown transatlantic voice, Laura turned to look at its owner. Eduardo was studying the text on the wall.

"Not an easy procedure" the stranger continued.

"Are you familiar with it?" Laura asked, interested. She

remembered now that she was supposed to be meeting her new professorial colleague instead of rummaging inside the abdomen of an overweight patient.

"Yes. More than once."

"Successful outcome?"

"Happily, usually yes."

"Professor Moreno-Dias I presume? Perhaps you'd like to join us? Laura Beechwood, but I won't shake hands."

"Delighted."

Julia had watched events with undisguised interest, especially the arrival of Professor Moreno-Dias. Not the dull donnish persona she had been expecting but someone much more attractive. Not good looking in any conventional sense – in any sense at all except for his hair through which she instantly wanted to run her fingers. He was undeniably quite short, stocky even, but sensual and so confident. Garth seemed so gauche in comparison. She was glad she always took such care with her appearance. Now all she had to do was make eye contact with him. Laura, on the other hand, could not care less. The only successful outcome she cared about was surgical.

James stood to one side as Professor Moreno-Dias took up his position as first assistant. The newcomer – "Eduardo, please. Professor Moreno-Dias is such a mouthful" – politely declined to assume Laura's position as lead surgeon which impressed. Strategic and well-mannered - Julia was intrigued.

The complicated procedure to attach the Roux loop began. Visibility and access were restricted to the point of exasperation but success was imperative. They manoeuvred the loop behind the colon without too much difficulty but then, using 5/0 PDS – sterile, synthetic, absorbable suture thread, for strength and manoeuvrability they had to, somehow, parachute the Roux down to join between the small bowel and the divided bile duct to correct the damage caused by the botched key hole surgery. Theoretically demanding, practically – apparently impossible.

“I just can’t see!” Laura’s frustration was unusual. “More retraction, please. Can’t we open him up any further? I keep losing sight of it.”

“He’s fully retracted with maximum exposure. More suction perhaps.”

Eduardo was speaking quietly; placid and reassuring. Then to James, “Suck … A little more … I’ll monitor and you do the suction.”

James nodded; they would work together. Laura would only achieve success with the most sensitive, informed, well-timed assistance they could provide.

Is that better?” Eduardo was consulting Laura who had visibly calmed.

“Much. Thank you. … Yes, getting somewhere.”

The fact that the imperturbable Laura Beechwood had been flustered had unnerved the team. Julia had watched them become unsettled with concern but now watched with admiration how Eduardo restored their equilibrium and confidence. Subtle, perceptive and proactive. This man would be worth knowing.

Laura’s hands were twisting and tweaking inside the stretched bloody orifice held open by metal pins and ratchets. God, the patient would be sore but at least he would be alive. James watched with suspended breath as she painstakingly wove a path through the pulsating pulp until the final moment when the last connection was made and the circuit was complete. The relief in the room sounded like air being released from an over-inflated tyre.

“There’s still a small amount of bile” Laura muttered self-deprecatingly as she bent over to inspect her handiwork. It was surgical craftsmanship she knew, but was it good enough?

"To be expected" Eduardo commented, almost casually. "A drain will sort that out; a small post-operative bile leak is almost to be expected."

He had deliberately repeated the word to emphasise and reassure, and it worked. The procedure had been successfully completed; the patient was no longer at risk of acute pain, peritonitis and possible death. His recovery would take time but there was no reason to think that it would not be complete and permanent. They had done a good job.

CHAPTER FIFTY-SEVEN

There was a new focus of interest now in Julia's life. Eduardo. She spent a great deal more time in the hospital, visiting parts of it previously eschewed as irrelevant or unsuitable. She had even been seen in the canteen, but not actually eating or drinking anything. It was frustrating that Eduardo did not seem to be as accessible as she would have liked and when he was discovered, was invariably with other people. What she really wanted was a one-to-one with him. That she had to work so hard to make this happen served only to resolve her determination and increased his allure. He was seen with Laura too often for Julia's liking, but the thin, androgynous Laura was no competition, that was obvious. Her interest in Eduardo was purely professional, something which fascinated him. He had never met anyone like her and, more fascinating still, was her obvious indifference to him as anything but a medical colleague. For the first time in his life, he found himself wanting to be liked by a woman. He wondered if there was a man in her life.

Arriving home one Friday evening, Julia kicked off her kitten heels at the front door and padded in her stockinged feet through to the kitchen, relishing the freedom in her toes. The Mulberry bag sat on the marble work surface and after lightly brushing imaginary dust off it, she headed straight for the fridge and bottle of Chablis. One elegant glassful then she would open the week's post. She only ever bothered with it once a week. Letters were so passé. No one sent letters now except outdated relatives and charities begging for funds.

Relaxed by the wine she picked up the pile of post that had been flung to one side over the past week. Junk mail, takeaway menus, blah blah blah. However, there was one item that caught her attention. A business envelope upon which her name and address had been hand written. By whom? No hand writing that she recognised. She discarded everything but the letter, then sat down with her wine to open it.

"What?"

The screech shattered the silence; ricocheted around the white room shading it red.

"This is outrageous." She reached for her mobile.

The letter was from the RSPCA and had been signed by the inspector who had visited a short while ago. It informed her that, pending further enquiries into an ongoing investigation of a case of animal cruelty under the Animal Welfare Act, she should be prepared for the likelihood of a prosecution being brought against her.

That same evening in their shabby, slovenly front room, Tiger Lily was nervous. The prospect of being a witness in court frightened her.

"What do I say, Fern?"

"Tell them the truth, from the heart. Clearly, simply, honestly.

And slowly. Don't gabble."

"Should I prepare something? Write something down?"

"No. Absolutely not. Too contrived. You need to be spontaneous and able to look at everyone, especially the judge. Eyeball him. You won't be on your own."

She wouldn't. The Facebook page had done it again. 'A presence' had been organised by a particularly vociferous contributor for the day of the trial. To date the numbers were unconfirmed but so much interest had been shown that even Tiger Lily was surprised and not a little apprehensive. A demonstration of support was wonderful but Tiger lily did not want a riot on her hands, particularly if the judgement went against Alex. A substantial media presence in the courtroom was guaranteed which further motivated the expansion and determination of 'the presence' to make their feelings known - outside the court building, inside the main entrance area and then inside the courtroom itself.

Tiger Lily had promoted the plan but was not directly involved in its growth. She wondered what she might have unleashed. But then, she reasoned, people have the right to speak and express their feelings. It's not up to me to tell them what they can and can't do.

"D'you think they'll have banners and stuff?" she asked Fern.

"Maybe. The media'll love it!"

"D'you think Mr Whiteley knows?"

"Only if he's been on Facebook. I wonder how he's feeling."

Nervous. As the day of the trial approached Alex became increasingly quiet, subdued; withdrawn. He spent long hours with Dave, stroking his soft ears, walking him so much that Lisa had to intervene.

"He's just a puppy, Alex. His legs are still growing and the vet said it's important not to over exercise him until he's strong enough."

His legs certainly were growing. It seemed that he went to sleep at night and in the morning was simply larger, but his sweet, gentle nature never altered.

Lisa's work had become more than a full-time occupation and she loved it; she was out of the house all day as well as some evenings to attend the events she had organised. Without Dave she would not have dared leave Alex, who refused to go to the soirees, exhibitions and lectures and she could not say she blamed him. Although she never admitted it, his absence was a relief in a way: no reason for anyone to raise the thorny subject of 'The Letterman'. She was not sure what he did all day but knew that as long as he had Dave, he would be active and have someone to talk to. Then she wondered, when had 'someone' become a dog?

Unknown to her however, she was closer to Alex's reality than she realised. Alex had tried writing a diary to expiate and make sense of his feelings and emotions. It did not work; he simply could not unload his inner self onto paper; it felt alien, cumbersome and hostile. Was it him? After a particularly long walk with Dave all through a windy afternoon into the chill of an early descending darkness, it came to him. If he found writing in the first person intimate to the point of paralysis, then why not write in the third person? In fact, why a person at all? What about a third party? He should write from a perspective that he understood and which protected his privacy.

So began 'Dog Days'.

Alex was tap tapping on his keyboard. It had not been easy at first and he would sit staring at the blank screen, oppressed by it, unsure how to say what he was frightened to confront. But Baldrick helped. As his alter ego, Alex could hide himself behind the voice of the little chap and it became easier to open up, confess, be wrong, flawed. It did not take long for him to start enjoying the daily escape into a virtual reality of his own making, where he had control and safety. Such was his occupation a couple of days before the trial. He had been sitting for most of the morning in his upstairs office on the arbitrary swivel chair, (they really should replace it but not at the moment) feet planted firmly on the floor for stability.

Lisa was at work, Dave was at his feet – keeping a safe distance from the chair which was prone to spin across the floor when least expected – when his phone chirruped with a What's App message. Alex finished the sentence he was writing, read it through, was satisfied, clicked Save and then picked up the phone. It was an unknown sender but he was curious and opened the message.

"Hi Alex

I am Jeff from Birmingham. After what has gone on you might be facing a custodial sentence.

If you was sent to prison we can protect you while you serve your sentence I have people currently serving time in HMP Midland West and other prisons.

Prison guards are also on my books.

You would be a vulnerable prisoner and be at risk from other inmates because of your profession.

Give me a call and we can arrange a meet. Also don't trust your barrister. Prepare for the worst.

Regards Jeff"

Alex was stunned. He read it again and ran for the bathroom where he heaved and spat, and heaved again and emptied his half-digested breakfast into the toilet bowl. As he flushed the acidic, foul-smelling spew away all he wanted to do was to go with it.

In Stroud, all hell had broken loose. Jayne was sitting in her office with Stephen. They had just received the defence's compulsory disclosure of evidence prior to the trial and were in a state of shock.

"But our whole case is based on this. What are we going to do?"

Jayne was appealing to Stephen who, perhaps for the first time ever in his long, wide-ranging career, was at a loss for an answer.

"I'm not sure. But we have to do something. I think a phone call to Kieran first, don't you?"

Jayne nodded and was dialling his direct line. Miraculously, he picked up and she did not have to leave yet another message on his voicemail.

"Kieran, it's Jayne. Have you seen the documentation from Alex Whiteley's legal team? ... Well, you need to have a look at it. Now. ... Yes, it is urgent. It rather looks as if we don't have a case."

CHAPTER FIFTY-EIGHT

The Trial

Judgement Day – cold, overcast but not wet. Dull but not bereft. Alex had not slept the night before so could not be said to have awoken with a sense of dread and fear; since the message from Jeff he had felt nothing else. Even writing had not helped; he had merely sat in front of his computer screen, with Dave at his feet, encased in horror.

Court proceedings were scheduled to start at 10.30 but Alex had been told to get there well before this to both meet his legal team and to avoid the media. However, the latter seemed to have received the same memo. Malcolm Piggott had made an especially prompt start to what promised to be a most exciting and rewarding day. He and his entourage of sound recordist and cameraman had even stayed overnight in the city at the expense of Midland Eye TV. It was not often his editor agreed to stay away expenses but this was a high profile case of global interest. Really, a comfortable night with a leisurely dinner in a decent hotel with a full English to line them against the cold – it had quite a festive feel about it. They were ready and waiting for Alex when he arrived at 8.30, clad in dark overcoat, scarf and cap, spectacles in his suit jacket pocket, million pound hands dug deep into those of the heavy coat which protected him against the chill but not the likes of Mr Piggott.

"Alex! Alex! Anything to say?"

Takeout coffee in one hand, microphone in the other, Malcolm was on the court house steps to greet his quarry. The steps were wide and shallow but there was no escape. Alex put his head down and soft focused his short-sighted eyes on his moving feet, hoping to God he did not trip and fall.

"Alex Whiteley, the surgeon who branded his initials on his unconscious patient is here at Midland Central Crown Court to be tried for his crime. What have you got to say to your patients, Alex? To everyone you've let down and hurt? What do you think will happen today, Alex? D'you think you'll go to prison?"

No reply. Derek had said to simply ignore all media attention and keep moving; Lisa the same. She was arriving later, unrecognised, with most of those who would be present in the court room. Alex knew he had only to reach the main doors for safety. The Press Gallery in Court Number Twelve would be full but Malcolm Piggott and those of his ilk were required to remain outside, thank God. The irony of being grateful to arrive inside a court house was not lost on Alex who fervently hoped that the obnoxious man and his crew from Midland Eye would freeze to death.

No such luck. They were far too busy keeping warm by approaching everyone in sight, keeping energetic vigil at the foot of the steps, darting between anyone of potential interest asking for comments, pictures, smiles, names, opinions, connections to Alex, anything that they'd like to say that might be of interest to the general public?

"It's a bloody nuisance that we don't know the identity of the patient" Malcolm lamented to the cameraman. "It could be any one of these people. We don't even know what sex he or she is so we'll just have to try and engage with all of them."

"Everyone else seems to have the same idea" his colleague responded glumly, eyeing the rapidly increasing numbers of reporters and their crews now thronging the area, posted like a motley guard of honour up and along the length of the steps, sound booms on poles extending over the arrivals like an arch of furry, technological swords. It had become a game of 'assail anyone not obviously in the media and get a reaction from them'. The sight of Arash with his trusty suitcase on wheels being hauled clumsily up the steps had elicited a few smiles but as he was undoubtably a legal sidekick dragging nothing but paperwork there was little to be gained from accosting him. The arrival a few minutes later of a large group of vociferous supporters carrying home-made placards and the occasional banner fell like manna from heaven on the proceedings. Cameramen and sound recordists now had something to film and record; reporters now had something to talk about; Malcolm would finally be able to justify the cost of his night away.

It was a welcome diversion for Fern, Tiger Lily, Lisa and James who were able to slide into the court house unchallenged and unnoticed as was, to his utter dismay, Carlos. Wearing a dark suit as befitted the occasion with a sombre tie and matching silk handkerchief carefully arranged in his top pocket, Carlos felt all the thrill and anticipation of an imminent stage appearance. Stage fright had never bothered him as an actor; one had a part to perform to the best of one's considerable ability. Appropriate recognition and attention were inevitable and very welcome. Truth be told, he had always felt that actors who suffered from stage fright were unprofessional and well, lacking. Being a successful actor was about living the part, being the character, not just playing lip service to it. One had to experience the performance, feel the pain, become the words. Clutching an unopened bottle of Evian he sauntered into the court house, knowing that this would be the performance of his lifetime and he wanted to savour every moment.

It was not until he had emerged through the large, heavy wooden doors into the central foyer that it occurred to him that he might encounter 'that man', Alex Whiteley.

Jayne and Stephen were determined to avoid such a meeting at all costs and had planned in advance. Jayne was positioned close by the door to steer her client out of danger into a side room where he could

"wait in privacy and comfort to compose himself for the rigours ahead" as she put it.

There was also something they needed to discuss with him but that would not be disclosed until he was securely closeted away. Alex had already been side-lined by Derek into a similar room on the opposite side of the building and the reception area was busy only with those playing bit parts and the extras. Like Tiger Lily but unknown to each other, James had also been called as a character witness by the defence and both were equally nervous, but for different reasons. Tiger Lily wanted to do Mr Whiteley justice. James feared for his career.

"And what's the worst they can do?" he had told himself . "Alex was cleared by the hospital hearing so you're not doing anything wrong by testifying for him and it's only a character witness you're giving. No one can reproach you for that, not even the Chief Executive. Even the Medical Director said it was okay and wouldn't compromise you or your career."

The unexpected quantity of people determined to sit in the public gallery had been noticed by the court house staff and frantic discussions were being held about transferring the case to a court big enough to accommodate the spectators. After a logistical juggling act, it was decided that the trial would be transferred to the larger Court Number Nine and a general announcement was made by a rather harassed court official for all witnesses to go there immediately. If everyone else could wait where they were until called forward that would be greatly appreciated. There was not enough room for everyone to wait outside the court room itself.

In his chambers, Judge Ian Hunter was holding counsel with the defence and prosecution barristers. The Clerk of the Court had just entered the room, a little breathless, having been summoned to M'Lud's chambers "immediately".

"Have the jury been sworn in?"

"Not yet, Your Honour."

"Then don't. Not yet. I need to talk to my learned friends first."

If he was surprised the Clerk hid it but as he noiselessly glided from the room his eyes were gawking. This was turning out to be quite a morning, what with the demonstrators, Press, assorted witnesses, spectators and now the jury had been put on hold. All they needed was a police presence to maintain order and then the chaos would be complete.

As soon as the door closed behind him the Judge began.

"Mr Morris. I take it that the Crown Prosecution Service has examined the documents and medical reports presented by the Defence in this case?"

"Yes, Your Honour."

"Examined them carefully?"

"Yes, Your Honour."

"And the case for the prosecution still rests on a charge of Actual Bodily Harm on the grounds of Post-Traumatic Stress Disorder, even though it is abundantly clear from every single one of these medical reports, including that of the CPS, that no harm was done and", here he referred directly to a document open before him, "the definition of Post-Traumatic Stress Disorder does not apply to the plaintiff, Mr Cardoso?"

Stephen had been anticipating such a question but even he was discomforted when it was actually delivered. It sounded so inept. In all his years with the CPS, loyally given, he had never felt so embarrassed and angry: this was not of his making. Bloody Kieran O'Connell and the CPS Special Crimes Division safely tucked away in Manchester. He had spent the last 48 hours of his waking life on the phone to them and had got nowhere; they would not budge. Kieran had stopped answering his phone and on the rare occasions when Stephen had managed to track him down, he had simply referred a final decision about the grounds for prosecution to his superiors, who, as far as Stephen could see, were distinguished only by their absolute inability to decide anything.

If Judge Hunter sympathised with the Prosecution barrister's awkwardness it did not ameliorate the situation one iota. He was pitiless. Relentless. He had a jury waiting in a side room, had had to change courts to accommodate all the interested parties and was also being required to decide a case that should never have reached his desk. And he wanted to know why. Then he would decide how to deal with it and as for the wasted public money ... well. He was livid.

"Let me recap for you, Mr Morris, to refresh your memory. I have in front of me a report from a Professor of Psychiatry, from one of our most illustrious universities, who is the recognised national expert in the diagnosis and treatment of Post-Traumatic Stress Disorder. She has treated all of the unfortunate veterans from Afghanistan and Iraq and she states, unequivocally, that the plaintiff, Carlos Cardoso, does not suffer from PTSD. In direct contradiction to the CPS report from a no doubt reputable but undeniably less well qualified psychologist, it is apparent that Mr Cardoso cannot possibly suffer from PTSD because he was unaware of the trauma when it occurred. He was anaesthetised, was he not?"

Stephen nodded miserably. It was unarguable.

"He was unconscious of the traumatic event therefore cannot, by definition, have stress from it afterwards." It was a legal body blow but Judge Hunter had more to say. He barely paused for breath.

"In addition to this report I have a further ... one, two, three, four, five, six ... yes, six separate medical reports all of which, I repeat, all, state that no harm has been done by the action of the defendant. These reports, Mr Morris, include one from the General Medical Council, two from the Midland Central Hospital Trust's investigative hearing, two from the defence team and, most remarkably, one from the Crown Prosecution Service. The authors of these reports include two Professors of Liver Surgery, a Professor of Hepatology from Cambridge, an expert from Kings College Hospital and two practising Senior Consultants in Liver surgery. They unanimously agree that the alleged initials on the organ in question caused no harm and would have disappeared within a few days to a maximum of two weeks with a normal blood supply."

His words hung sword-like around the room, waiting to fall. Even Charles Somerton seemed shocked.

"May I ask, Mr Morris, upon what grounds the Crown Prosecution Service propose to continue the pursuit of their case against Alexander Whiteley?"

He had to reply, he knew. Stephen set off, trotting out the line that the CPS Special Crimes Division had decreed, knowing that it was an almost impassable track leading nowhere and hating it, every step of the way. But he was a professional and employed by the CPS. He would do his best.

"The Crown Prosecution Service maintain that, in spite of their medical expertise, it is not for any doctor to decide the level of harm in law that has been committed. Only a jury can determine whether the harm is trivial or more serious. If it is trivial then a crime of Common Assault has been committed but if, as we believe, it is more serious, then the defendant must be found guilty of the crime of Actual Bodily Harm and sentenced accordingly."

Judge Hunter looked straight through him and leant back in his chair.

"Your Precedent for such an argument?"

"DPP v Smith."

"Cutting off a girl's ponytail against her will thereby causing harm serious enough to amount to Actual Bodily Harm?"

"Exactly."

"You are aware that this was a contentious case?"

"I am."

"And the CPS is relying on a jury to reach a verdict of harm serious enough in the case of Alexander Whiteley to warrant a ruling of Actual Bodily Harm?"

"Yes, Your Honour."

"Even with the quantity and level of expert evidence that will be put before the jury?"

"Yes, Your Honour."

"It is a highly speculative strategy on the part of the CPS. Why is a more sustainable charge of Common Assault not being brought?"

"The lesser crime of Common Assault by Battery is included in the more serious charge of Actual Bodily Harm so there is no need to bring a separate charge. Should Your Honour deem it appropriate, the jury could be instructed to return a verdict of Common Assault if they did not believe that the threshold for ABH had been crossed."

"Your Honour, may I comment?" Charles had almost been forgotten in the intensity of the exchange between Judge and Prosecution counsel. Both looked at him as if seeing him for the first time.

"Please do."

"In the light of the plethora of expert medical and psychiatric opinion, the Defence would like to plead for a charge of Common Assault and Battery."

"It is a sensible plea, Mr Somerton and begs the question, Mr Morris, as to why the CPS has brought this case to trial by jury in a Crown Court when a charge of Common Assault could have been heard in the Magistrate's Court at far less trouble and expense to the taxpayer and Her Majesty's legal system."

"It is matter of public interest, Your Honour. The Special Crimes Division of the CPS felt that this was a test case in terms of medical malpractice and stand by their belief that the level of harm can only be decided by a jury."

"Is there a representative of the Special Crimes Division here today?"

Stephen wanted to spit.

"Unfortunately not, Your Honour."

"That is unfortunate, Mr Morris. The CPS are determined to press charges of ABH against Mr Whiteley?"

"They are, Your Honour."

"I would respectfully like to suggest that the CPS change their charge against my client from Actual Bodily Harm to Common Assault." Charles, genially flicking his hair from his eyes, pressing home his point, a smiling assassin pressing the tip of his knife into the CPS jugular vein.

Judge Ian Hunter finally showed some humanity and took pity on his erstwhile legal colleague.

"Mr Morris. Perhaps you would like to consult the Special Crimes Division and share with them the content of our discussion? There is a telephone at your disposal next door. I suggest you convey to them my advice that the CPS need to think very carefully about their decision to prosecute Mr

Whiteley for Actual Bodily Harm. We will reconvene in, say, twenty minutes. Is that sufficient time for a decision to be reached?"

"It is, Your Honour. Thank you."

Stephen had little doubt what his Honour was saying – Common Assault not ABH, whether they liked it or not.

In the corridors, on the landing outside the court room, perched on the stairs, in the central reception area and in the side rooms people were becoming impatient.

"It should have started by now." Court officials were looking increasingly harassed and doing their utmost to avoid any contact with the questioning public, especially the group of enthusiastic supporters who were not a little riled to have been forced to relinquish their placards and banners to the care of the receptionist. "Collect them on the way out but do not take them into the court room" they had been told.

"That defeats the object of the exercise" they had complained but then cheered up considerably when they remembered that they still had their voices.

Meanwhile the witnesses had gathered and were getting to know each other. Alex's Defence Team had amassed an assortment of testimonials – Tiger Lily, James, an Emeritus Professor of Hepatology, an army doctor seconded to the MCH Military Wing, a representative of a national liver charity and several other patients. All had either worked with or been treated by Alex. All were keen to speak up on his behalf. The Clerk of the Court was struggling with where to place all the participants in the drama; maybe the unprecedented number of witnesses who were to be permitted to hear the proceedings could occupy the Press gallery? The Press could move to the Spectator's Gallery but then where would the sizeable and recalcitrant group of spectators go? The proceedings were running late, the jury were full to bursting with caffeine and biscuits, keen as mustard to get going; it was all getting out of hand.

In one of the side rooms Jayne had problems of her own.

“What do you mean I haven’t got Post-Traumatic Stress Disorder? That’s utterly ridiculous! Of course I have! I’ve got all the symptoms, the pain, the flashbacks, the night terrors. I can’t sleep or eat or even close my eyes without reliving the experience. My life is in pieces!”

“Mr Cardoso, please. Be calm.”

“Be calm? Be calm? Are you out of your mind? I’m here for the trial of the man who tried to kill me when I was helpless and vulnerable and you tell me to be calm!”

“I’m afraid that’s the point.”

“What is?”

“You were under anaesthetic when the event occurred and therefore cannot have any recollection of the experience. According to the medical definition of PTSD you have to be aware of the traumatic event as it happens in order to get the stress disorder afterwards.”

“But that’s ridiculous! Just because I didn’t know at the time doesn’t detract from the pain and suffering I’ve endured since I found out.”

“Yes, I understand, Mr Cardoso. But unfortunately the recognised medical definition is the criteria against which the case will be measured so we have to accept that there is no PTSD.”

“But the expert, the psychologist lady said I had all the symptoms!”

“I’m afraid the Defence have consulted a different expert whose report states that you don’t ...” here she hesitated, intimidated by Carlos’ venomous look, ”well, not that you don’t have the symptoms but that they can’t be attributed to the actions of Mr Whiteley."

There was worse to come; she ploughed on. "In addition, it wasn't Mr Whiteley who told you about the initialling so the chain of causation has inevitably been broken."

"But I was promised! Kieran promised me that I would get justice for my suffering. He told me it was PTSD!"

There was a slight pause while Carlos clenched his bottle of Evian water and breathed dramatically, deeply, furiously. "Where is he? I'd like to speak to him."

"I'm afraid Kieran could not be with us today."

Composed as she said it, Jayne wanted to blast Kieran O'Connell and his Special Crimes Division to hell and beyond, wherever that might be.

"He's not here?" Carlos was now genuinely outraged. "Why not? He said this was an important test case."

The door opened and Stephen appeared, black-robed and bewigged. Jayne wanted to hug him.

"Ah! Mr Cardoso. Not nervous I hope?"

Jayne thought Carlos was about to combust. Stephen took no notice.

"Not long now. Jayne, will you stay with Mr Cardoso throughout the proceedings please? To explain anything he might not understand? Thank you."

A euphemism for keep him quiet and well behaved; no theatrics or we're in even more trouble. Jayne understood perfectly.

"The Clerk of the Court will send someone to fetch you and show you where to sit. Judge Hunter is an excellent man; we're in good hands, Mr Cardoso. He'll explain why there's been a slight delay so I don't need to go into that now. Suffice it to say that there has been a slight change in the form the proceedings will take but your claim for justice is still my paramount concern and priority as your barrister. I am confident that there will be a conviction in our favour. We'll catch up after the trial."

And he was gone, the door closed and Carlos stunned into silence. Jayne girded herself for a long, long day.

On the other side of the building Alex was waiting no less nervously in his side room. Derek was with him but neither was speaking. The solicitor suspected he knew the cause of the delay but did not want to say anything in case he was wrong and gave Alex false hope. Better to wait for the judge to speak and then, hope against hope, that he dismissed the jury and instructed a trial for the lesser crime of Common Assault. The argument as to whether or not Alex had actually committed a crime of any sort was irrelevant at this point. Justice was a funny business and sometimes seemed to have so little to do with the law. The waiting was always worst. He looked at his client, who seemed to be coping. He was quiet and apparently unruffled, but who knew what was going on within? The truth was, not much. Alex was in a state of emotional paralysis, a prelude to what was to come. His reverie was interrupted by the sound of the door opening and the entrance of Charles.

"Alex, there's been a development. We need to have a chat."

CHAPTER FIFTY-NINE

"Court is in session. Judge Ian Hunter presiding. All rise!"

All rose; it was standing room only anyway. The Press had categorically refused to sit anywhere except in their designated gallery on the grounds that they had to see and hear properly in order to report accurately and the Clerk had not argued. The jury were in their seats, the Public Gallery was packed and the witnesses were ranged along a wall behind the Press. In desperation the Clerk had placed Carlos and Jayne in discreet positions alongside the jury; it had been impressed upon him that the plaintiff had, at all costs, to be inconspicuous and anonymous. Only Alex had plenty of room as he sat, isolated, behind a transparent security screen in the centre of the room directly opposite the judge. Boxed; caged like a dangerous animal. Between the two of them in the well of the court were Charles, Arash and his suitcase, Stephen and other court officials: a legal chasm. Alex had never felt so alone. Lisa he knew was in the Public Gallery immediately beside him but obscured by an opaque wall. She was there, but not there. Not even able to throw him a loving look or a supportive glance. He wanted to weep.

Judge Ian Hunter sat. Then everyone else shuffled, shifted and settled into their seats. In the Public Gallery there was a lot of head bobbing and neck stretching for a better view; the Press had their phones on record, iPads and lap tops open, fingers poised over the keys, ready to write their releases and articles, all eager to be the first with the news – whatever it was. Carlos half unscrewed the top of the bottle of spring water so that discreet sips would be possible as anxiety dictated. Only when the room was still, did the Judge begin.

"This is an unprecedented situation. For the benefit of the jury, who have not been sworn in, I would like to explain that in law there are two similar offences: Actual Bodily Harm, known as ABH, and Common Assault. The difference between them is determined by the level of physical harm caused. Anything more serious than trifling or trivial is regarded as ABH or worse."

At this point he glanced at the Press who were goggle-eyed with anticipation and feverishly texting. The jury - not sworn in? Something juicy was coming. Judge Hunter paused, just long enough for them to catch up, then continued.

"The Crown Prosecution Service has asserted that the charge of Actual Bodily Harm should stand in this case and that the level of harm should be determined by you, the jury. However, I have in my possession no less than six separate expert reports that all agree that the level of harm is no more than trivial and trifling."

A combined gasp percolated around the room like a Mexican wave which began and ended with Carlos.

"One of these reports comes from the Crown Prosecution Service itself."

Deadpan; dramatic pause; let it sink in then release the blade on the guillotine.

“So on that basis, I am dismissing the charge of Actual Bodily Harm and discharging you from your duty. I would like to thank you for your service and sincerely apologise for the inconvenience this has caused. No doubt the Crown Prosecution Service will share my concern about the time and public money that has been wasted.”

Stephen as the sole representative of the CPS nodded apologetically towards the jury who stared at him. Verdict? Unanimous: a fiasco.

“Court is adjourned for the jury to be discharged and will reconvene in 45 minutes.

As soon as the door closed behind the judge the noise erupted, born at crescendo level and climbing. By the time half the Press had scuttled off and the jury had been escorted out of the room, the noise was trapped in the room and swelling the walls. Loud jubilation burst from the protesters until someone reminded them that Alex Whiteley was still almost certain to be convicted of something; Lisa sat silent and stunned amidst the maelstrom. The witnesses grouped together in a huddle: what now? Would they be needed? Arash came over; yes, they would be needed and could now sit down in the room; they would be told where. Sentencing would be influenced by their testimonials and in the light of todays’ events there was no way His Honour was going to extend the case into a further hearing. It would all happen today.

The barristers had disappeared immediately after His Lordship so apart from Arash’s suitcase, the centre of the court was now abandoned. Jayne hurriedly checked that Carlos was okay? No, he most certainly was not but yes, he would wait where he was. What else could he do? She then set off in pursuit of Stephen and Patient C was left, in a state of suppressed hysteria, to sweat and sip water. Alex too was alone in the dock behind the bullet-proof transparent wall; a legal freak show, locked in to prevent escape while the security man 'stepped out for a minute' and a quick smoke. No need for Alex to confer with his legal team; he already knew what he had to do. He sat down, parallel with Lisa but worlds away from her and gazed incredulously around the room. It was surreal. How had it come to this?

Carlos and Alex's eyes met over the cavernously empty well of the court.

Time held its breath, suspended in the noise but not part of it. Insubstantial, overwhelming, a clamp on reality.

So much to be said but nothing to say. Alex half expected his life to flash before his eyes but instead he saw only Carlos. Fit, healthy, dapper dark, white with holy anger.

And what did Carlos see? A blighted life, pain, o'er weening ambition, attempted murder; revenge. He had hope; Alex had none.

Court scene - Take Two. "All rise."

Tense expectancy now instead of excited chatter, even from the hardened Press whose editors and outside reporters awaiting the next instalment. Everyone sat, except Alex.

Judge Hunter began.

"This is an unparalleled case in that there is no Legal Precedent for the alleged crime committed. I am therefore directing that the Defendant, Alexander Whiteley, be charged with Common Assault by Battery to which he should plead guilty. The jury would have been instructed by me to find him not guilty of Actual Bodily Harm, but guilty of the lesser offence, Common Assault by Battery. Alexander Whiteley. How do you plead?"

"Guilty."

Quietly, sadly, utterly alone. Every syllable a tear. The most lame and impotent conclusion to a life in medicine.

Silence. No one moved. Carlos smiled.

"Be seated."

As if in a trance Alex did as instructed, but would never remember what the judge said next. He was told about it sometime later but it meant nothing. All he would ever know was that he had never been able to put his side of the story, never been heard or given a chance to explain. He would forever be Guilty.

"This case should never have come to the Crown Court but should have been heard in the Magistrate's Court. The Defendant will therefore be sentenced accordingly. Mr Morris, does the Prosecution have anything to add?"

Carlos stiffened with excitement, felt the familiar flutter of pre-performance nerves in his belly. He could almost smell the greasepaint and feel the warmth of the lights as he prepared to make his entrance. Don't walk in front of the Judge, go round the back of the lawyers he reminded himself and straightened his perfectly vertical tie. He hesitated for a second then decided against taking the bottle of water with him; easier to make a dramatic appearance with free hands – the use of hands always marked out the good actor from the bad who stopped playing their parts at the wrists.

"Yes, Your Honour. My client, known as Patient C, would like to be able to take the witness stand."

Carlos sighed happily. In all the legal catastrophe leading up to this moment when everything had gone wrong for him, the one saving grace was that Stephen had finally consented to allow him to take the witness stand. Jayne apparently was opposed to it but she was only a solicitor and he understood that Kieran, for all his faults, had agreed with Stephen. What a pity he would miss the performance.

Judge Hunter started to speak. Carlos prepared to rise.

"I have studied your client's detailed and emotive witness

statement and do not feel that there is anything to be gained by the plaintiff taking the witness stand. In addition, it is essential to preserve the anonymity and privacy of your client. To that end I am making it a legal requirement that the name of your client is not made public, now or in the future, to ensure the permanent protection of their privacy and reputation. I emphasise that point for the benefit of the Press." A narrow-eyed look at the Press Gallery to underline his words. They got it.

"What?" Carlos hissed at Jayne sitting beside him.

"Shh!" She rejoiced; able to silence him at last.

"You may read aloud the Witness Statement of Patient C in full for the benefit of those present, Mr Morris."

"Thank you, Your Honour."

Without so much as a glance at his client, Stephen stood, holding a sheaf of papers in his hand and prepared to deliver Carlos' speech. Stephen! The understudy! Carlos wanted to weep but instead sat back, a picture of Academy Award-winning nonchalance and disregard.

As Stephen began the Statement of Patient C about that fateful day in August 2013, the audience settled back to listen. Such eloquence, such emotion, such power of description, even Carlos was impressed all over again as he surveyed the room like a camera panning a landscape. Stephen was doing a passable job of the rendition. Perhaps there was something to be gained from such a stolid delivery - after all, the words spoke for themselves. The Press were actually paying attention, making only occasional notes. The public were quiet and attentive – even the protestors. What a motley collection of spectators they were. Just the kind of fringe society nutters Carlos would expect to support the likes of Alexander Whiteley. And what was that monster doing? Listening? Yes. Good. So he should. White faced and tight lipped; hopefully holding back the tears. No more than he deserved for all the suffering he had caused.

Carlos' reverie was disturbed by a whisper from one of the character witnesses sitting immediately in front of him. She was quite young judging by her clothes, with dangly earrings and she was muttering to her neighbour, a tall chap badly in need of a hair-cut, wearing a jacket and tie when he ought to have worn a suit. They were ... surely not ... giggling? Carlos was outraged and wanted to say something, to slap their heads, bring them to order. Had he known it was Tiger Lily in front of him he would have happily drenched her in his spring water. She was talking to James who did not know that Patient C, on whom he had operated but with whom he had never spoken and certainly did not recognise now that he was healthy, was sitting directly behind them. They were scoffing at the absurdity of the claims made in the witness statement. It was highly descriptive, entertaining, purple prose, the language of the absurd. The barrister's bland delivery made it nothing short of hilarious.

"... My life is destroyed, my mental health ruined. I can never trust anyone again. I have been violated. Raped. Despite what people say, I know that the first liver failed because of the letters branded on it and I could have died. As far as I am concerned, it was attempted murder and I have been condemned to a life blighted by the effects of the trauma inflicted upon me. All I want is justice and recognition of my suffering. Justice."

"Money" hissed Tiger Lily to James, "and lots of it."

Stephen had finished. He put the papers down on the bench before him and then sat, looking only at the judge who nodded and turned his attention to the defence.

"Mr Somerton?"

"Thank you, Your Honour. My client would like to apologise, unreservedly for his actions. He deeply regrets the pain and suffering he has caused the plaintiff. He knows what he did was wrong and has never denied that. He has pleaded guilty to the charge at the first opportunity and expressed extreme remorse."

All eyes were on Alex, watching the silent tears on his fixed, marble face. In the Public Gallery Lisa was shredding a tissue into minute pieces.

"Had the liver been healthy, as there was every reason to assume was the case, the initials would have faded within days. No harm was done. We have, as you already know, expert testimony to that effect. The claim of Post-Traumatic Stress Disorder is unfounded as the plaintiff was anaesthetised at the time of the action and cannot therefore be said to have experienced a traumatic event."

At this the Press hit their keys as one body and a stifled group exclamation emanated from the Public Gallery. Charles waited for silence before he resumed.

"My client is a world class surgeon with an exemplary record. He has saved hundreds of lives over a working life of more than 30 years. His whole career has been dedicated to improving the quality of life of others. The presence of so many in court today indicates the depth of loyalty and gratitude felt by his patients and their families, friends and relatives."

A dramatic pause as he gave His Honour the opportunity to digest the scale of the crowded courtroom.

"I believe Your Honour has received letters and testimonials in support of my client not just from patients but also colleagues in all walks of his medical life, past and present."

He indicated to the bulky red file on the judges's bench containing over 270 written statements. Fern twisted her head round at an uncomfortable 180 degrees angle to catch Tiger Lily's eyes and they beamed at each other. Charles continued. Alex, condemned by admitted guilt to silence, could only hope that his barrister would choose the right words.

"There are mitigating circumstances for my client's actions. He had been operating for nearly twelve hours under the most stressful conditions when the incident occurred. The procedure itself was complicated and, at times, life-threatening. My client was fatigued and stressed. His situational awareness was undermined as a result of cognitive overload; decision making was compromised. He is truly sorry for his actions. He has tried to apologise to the plaintiff but this was rejected. He has had to resign from a job he loves. He has been hounded and vilified by the press, received malicious letters and someone has even tried to poison his dog, which, as a result, has since died."

A loud, corporate gasp of horror ran round the room. Real horror. The Press could not believe their luck; this story had everything. Even hoary old Judge Hunter showed uncharacteristic shock. He was a Black Labrador man himself and could only imagine the pain of losing any one of his three girls.

"Thank you, Mr Somerton. I am aware that there a large number of witnesses present who wish to testify to the good character of the defendant. Do you wish to call three of them to the stand?"

Tiger Lily, the Army Doctor and the Emeritus Professor were the chosen ones. James was relieved not have been called forward; he would have done it gladly but life in the MCH would be a damn sight easier now that he was off the hook. Tiger-Lily, nervous and a little hesitant at first, described the reason for setting up the Facebook Page and how it had evolved, burgeoned, taken over her life. The judge had clearly visited it and smiled encouragingly at her as she listed data about the number of hits, comments, likes and views. To her surprise he knew what she was talking about but declined her offer to read out a sample of the comments posted, saying he had already been supplied with the information and had read them with interest. Quite a nice man, really, she found herself thinking, and surprisingly computer literate for someone of that age.

Then the Army Doctor, a Colonel of some standing and even more combat experience testified to the expertise of Alex, his dedication, innovation and value to injured Service personnel. "Arguably the outstanding surgeon of his generation" he concluded. Tiger Lily wanted to applaud; Carlos wanted to spit. The Emeritus Professor endorsed the Colonel and lost most of the room in a litany of acronyms, medical jargon, procedures and surgical outcomes but the message was clear. Alexander Whiteley was a fine surgeon who had destroyed himself by a single act of stupidity. Shouldn't that be punishment enough? Not to mention the patients that would not now benefit from his skill?

Not according to the law. Judge Hunter did not say as much but it was implied.

"The defendant has written a letter to the court in which he acknowledges his wrong doing, without a trace of self-pity. It is to his credit that he has demonstrated such contrition and regret. The court will adjourn until 2.30 pm when it will reconvene for sentencing."

Just enough time for a coffee and a sandwich. There was a stampede.

The desire to hear the sentence brought almost everyone back into the courtroom for the Final Act. The Press could hardly wait. During the recess there had been a great deal of feverish speculation and discussion across the airwaves about the possible punishment 'The Letterman' - now a convicted criminal - would receive. The maximum was five years imprisonment as the case had been heard in the Crown Court. What would happen?

How would the guilty man react to incarceration? Did he deserve it? They would love to know how the plaintiff felt but alas, reporting restrictions prevented any such information. Back in their offices their editors were already consulting lawyers about the possibility of 'anonymous' interviews with the mysterious, victimised Patient C.

Carlos was confused. He had been vindicated and that felt good. The beast who had tried to kill him had been branded a criminal but why had he, Carlos, who had suffered so much, not been given the public recognition and approbation that he so richly deserved? It felt not so much like a victory but a robbery. His glory had been stolen from him.

Perhaps the punitive sentence that the criminal was bound to receive would make him feel happier? He settled himself in his seat alongside Jayne who, quite rightly, had paid for his sandwich and sparkling water repast. He could hardly eat of course, but it was essential to maintain his energy levels at such a time. There was an air of expectancy when Judge Hunter entered.

Carlos listened intently to the Judge's preamble to the main event, nodding sagely in sad agreement with everything that was said. He especially liked the reference to the crime as an unacceptable breach of trust and an abuse of the sacred relationship between doctor and patient. Yes, Judge Hunter was indeed an excellent man. Even more so when he described Alexander Whiteley's actions as those of an arrogant man whose ego was out of control. Couldn't have put it better himself. He was not so sure about the notion that a great surgeon had let himself down but he most certainly had let down his profession. And how did we know that it was just one stupid action for whatever reason; a moment of madness that had undermined all that had been achieved in an otherwise illustrious career? He might have done it countless times but never been discovered. Carlos now found himself mournfully shaking his head.

"Having heard both sides of the argument, I am now ready to

rule. Will the defendant be upstanding?"

He would. He did. A solitary figure behind a transparent wall. No-one breathed.

"Alexander Whiteley. You have pleaded guilty to a charge of Common Assault by Battery. You are sentenced to 120 hours of Community Service and fined the sum of £10,000, to be completed and paid within 12 months from today."

Carlos could not believe it. Nor could the Press or indeed, anyone else. It was almost as if the Judge was letting him off. Stephen glanced at Jayne who placed a calm but undoubtably restraining hand on Carlos' arm. It worked; there was no outburst but the bottle of Evian began to buckle in his clenched fist. Jayne hoped the cap was securely fastened.

Stephen was on his feet putting forward a case for full costs and compensation for the not inconsiderable pain and suffering of his client. Following the conviction of the Defendant it seemed only fair and appropriate that a substantial sum should be awarded to his victim. Yes, the Judge had considered the matter carefully and decided however, that in the light of the Crown Prosecutions Service's reprehensibly inefficient handling of the case, full costs would not be awarded against the Defendant.

"Patient C will be awarded 10% of the costs which, I believe amount to £13,000 in total. As for compensation, that is for another court in another place. No damages will be awarded by this court."

CHAPTER SIXTY

The reaction to the court case soon became old news. Opinion was divided but most of the Press were outraged about the leniency of the sentence and much was said and written about the suffering of innocent, hapless Patient C. The tabloids shared his pain; his anger was their anger; if only they could speak to him, get to know him, print his words.

Eventually Carlos was persuaded to give an anonymous interview for an undisclosed sum, part of which was to be donated to a good cause. 'Patient C' spoke at length about the agony of the ordeal and was widely quoted, but there it ended. Malcolm Piggott had managed to waylay Tiger Lily and Fern on the steps of the courthouse but they had ignored him he had had to resort to an impromptu but lively interview with the Alex Whiteley supporter's group. Most of the footage was not fit to broadcast.

There was a storm of posts on the 'Save The Letterman' page when Tiger Lily announced the outcome of the case but that too quickly quietened. Immediately after the trial Alex posted a heartfelt message of thanks to everyone who had shown support. There had been an outpouring of praise for him, particularly in the light of what was perceived as ill-informed, biased Press coverage but now, all was silent.

"D'you think I should close the page, Fern?"

"No. Not yet. You never know. Just let it go dormant."

"I hope we don't need to do it again. I wonder what Mr W's doing now?"

What was he doing?

Unemployed and notorious. A convicted criminal, wondering how to earn an income. He was ashamed, humiliated and full of self-loathing. Had it not been for Lisa and Dave he might have given up. But then, as Lisa had pointed out, there was the Facebook page and all the people on there who believed in him, the witnesses in the court, the patients whose lives he had saved, the colleagues who had kept in touch and were still texting him, even from the MCH. She was earning so they would manage. It was only money; they had each other and Dave had them both.

Alex spent the short days and long, dark evenings sitting at home in front of his computer screen, tapping out 'Dog Days' because there was nothing else to do. He drank too much coffee and filled the grey, wintry silence by talking to the dog and reading his work aloud. He had heard somewhere that 'if it sounds right, it probably is right' and while the Goldendoodle was not perhaps the most informed of critics, he seemed to enjoy the renditions. To his astonishment, Alex began to occasionally enjoy himself; he liked the way he could comment on the perplexities of the world from a dog's eye view. His writing became more lively, less introspective and sometimes quite amusing. As Baldrick's voice became more assured, idiosyncratic and confident, Alex began to heal. Lisa asked to read a sample of what he had written and to his wonder actually seemed to enjoy it; she laughed out loud and even let her tea go cold while she insisted on reading to the end.

"Alex, It's good!"

They were both amazed.

"It might make a radio play" she said. "It's just the sort of thing people listen to in the car, especially on a long journey. Why not send it to the radio drama people? What've you got to lose?"

Nothing. As far as he was concerned it had all gone. So why not take a risk? He googled how to write a radio play and slowly, painfully began to try and bring his text to life.

It was the hardest thing he had ever done. It only became manageable when he approached it as a surgical procedure: identify the conflict, the action, the desired outcome then plot the way carefully towards it. Incision to start? Or maybe a laparoscopy? it did not matter, as long as the subject was opened up, made visible, exposed. Then lay it bare and expose the details: fleshy layers, sinewy strands, ligament, nerves, muscles, bone and blood: the energy of the drama which had always to be a living thing. It had to pulsate and throb with life as a body on the operating table; an innate physical voice without words. Probe, delve, finger a way through the visceral pulp to the central conflict and reveal its tainted ugliness, discoloration, twisted sinfulness. Unmask it. Take decisive action to win the battle; he who dares wins. Remove the cancer, reinvent the organ. Purge and sculpt. Create something new. Rewrite it. A different drama now, with potency and hope, a life restored. Then close, deftly, swiftly, leaving little damage but a permanent mark like an afterthought or a visual image.

The pain fades away but the scar remains – lesson learned; dramatic conclusion. Curtain falls, theatre empties.

As soon as he sent it off to the radio drama department Alex forgot about it partly because he was living only in the present and partly because he did not rate it. Who in their right mind would want a play written from the perspective of a Jack Russell? Besides, he was a surgeon, not a writer.

Carlos grieved that interest in his case had died so quickly. He found himself alone in Stroud, anxious to stop 'resting' and resume his acting career. His agent in London was pleased to hear from him.

"Where've you been, Carlos? I know you were ill but you're okay now, right?"

"Physically back to normal but it's been a long, hard journey. Very emotional. Traumatic, but I won't burden you with my troubles. What have you got for me?"

"Nothing much on the books at the moment but now I know you're back on form I'll put out some feelers, make a few calls. It's a quiet time though. Same old, same old."

This was not what Carlos wanted to hear.

"I'm ready to get back into harness; to put my hand to anything."

"There might be a voiceover coming up. I'll let you know. Keep well."

He was gone. Carlos was left alone with only anger and resentment for conversation and company. He stared at the eternal rain out of the narrow kitchen window over the Belfast sink, original not designer, the dripping tap and the mildewed corners of the window sill. His cottage, Cotswold Stone, inside and out. Picturesque, damp, prone to mould, draughty, and clammy, full of woodlice and silver snail trails at dawn. He was residing in his own life and he hated it.

His phone chirped beside him. Thank God! His agent. A job! Money. Escape from Stroud and maybe permanent exile to somewhere more civilised. Even Cheltenham would be preferable – a Literary Festival, intelligent company, a theatre. The caller information came up. It was Jayne.

"Hello Mr Cardoso. How are you? ... Oh. ... I'm sorry to hear that. Yes, it was disappointing, however, I may have some news that will cheer you up... No, we're not going to appeal. Mr Morris explained all that to you after the trial... As he told you then, a claim for compensation through the civil courts would be risky and expensive and not something the Crown Prosecution Service would be involved in. This is about Alexander Whiteley. As a result of his criminal conviction the General Medical Council are reopening their case against him and plan to have him struck off the Medical Register."

EPILOGUE

Eighteen Months Later

Her immaculate flat but now was too small, too cluttered and too white. They would have to move. Julia sighed and shifted the almost asleep baby onto her other shoulder, praying that it would not start crying again. They would have to get a nanny and then she could go back to work – not a moment too soon. And there would only be one baby, she would see to that. Her husband wouldn't object. He had known her long enough. She had wanted a baby before it was too late and he had obliged. It would do for the time being. Garth in India, Eduardo Moreno Dias and the RSPCA prosecution, which had come to nothing, were irrelevant.

The muted tv was on in the corner of the kitchen. Julia glanced at it as the baby settled, then cried out. Her husband came running into the room as the baby began to howl.

"The bastard!"

"Julia! What's happened?"

"Look!"

She pointed at the television screen.

Bright, hot, white light burning into his eyeballs. Smaller explosions and incendiary flashes out in the deafening darkness. He wanted to shade his eyes and focus into the distance. Somewhere out there was Lisa but she was obscured by the inky noise. He was alone, on a scratched worn surface behind a blazing lip over which the ground fell away into people and seats. He blinked again and again as if to clear the view but nothing changed except the noise which began to recede. His mouth was parched dry, arid, framed by cracked lips that wanted to curl into laughter and disbelief.

Silence.

He cleared his throat. It echoed throughout the theatre and round his ears. Come on he thought, willing himself to be intelligent. Say something.

"Thank you, but I'm really not sure why I'm here."

Pause. Titter of polite interest from the darkness.

"If you're surprised to see me here, you're not half as surprised as I am. For those of you who don't know – all one of you – I used to be a surgeon."

Genuine laughter now.

In his cheerless, dimly-lit living room Carlos is watching the ceremony on television. Only an overhead ceiling light illuminates the cheerless room. Outside it is still light and the sun has been warm but the thick stone walls of the cottage have kept the room shaded, cool, ever moist. There is a faintly dank odour. Carlos sits alone in an easy chair in the centre of the room; the only chair. No need for others as no one visits. Fortunately, the room is small so needs little furniture and Carlos has presence enough to make it seem full. He is sitting forward in his seat, his hands white-knuckle gripped on the arms of the chair. There is no bottle of spring water.

On the screen before him the travesty continues.

"And now I find I am a writer, signing books."

Applause. Alex smiles, not entirely happily. He had hardly believed it when the radio play had not only been accepted but performed, to modest acclaim but sufficient for an agent to contact Alex,

"Just to see if you've written anything else."

She had been told about the rest of 'Dog Days' and asked to see the text; had liked it; said it might be of interest and that she could offer Alex a good deal as his literary agent. Alex had signed a contract and expected nothing. When the book was published, he was pleasantly surprised; when it became a best seller he was astounded. To then be recognised at an awards ceremony for his endeavours was absurd. Had the world finally gone insane?

The General Medical Council had been taken to a Judicial Review after they attempted to reopen the case against him and he had been cleared, free to practice medicine but unemployable. He had completed the community service and paid the fine but his criminal record had made him a medical pariah and no one would let him work. So, he had carried on writing, slamming words onto the laptop screen until he had written out the rejection, anger, humiliation, bitterness, guilt and shame. Catharsis.

"Instead of wearing scrubs I'm dressed up like a dog's dinner, which is appropriate and I know Baldrick would approve."

Dramatic pause. Mirth.

"Apart from Baldrick, obviously, there is someone very important I must thank."

Alex stops and gazes out into the darkness ahead, through the screen, into Carlos' eyes.

"Patient C."

A rather tacky trophy is held aloft; shards of light dazzle from its metal surface and refract into the dimly lit Stroud sitting room, splintering the gloom and reflecting on Carlos' face.

"From the Letterman".

ACKNOWLEDGEMENT

We owe so much to so many, but mostly, as always, to our wonderful families for their love and support.

Thank you.

Printed in Great Britain
by Amazon

39577700R00195